A Knight Like No Other

Realm of Honor

MICHELLE MILES

This is a work of fiction. All characters, organizations and events portrayed in this novel are either products of the author's imagination or used fictitiously.

A KNIGHT LIKE NO OTHER

This title was previously published.

Cover Design by Erin Dameron-Hill

Copyright © 2016, Second Edition

ISBN: 978-1-7333887-7-1

Chapter 1

Sir Drake Attenborough watched as Princess Allanna rode away from the Queen's Palace, his heart breaking more with the expanding distance between them. She was returning to her home high atop the trees in the Woodlands and he hadn't even had a chance to tell her goodbye. Her father and her royal brothers flanked her as though they were a shield or a barricade to keep her from him.

Drake was aware the king and all the others at court knew of his fancy for the Elven princess. And she for him. He hadn't kept his feelings secret, nor she hers. They had spent as much time as possible together. They had danced with each other every chance they could get. He had hoped he would have another opportunity to be with her at the coronation that day. But no. They were riding back to the Woodlands. He was certain her father did all he could to get her back home—away from Drake.

"Will you let her go so easily?" Elyne asked.

He hadn't realized the Fae queen stood beside him, watching him watch the princess. Allanna kept her back rigid and straight as she rode. He memorized everything about her, burning it into his mind so he could conjure it any moment he wanted. It pained him to think he may never see her beautiful face or her brilliant smile again. She wore a silk gown of pale blue, an ivory sash at her tiny waist. An opaque veil draped her head, cascading down her back and hiding the length of her hair which was the color of spun gold. Aye, he memorized the way she looked, sitting astride her white horse. The horse she'd named Moonshadow.

Moonshadow. How delightful and fanciful was the princess.

His chest ached as she looked at him over her shoulder one last time. One last look of longing. Their gazes locked. But the moment didn't last long when the king noticed. He glared at Drake. Allanna faced forward in the saddle once more.

"Shouldn't you go after her? I believe that's what she wants."

Aye, he should. And he wanted to but knew the king of the Elves frowned upon their match. He knew it was forbidden in their culture. Yet the young princess made it clear by the fluttering of her eyelashes and the way she blushed she was interested in his affections. He knew it as surely as he knew he would never be happy without her.

They hadn't so much as kissed. He wanted to taste those perfect, blood-red, heart-shaped lips. To feel if they were as petal soft as they looked. Oh, there was one time they came close only to be interrupted by Lord Eldrin.

Drake would never forget the way her tiny body fit against his as he held her, leading her through the steps of his medieval dance. The velvety skin of her hands as she held his. The way her waist curved inward as he held her close. The feel of the small of her back while they swayed, their heads close together. He could still feel her warm breath on his cheek and smell her honeysuckle-scented hair.

By Saint Mary, he loved her.

"It is forbidden," he said at last. "The king will not allow it."

"A lot of drivel that," Elyne said, her voice airy. "There has to be a way. Look at my mother and Henry after all."

Henry was a human who had crossed the veil into the Otherworld to find his missing daughter, Maggie. When he met the queen of the Fae, he fell madly in love with her. He'd helped save her from the Goddess of War and won her heart. The queen, in turn, gave up her crown and immortality to be with him in the human realm. A love story the bards would sing about for ages yet to come.

"Need I remind you that your mother was queen of the Otherworld and could do what she pleased," Drake said. "I daresay our situation is vastly different."

"Nonsense," Elyne said with a wave of her hand. "What would it hurt to try?"

Rejection, that's what. Drake didn't know if he could suffer the indignity of losing Allanna for good. Of having the king turn him away. But the Fae princess—nay, the newest queen of the Otherworld—had a point. He could try. Mayhap he could win Allanna's heart and her hand in marriage.

"Suppose I provide you one of my fastest horses," Elyne continued. "And you rode to the Woodlands. And suppose you had a message…no, a *gift* from the Fae queen to bestow upon the Elven king."

Drake gave her a surreptitious glance. He could see her mind working as she tapped the tip of her finger on her chin. She must be concocting a way for him to gain entrance to the Woodlands. Her blonde hair tousled in the slight breeze and her cornflower-blue eyes snapped to his as she looked at him, a glint of mischief in her gaze.

"Aye, that's what we'll do. I have a token of thanks to bestow upon the king. And a letter expressing my regret he couldn't stay and attend the coronation and the celebration of my wedding to Lord Derron."

"Your majesty—"

She held up her hand. "Sir Drake, do you wish to see the princess again or not?"

"I do, but—"

"Good. I can't have a lovelorn human moping the halls of the palace indefinitely."

"I had thought I would return to the human realm, your majesty."

"Bollocks. I'm not letting you go back there. You have a princess's heart to win after all."

He grinned and ran a hand over his bristling chin. Since he'd been in the Otherworld, he'd allowed his beard to grow. During a dance one evening, Allanna had flushed and said how handsome he looked with it. He had been resistant to shaving after that. Anything to keep her looking at him with those adoring gazes.

Elyne had become quite the matchmaker in the last few months. She'd helped arrange the romance between his Scottish friend and knight, Finn McCullough, and Maggie. She'd also had a hand in the arrangement with Queen Maeve and Henry.

"Your majesty, forgive the intrusion, but the time has come." Lord Vaughan, one of the Fae council members, joined them on the hill outside the gates.

"Sir Drake, shall we?" Elyne motioned toward the courtyard. "You must join the celebration. Afterward, I'll send you with the message to the king."

"What message, my love?"

Lord Derron, Guardian of the Sword of Light, Knight of the Realm and Protector of the Otherworld. And now king. Sir Drake had fought alongside him in the battle against the dark lord Kieran. He had gladly traded in his jousting lance for a chance at a real battle—a battle that mattered. The war between England and France had never interested him, which was why he chose to joust instead. And was quite successful at it, too. Until he'd been pulled into the realm with Finn and his woman and the Fae.

Derron was dressed in his finest clothes with a deep-garnet tunic sewn with gold thread. He wore black pants tucked into shiny knee-high boots. His gloved hand rested on the hilt of the Sword of Light strapped to his side. And around his shoulders he wore the royal garnet velvet cloak trimmed in gold.

"I intend to send King Urdithane a token of thanks as well as a letter regretting that he could not stay for the coronation. Sir Drake has volunteered to deliver the message."

Derron must have known his wife was up to something for his brows knit. "Has he?"

"Aye, my love. He has. Now come. We mustn't be late for our own coronation." She hooked her arm in Derron's and led him away.

Vaughan and Drake fell in step behind the two Fae royals. He hadn't intended to stay for the coronation. He'd intended to ask Elyne to send him home. But now that she'd planted the seed of hope in his mind, he found it difficult to ask her.

Could he win the princess's hand? Would the king overlook their differences and allow them to marry? He could try.

Work to repair the Queen's Palace was still underway. It had been damaged when the Goddess of War, Morrigan, attacked trying to kill Maeve. The Fae had worked tirelessly to rebuild. But on this day the queen regent had ordered a halt in all work to join in the celebrations.

In the courtyard, lists had been erected. There was a viewing gallery along one side for spectators. He hadn't realized the royals intended to host a jousting tournament.

"I do hope you'll join us in the games, Sir Drake," Elyne said over her shoulder.

"I had no idea you were planning them, your majesty. I'm afraid I haven't any jousting armor."

"Oh, don't worry about that. I'm sure we can find some to suit you at the armory," she said. "It would be wonderful if you could be a part of it. Sir Finn has agreed to participate."

"Sir Finn?" Now his interest was definitely piqued. He and Sir Finn had unfinished jousting business. He would love to have another chance at jousting with him. "Then I suppose I cannot refuse."

"Wonderful! We'll get you outfitted after the coronation."

"Aye and I intend to joust as well," Derron said.

"You? Are you certain?" Elyne didn't hide her surprise.

"Fear not, my sweet Elyne. I'm sure no one is out to kill me here." He winked. Derron had once been a jousting hero as well. He had used glamour to hide his Fae appearance to participate in the tourneys. No one had known his true identity until he nearly died in the lists.

"You must promise me you'll be careful," she said.

"Always." He kissed her hand.

Witnessing the simple gesture sent a pang of longing through Drake. He wanted to be able to kiss his princess's hand. He wanted her to worry about whether he would make it out of the lists unscathed. He wanted her to look at him with that same adoring look as Elyne gave her husband.

He just wanted her.

When they arrived inside the palace, Elyne left Derron to dress in her coronation gown. Sir Finn and Maggie spotted him then. With her arm hooked in Finn's, she bustled toward him. Maggie was all smiles as they approached.

"Sir Drake, I'm so glad you decided to stay." She stood on tiptoe and kissed first one cheek and then the other.

"Aye, me as well," Finn added. "I'll finally get a chance to best ye."

Drake laughed. "Is that your plan, my friend? We shall see."

"My husband and I intend to return home after the festivities," Maggie said. "Will you be returning home as well?"

"Lassie, dinna be asking the man such questions."

"Why not? It's a fair question." She gave Drake her full attention. "What say you, Sir Drake?"

He rested his palm on the hilt of his sword. He knew Maggie was much like the Fae queen—a matchmaker. A slow smile spread as he realized the two must have conspired.

"I'd thought I might stay a bit longer," he said.

Maggie clasped her hands, an expectant look on her face. "Good, good. And…?"

"Lassie…" Finn groaned.

"Shh. He'll answer. And, Sir Drake?"

One eyebrow arched. He knew what the lady was trying to pry from him. She and Elyne were definitely in league. "Her majesty the queen has asked me to deliver a token of thanks to King Urdithane."

Maggie clapped. "Wonderful! Then you will surely see Princess Allanna again."

"Maggie, dinna be meddling again. 'Tis nothing but trouble."

"It's all right, Finn. I daresay your wife has my best interests in mind."

"I do. And I would love to see you and Allanna together. It would do my heart good. Oh!" She pressed her hand against her abdomen and turned to her husband, leaning into him. "Finn, I'm afraid I…feel sick again."

"Come then, lass. Let's get ye to the privy."

She flashed Drake a sheepish grin. "Morning sickness. See you at the coronation, Sir Drake."

Finn wrapped an arm around her shoulders and led her away. But as he did, Fae nobles and others trickled into the Queen's Palace, all heading for the throne room. Drake fell in step with them, following along with the wave of people. As he took his place, he waited with the others.

A small group of musicians played quietly off to one side. The coronation had drawn Fae and Elves alike dressed in their finery. Maggie and Finn joined the crowd and Drake could see the lady was pale. Finn had an arm wrapped around her shoulders to hold her up. She needed rest but knowing Maggie she would not miss the crowning of her best friend for anything in the world—or Otherworld.

The High Druid entered dressed in white robes. He was led by two young squires. One carried an ornate pillow with a silver scepter resting atop it while the other boy carried an ornate pillow with a gleaming broadsword. These must be gifts of power for the two monarchs.

Two more squires walked behind the High Druid, each one carrying a small cushion with a crown for the king and queen.

Several other Druids followed the High Druid. Drake heard the whispers this was the Council of High Druids. One of their responsibilities was to record the history of the Fae, so it made sense, then, they should be in attendance.

The High Druid walked with unhurried steps toward the front of the throne room where the two silver thrones sat empty and waiting. He turned and faced the crowd, waiting for the monarchs. Elyne stepped into the doorway.

Her golden hair hung down in long waves over her shoulders and back. She wore a gown of pale pink with a scooped neckline and a gold braid belted at her waist. She had a sort of ethereal beauty about her that reminded Drake much of her mother, Maeve.

Derron stepped next to her and together the two walked down the aisle toward the High Druid. They paused in front of him and he raised his arms above his head.

"Welcome, honored guests. Today is a momentous day as we crown Elyne, daughter of Maeve, and Lord Derron, son of Lord Malcolm."

The High Druid turned to one of the boys standing next to him and removed the scepter from the cushion. He turned back to Elyne.

"Kneel," he ordered.

She dropped to her knees. The High Druid placed one hand on the crown of her head. "Do you, Elyne, daughter of Maeve, swear to protect the Queen's Palace and all those residing within its walls?"

"I so swear."

"Do you, Elyne, daughter of Maeve, swear loyalty to the realm as well as swear to protect the realm by any measures necessary?"

"I so swear."

"As Queen of the Otherworld, do you swear to act with honor and duty above all else?"

"I so swear."

"As High Druid of this realm, I proclaim you Queen and Ruler of the Otherworld. Rise, Queen Elyne."

She rose and faced the High Druid. He passed her the scepter.

"As Queen and Ruler of the Otherworld, I bequeath the Scepter of Power to you as a symbol of your position and your duty."

He extended the scepter and Elyne took it from his hands, holding it to her chest.

The High Druid turned to the second boy and removed the broadsword.

"Lord Derron, Protector of the Otherworld, Knight of the Realm and Guardian of the Sword of Light. Have you chosen successors to your titles, my lord?"

"I have, your grace."

"Please announce your selections."

"As Protector of the Otherworld, Lord Ranaan. As Knight of the Realm, Lord Kevon. As Guardian of the Sword of Light, Lord Toren."

"So it shall be," the High Druid said. "Lord Toren, please step forward to claim the Sword of Light."

Derron removed the Sword of Light from its sheath and turned as Lord Toren came to him. He knelt as Derron tapped him on one shoulder then the other.

"I name you, Toren, son of Malvin, Lord and Guardian of the Sword of Light. Henceforth, you shall assume all responsibilities and duties of Guardian forthwith. Do you accept this title and duties?"

"Aye, I do." He took the Sword of Light, bowed to Derron, and sheathed the sword.

Derron turned back to the High Druid.

"Kneel, my lord."

Derron bent to one knee. The High Druid placed his hand on Derron's head.

"Do you, Derron, son of Malcolm, swear to protect the Queen's Palace and all those residing within its walls?"

"I so swear."

"Do you, Derron, son of Malcolm, swear loyalty to the realm as well as swear to protect the realm and the queen by any measures necessary?"

"I so swear."

"As King of the Otherworld, do you swear to act with honor and duty above all else?"

"I so swear."

"As High Druid of this realm, I proclaim you King and Ruler of the Otherworld. Rise, King Derron."

He rose and the High Druid passed the sword to him.

"As King of the Otherworld, I bequeath the Sword of Justice to you as a symbol of your position and your duty."

Derron took the sword by the hilt.

"Queen Elyne, King Derron. By accepting these gifts you are accepting your titles as rulers of the Otherworld. Do you swear allegiance to the crown, the realm and to each other as you rule together?"

"We so swear," they said together.

The squires carrying the crowns stepped next to the High Druid. He picked up a delicate gold crown encrusted with fine jewels. Elyne bent and he placed it on her head. The second crown was larger, a little more ornate and definitely kingly. He placed it on Derron's head. Then he waved toward two more squires who brought forth the royal cloaks. Fur lined the inside as well as trimmed the edges. They slipped them over Elyne's and Derron's shoulders.

"The crowning is now complete. Queen Elyne. King Derron. Ascend your thrones and face the people of your realm."

The High Druid stepped aside. Elyne took Derron's hand and together they stepped to their thrones. They sat for the first time as king and queen. Cheers erupted in the room as everyone clapped for the two. Elyne was all smiles. Derron looked more serious than ever.

As the cheering died down, Elyne addressed them for the first time as queen. "Today is a momentous day and one we shall not soon forget. Today we rejoice, we honor each other and we begin a new era. Let us not waste another minute. Let the tournament begin!"

Another round of cheers and the two monarchs rose and watched as the Fae left the throne room for the lists. Maggie and Finn, however, made their way toward them to offer their personal congratulations. Not to be left behind, Drake followed.

Maggie hugged Elyne. "I'm so happy for you both."

"As am I," Finn added. "'Tis a new era for yere people indeed."

"I'm glad you could both stay," Elyne said. She practically beamed.

"Aye, but the lass is feeling poorly," Finn said. "I dinna think we can stay for the tournament."

Maggie did look faint and pale. She leaned on Finn to keep herself upright.

"I understand, of course. Though I will miss you terribly," Elyne said. "Will I be sending you back to Finn's time?"

Drake recalled Maggie had come from the future and was a modern woman. She'd met Finn in the 1300s—Drake's own time as well. Despite that being his true home, he was at ease in the Otherworld. Almost as though it were a second home to him.

"Yes, please," Maggie said with a nod. "That's where I belong. My father wants me to be with Finn there."

Elyne glanced at Drake. "And you, Sir Drake? Will I be sifting you home as well or will you be able to stay and go to King Urdithane as we discussed?"

"I'm happy to stay and visit the king for you, your majesty." He gave her a bow of respect.

She smiled approval. "Very well then. Derron, I'll sift them home. You and Drake should go on. I won't be a minute." She kissed him on the cheek.

"Aye, then. Drake and I will head to the lists," Derron said. "I'll inform the list marshal Sir Finn is unable to participate. I'll take his place instead."

"Do you think that's wise, husband?" Elyne asked.

"I'm sure Sir Drake will go easy on the new King of the Otherworld." He patted the English knight on the back. "Won't you?"

"Aye, your majesty. I will."

"I may be a bit rusty at the joust but I'm rather looking forward to getting back to the lance."

"Do be careful," Elyne said.

"As you wish, my queen." Derron bowed to his wife.

"Are you sure it's wise to participate, your majesty?" Drake asked as they left the throne room.

"Most likely no," Derron answered. "But I wouldn't pass up the chance for anything." And he grinned, well pleased with the thought of jousting once again.

Drake had to concur. It had been a while since he'd sat his horse with lance in hand. He too looked forward to it. He wished Princess Allanna could be a part of it as well.

Later that evening, Drake was at banquet with a tankard of ale in hand. The buffet spread over several tables with piles of fruit, cheese, bread, tarts and pies. The roasted meats included everything from boar to fish to fowl. Wine and ale flowed freely and there was nothing short of gaiety in the great hall. The many Fae and Elves assembled feasted until they could no longer feast. And then danced until they could no longer dance. The musicians would be playing long into the night.

He'd jousted most of the afternoon and come out the winner, besting the new Fae king. Derron had taken the defeat with grace, though, as he proclaimed Drake victorious. For his win, he received golden armor—Fae armor made from the hardest steel he'd ever seen—a horse, as well as several pouches of gold. If he chose, he could return to the human realm a very rich knight.

He wasn't interested in returning to the human realm. All he could think about was riding to the Elven king's home in the Woodlands. Where his princess waited. They hadn't even been able to see each other before parting.

But she'd turned to look at him as she rode away. She'd met his gaze with a look full of longing.

He wanted to seek out Queen Elyne and ask her when she would have the letter to the king ready. But he didn't want to bother her in such a time of celebration. He'd watched as she greeted each and every one of her nobles, as they had taken her hand, fallen to a knee and kissed her knuckles. And all the while her king stood by her side, his hand on the Sword of Justice.

Weary from the day and from waiting, Drake rose. He would retire and find the queen in the morn. As he made his way through the great hall, Elyne caught sight of him and excused herself. She weaved through the crowd—which wasn't all that difficult since her subjects quickly moved out of her way—and intercepted him.

"Sir Drake, a word with you, if I may."

She hooked her arm in his and led him from the noisy banquet into the relative peace of the hallways.

"I know you've been waiting for me to give you the letter to the king as well as my token of appreciation," she said. "Come with me now to my private chamber and I'll write the letter and send you on your way."

"Thank you, your majesty. But the day is long. I'm sure you do not wish to leave your celebration so early."

"Nonsense. This is much more important. You need to get to your lady love, aye?"

"Well…aye. But I'm not so certain it will do any good. Her father doesn't care for me."

"Aye, I know. And you and I have discussed this numerous times. Have faith, Sir Drake. I do."

Once in her chamber, she waved him to a chair. She sat behind her desk, grabbed a quill and dipped the tip in ink. She scrawled on a parchment paper, her pen scratching along the surface for what seemed like an eternity in the silence. When she at last finished, she folded it, poured hot wax on the seal and stamped it with her royal crest. She placed the letter in a leather pouch.

She rose from the chair, tapping her finger on her chin and looking deep in thought. Drake waited patiently as she clutched the leather pouch in one hand. Then her face lit up with an idea.

"Wait here, Sir Drake. I'll be right back."

She dashed from the room, leaving him alone. He shifted in his chair and counted the seconds in his head. A moment later she returned with something clutched in her free hand, the leather pouch still in the other. She extended her fist.

"Open your hand."

She dropped a large sapphire stone cut in the shape of a square into his palm. It was huge—the same size as his fist.

"A token of thanks for the king," she said. "A sapphire from the Fae mines. And here is the letter."

"Your majesty…it's amazing."

"I know I can trust you to deliver it to the king, Sir Drake," she said.

"Aye, you can."

"Lord Navin will try to bar your way. Tell him you must deliver the sapphire and the letter to the king personally. Insist upon it."

"Are you certain I will be able to get by Lord Navin?"

"You *must* insist. If I could send word ahead of time I would but I don't think it would reach the gates before you. I intend to give you my fastest horse."

"You honor me, your majesty."

"It is the least I can do after all you have done for us. There is one more thing."

She returned to her desk and opened a top drawer. She pulled out something wrapped in a fine linen and came around the desk. She extended it to him.

"Please give this to your lady," she said.

"What is it?"

"A fire pendant. It was my mother's."

"Oh no, your majesty, I couldn't—"

"I insist."

"But…wouldn't you want that for your daughter?" he asked.

"My father gave it to my mother long ago. When they were betrothed. I want you to have it."

He stared at the folded linen in her outstretched hands. Stunned. "But…why?"

"Because this is a symbol of love and purity. I have plenty of other jewels that belonged to my mother but I want you to have this. For your princess. She is a lovely girl. And mayhap it will help you win the king's favor."

He placed the sapphire inside the leather pouch with the letter then rested it on his knees. He took the linen from Elyne and, holding it in one hand, flipped open the cloth. The pendant was breathtaking. A fiery jewel was surrounded by what looked like Celtic knotwork on a golden chain. When he tilted the pendant, candlelight winked off the facets, throwing out what looked like streaks of fire.

"See how it catches the light?" she asked, sounding delighted. "I don't know how my father came to have it, but it came from the land of the Fire Elves. It is said it was forged from the lava of the volcanoes in the Hin'dar Rhule. That's where the Fire Elves live. King Urdithane will recognize its worth."

"Is that why you want me to have it?"

"Aye. That and it belongs with the Elves, not me. All it will do here is collect dust and has for the last few thousand years. If you give the princess an Elven jewel…well…the king's certain to allow you to court her, if not marry her." She smiled, pleased with herself.

"Thank you, your majesty."

"Please call me Elyne. We have, after all, fought side by side more than once."

"Elyne, then." Yet he bowed out of propriety.

"Now, go to your princess, Sir Drake. And I wish you both the best of luck."

He covered the pendant and clutched it against his chest. "I don't know how I can ever thank you."

"You can thank me by inviting me to the wedding." She gave him a hopeful grin that all would work out between him and Allanna.

"I do hope you're right in that," Drake said. "But even that is not payment enough for this." He held up the linen.

"You are a noble knight, Sir Drake. Knowing you're in my realm to protect my people and Allanna's is enough. I promise. One last thing. Elven magic hides the gate. Even a Fae cannot see it without being in the presence of an Elf."

"Then how do I see it?" he asked, perplexed.

"My advice is to see with your heart. Your love will be waiting for you on the other side. Even magic cannot hold up against true love." She placed her hands on his shoulders, then kissed each cheek. "I believe it's customary to say 'Godspeed' in your human realm. Is it not?"

"It is," he said.

"Aye, then. Godspeed, Sir Drake. Go to your princess and profess your love to her."

Clutching the items Elyne had given him, Drake strode from the queen's chamber toward the stables. He would not wait until morning to leave. Nay. He would leave tonight.

Chapter 2

Princess Allanna could not stop the well of tears behind her eyes, much as she tried. She blinked furiously to keep them at bay but still they came. One warm tear slid down her cheek as they left the Queen's Palace. As the distance expanded between her and Drake, she couldn't help but glance over her shoulder to see him standing with Princess Elyne, watching them leave.

He stood rigid, one hand clenched at this side and one on the hilt of his sword. As though he might brandish it and run after her, demanding she stay. Demanding she never leave his side. A slight breeze ruffled his dark hair. His gaze of longing would forever linger with her.

And her heart ached.

Nay. Her heart broke. Sliced in half as the one man she'd ever loved was lost to her. She would never see him again and the thought was like an Elven dagger through her heart. Shredding the tender organ. Making her bleed. Leaving an ache deep in her chest. An ache, she knew, would not be assuaged by anyone other than her knight.

She tried to talk her father into staying for the coronation and subsequent festivities—hoping to get one last dance with Sir Drake—but he had refused. And she knew it was because he wanted to get her as far from Sir Drake as possible. He did not approve of him because he was human. Though he hadn't spoken the words to her, she knew. She could tell by the way he glared at Drake and by the scorching glower he gave her as they rode away.

She faced forward again, trying to stop more unshed tears from falling. To no avail.

"'Tis best to find other interests, daughter," Urdithane warned, his tone hard.

By other interests she knew he meant someone who was not Sir Drake. Someone who would be a more suitable match. But there wasn't anyone else in the Otherworld she wanted. There was no other Elven warrior, noble or ranger she wanted to give her heart.

She stared at the landscape ahead, the rolling hills, the pink sky. The days she'd spent with the Fae and their human friends had been some of the best days of her life. Even though her brother Eldrin wanted her to return to the Woodlands where it would be safe, she had refused.

She'd been born a princess but had wanted to be a ranger like him. She had countless skinned knees from climbing trees. She could shoot a bow and arrow better than most of the rangers, thanks to Lord Derron's tips. She helped fight against Lord Kieran's attack at the Stone of Destiny. And she'd lost her heart to the human knight.

She would gladly give up her wild ways, her skinned knees, her bow and arrow for him. She'd trade it all for gowns and banquets and stolen kisses. Not that he had ever stolen a kiss. He'd been nothing but the most proper gentleman every time they were together. Every time they danced. There were never any unsupervised walks in the moonlight. All they had ever done together was dance. And talk. And dance some more. And exchange long, adoring looks.

The feel of his hands in hers…his hands on her waist…the closeness of his body next to hers would forever be burned into her memory.

She did not want to return to the Woodlands but she had no choice. Her father would have no more excuses or delays.

Even though she'd been somewhat of a rebel, she knew not to push her father too far. For if she did he would never speak to her again. He would banish her from court, from her life, from her family. She could not live without contact with her brothers, especially Eldrin. Everyone knew he was her favorite sibling.

She whisked away the tears. Mayhap she would find a way to see Sir Drake again. Somehow.

"Am I not allowed to choose, Father?" She couldn't help the barb.

Anger flashed over his face before he regained his composure. "Of course you are. But it will not be him. I won't allow it. He is *human*. And you are Elven royalty. My only daughter. You are free to choose someone else."

Despite his assurance she could choose another, she knew that was not to be. There were far too many other royals to whom she could be betrothed and most likely would be once her father found a suitable match. It would be his way of removing Drake from her once and for all.

But Allanna would always love him. And her father could not take that away from her. Her father could never kill those feelings inside her and she would hang on to them until she gasped her last breath or the end of the Otherworld, whichever came first.

"You mean someone else of *your* choosing, don't you?" The acid words slipped from her before she could stop them.

"Mind your tongue," he warned.

She wanted to continue to retort but knew it was wiser to remain silent. Her father had never raised a hand to her but on this subject, one he was most passionate about, she feared he might.

The rest of the journey was in relative silence. They were able to make it back to the gates of the Woodlands by nightfall where her brother and gatekeeper Lord Navin opened the gates for them.

As a Wood Elf and part of the nobility, she lived high in the trees. Other Wood Elves lived along the ground, taking care of the horses and other animals, as well as harvesting their fruits and vegetables. Eldrin assisted her from her mount and she relinquished the mare to the stable boy. He had been injured in the battle against Morrigan but showed no signs of it. She suspected he still carried some pain but hid it well.

They entered the wide trunk of the Elven oak tree, where a winding staircase carved into the wood led them up to their royal domain. Allanna kept her gaze lowered as she followed her father and her brother, Prince Andahar. Eldrin walked next to her and though she sensed he wanted to speak to her, he remained silent.

There had to be some way to leave the Woodlands and get back to Drake. She knew she shouldn't run away. Her father would never forgive her. But how else would she see Drake again? She must have one last moment with him, one last day to say goodbye once and for all and try to put him out of her mind.

Aye, she would plan her escape carefully. She knew all the ways out of the kingdom without being detected. She had slipped out of the gates on numerous occasions without her brothers or her father knowing. When Lord Kieran had threatened their lives, she had snuck out to join her brother in the fight against his darkness.

She could do this. A small smile lifted the corners of her mouth.

"What are you smiling about?" Eldrin whispered.

Caught. She immediately stopped smiling and gave him a sideways glance. "Nothing, Eldrin."

"It's not nothing. You're up to something."

"No, I'm not."

His hand wrapped around her upper arm and he leaned in as they continued ascending. "Whatever you're concocting, forget it. Father will be watching you like a dragon watches his treasure."

Her head swiveled in his direction. "What makes you think I'm concocting something?"

"Because I know you. You didn't get your way with Father, so you're going to do something foolish."

"Eldrin—"

"It's not worth it, *nethielle*."

Nethielle. The Elvish word for *little sister*. He often called her that when he wanted to get her attention. He had it. But what he didn't understand was it *was* worth it. *He* was. Everything about Drake was worth it. Worth the risk. Worth her heart. Worth her life. "But I love him, El," she whispered.

He clenched his jaw tight and she could see the muscles working there. "I know you do."

Then what was she to do? Eldrin was right though—her father would be watching her closely. He would know if she was up to something. Such as slipping out of the Woodlands to find Drake. If her father were truly savvy—and she knew he was—he would post extra guards at all the gates. So she would wait until he stopped watching her. Until he was sure she would do as he bid her. Until she was certain she could slip away. Her fear was Drake would have returned to the human realm.

They arrived at the top of the giant sequoia where their home was built around the trees. She continued to be the good daughter and follow the procession to the palace where the bridge ended in front of two giant wood doors in the shape of an arch. Guards in full dress flanked the doors, each one with a quiver on his back, a bow in one hand and a sword strapped to his belt.

The guards opened the doors for them and they proceeded inside. The polished wood floors, the smooth wood walls and smell of the earth, damp leaves, freshly cut grass and sunshine were the comforting smells of home. She'd forgotten how she missed it. The entrance to the great hall was lit by numerous white-flamed torches in iron brackets that lined the walls and columns.

Once her father and Andahar were greeted by the royal advisors, they whisked them off to the council chamber to update the king on the state of the kingdom while he was away. Her father still had a slight limp due to that injury he'd sustained in the battle with the Goddess of War. She could tell he still had some pain.

As they disappeared out of sight, she walked back out to the rope bridge. The view from up here was breathtaking. And despite her sadness at leaving Drake behind, being here and smelling the scents of home made her feel at ease. She gripped the rope handhold, gazing out across the kingdom of treetops where the Elven nobility went about their business. She wondered what to do next. Eldrin joined her, standing beside her.

"What am I going to do?"

"You should forget him," Eldrin said. "There is nothing to be done about him now. We're home. The Treaty of Separation has been broken. We are facing a new era, Allanna. Do you understand that? Father will not allow you to be distracted by a human. Warrior or not. It doesn't matter to him."

"Father doesn't like humans, El," she said. "You and I both know that is the true reason."

"That's not it. You know what will happen to you if you leave the Woodlands for him."

She gripped the rope tighter, the coarse fibers biting into her skin. She knew all too well what would happen. Her father would abandon her. She would be disowned. Outcast from her own family. They would not be allowed to speak to her and she would not be allowed to speak to them.

Eldrin placed a hand on her shoulder. "Do you want that?"

Did she? In her heart, she knew she loved Drake. She would always love him. But her duty and her life was here in the Woodlands with her brothers and her father. She was the only princess. Her father's only daughter. If she went through with it, she would break his heart. He would never forgive her. He would never accept her back into the kingdom.

"No," she whispered. "I don't."

"As I said, it's best you forget him."

Knowing her brother was right, she nodded. She started down the rope bridge.

"Where are you going?" Eldrin called.

She paused, looked at him over her shoulder. "To my chamber." To sulk. To nurse her broken heart. And to weep.

"Why don't you meet me in the grove on the morrow? We could practice shooting."

By shooting she knew he meant arrows. She'd not held a bow and arrow in her hands in a while. She'd been trying to be the proper lady for Drake. Now that her dream of loving him was over, she could be herself again.

"I'd like that."

It'd been a while since she had that to look forward to. She could hit a bull's eye as well if not better than Eldrin. She looked forward to trying to best him again.

Allanna had decided to emulate Eldrin to become a ranger, even though she knew it was never possible. She'd shocked the nobility by wearing trousers and carrying a quiver of arrows. She wanted to do everything her big brother did. She followed him everywhere as his constant shadow. And she was scolded by her mother for not acting like a lady.

When her mother died, her father allowed her to continue her wild ways without intervening. Her brother had taught her how to use a bow and arrow and a dagger. How to hunt. How to protect herself. She was an explorer. A hunter. A fighter. But she was willing to give up all that.

When she'd met Lord Derron for the first time, she had begged lessons from him, even though she already knew how to fire a bow and arrow. She admitted now she had a girlish crush on the man. He was quite dashing. But then she met Drake and everything changed. He had captured her heart.

She entered the palace to a bustle of activity. The Elven people were happy they had returned from the Fae court at last. And the servants prepared a welcome-home feast in their honor. She knew her father would insist she be there. She passed through the halls to her chamber.

She had missed her room—a spacious room with a balcony overlooking their kingdom. She had one of the best views in the palace. Her four-poster bed had fresh linens, her balcony doors opened to let in the cool evening air.

"Your highness, welcome home." Her lady-in-waiting, Igraen, greeted her with a deep curtsey. "We have missed you."

"It's good to be home," she said, though she wasn't sure she meant it.

In some ways, she was happy to be here but in others, she wasn't. Her heart still longed for the English knight.

"You look tired, my lady. Shall I prepare a bath for you and then help you dress for dinner?"

"No bath, Igraen. Mayhap on the morrow."

"As you wish. I've laid out a fresh gown for you."

"Thank you. I can manage on my own. I'll send for you when I need you."

With a nod, the girl left. Silence descended and she stood in the middle of her room, hearing nothing more than her own ragged breathing as she tried to control her emotions. She stepped toward the balcony, inhaling the crisp air.

She needed to be alone to collect her thoughts. She closed her eyes, listening to the breeze rustle the leaves high in the trees. It helped calm her emotions.

As she stood there, listening to the night sounds, the vision burst through her mind's eye. So vibrant and vivid. She saw her own wedding as she stood in a gown of pale blue, a veil draped over her head cascading to the floor behind her. She gazed toward the two giant wood doors at the exit of the palace, waiting. Her heart in her throat.

And then they opened, the light slanting through the doors. The man—her groom—stepped through, but the light blotted out his features.

The doors closed and then she could see him. She could make out his face. And her heart skipped a beat. Her breath caught. Sir Drake walked toward her, dressed in a polished golden breastplate. His sword was strapped to his waist, swinging with every step. He wore black padded pants tucked neatly into shiny black boots. He hadn't shaved and still wore the beard. His dark hair hadn't been trimmed and the tips brushed his wide shoulders.

He was handsome and breathtaking.

And he was hers.

Allanna's eyes flew open and she gazed out into the darkness.

She often had visions as she had the gift of foresight. They often came true. Or sometimes they showed her what the future could be. The wedding with Drake was the future she wanted. Mayhap her emotions were running so high that her mind conjured this vision. Or was it true? How would she gain approval from her father to marry Sir Drake?

A brisk knock on the door interrupted her thoughts. Before she could grant entry, it opened and Andahar entered.

"Allanna, Father sent me to fetch you. Why haven't you changed your dress?"

"I'm not going, Andahar."

"You are going. Father will be unhappy. The High Nobles will be there."

"I don't care about the High Nobles. Tell Father I'm ill or something. I don't care what you tell him."

"I will not. Change and let's go. Father will be displeased to see you still dressed in your riding gown. Where is your chambermaid?"

"Andahar...please. Don't make me go. I don't want to. I'm tired." She scrubbed her hands down her face.

He took her by the arm. "Don't make me drag you there."

She met his stern gaze and knew he meant business. She wasn't getting out of this. She knew it. She had to go and Andahar was right. Father would be very displeased with her. She wished Eldrin had been the one to bring her. She could talk him into fibbing for her. He'd tell their father she wasn't well.

"Fine then. Give me a moment to change my gown."

"I will wait outside."

He closed the door with a snap. Allanna heaved a sigh. She hated formal events.

Allanna was right. The formal feast was long and boring. Her father caught her mid-yawn once and gave her a steely glare. She straightened in her chair, her hands in her lap. Politics didn't interest her and she tired of listening to her father, Andahar and the other High Nobles drone on and on and on about the state of the Elven domain. Who cared? She had more important things to think about.

Like Sir Drake.

Sir Drake with his piercing blue eyes. Eyes that seemed to look into her soul, reaching down deep into her and igniting a sensual flame that burned as bright as his gaze. Gooseflesh broke out on her arms thinking about him. Thinking about kissing him. Touching her lips to his. What would it feel like? Her fingertips brushed over her lips then as she dreamed about kissing him.

And then her father caught sight of her and glared. Again. She dropped her hand back into her lap.

Allanna knew she should not be thinking such things at an important function such as this. But she couldn't help it. Her father hadn't even allowed her to tell him goodbye. What had Sir Drake thought when he saw her riding away? Did he think she no longer cared for him? Certainly not if that longing look he gave her was to be any indication.

"Princess Allanna."

Her father's sharp voice broke into her thoughts and made her jump. "Aye, Father?"

"You clearly have no interest in our discussion, as evidenced by the way you're daydreaming. You may be excused."

"Thank you, Father."

She didn't miss the look of disapproval he gave her as she rose from the table and practically skipped from the room. All eyes had been on her. Even her brother's. The only person who really understood her feelings was Eldrin. He would be with the other rangers now. How lucky for him he didn't have to be bored to death with political matters as the youngest son and third in line for the throne. She envied his freedom. Curses of being the only girl.

Clutching her gown in her fists, she made her way down the winding tree staircase. She thought to look for him at Ranger Hall, but instead found him in the grove with the others around a bright campfire drinking ale and telling war stories. They all quieted when they saw her approach.

"Allanna, what are you doing here?" Eldrin rose to greet her. "I thought you were at the feast."

"Politics is so boring," she said. "Can't I stay here with you?"

"Begging your pardon, your highness, but this is no place for a lady," Firdaras, one of Eldrin's rangers, said. "A lady who happens to be the princess."

"Firdaras is correct," Eldrin said. "Let me take you back to your chamber."

"No." She frowned. "I don't want to go back up there. In fact, I don't want to shoot arrows with you either." She folded her arms over her chest.

His eyebrows shot straight up. "You don't?"

She shook her head.

Eldrin narrowed his eyes. He knew her well enough to know something was amiss. "Gentlemen, if you'll excuse me? Come, Allanna, let's walk."

She hooked her arm in his, triumphant she managed to garner her brother's attention. They walked from the others. Night sounds were all around. She could hear the faint song of the shadow-bird—a black bird that spent its nights hunting and singing. Fire pixies flitted through the air, blinking with flashes of bright yellow light. Eldrin led her to the loch not far from their campfire.

"Now what's this all about, *nethielle*?"

"Nothing. I…I'm not ready to go back up there, El."

"Something is bothering you. I can always tell. You can't hide it from me."

"How can you tell?" she asked.

"You always find me when something's bothering you. Otherwise, I never see a hair on your head."

Curse her brother for knowing her so well. She squatted at the water's edge, picking up a loose stone. It was smooth on both sides. As she rose, she flicked her wrist and skipped the rock across the glassy surface. Moonlight flickered in waves of the surface she'd disturbed.

"Did you have a vision?" he asked.

Her heart sped up. "Aye," she said, the word icy against her lips. "I had a vision."

"Would you like to tell me about it?"

Eldrin was the one person who encouraged her to talk about her visions. Oh, her father knew she had the gift of foresight. She'd used it before the battle for the Otherworld. She'd seen the deaths of Queen Maeve and Princess Elyne. Deaths they ultimately managed to cheat. All because she'd been able to give them enough information to keep them alive.

A fire pixy fluttered by. Cattails swayed above the surface in the breeze. A mournful wail emitted from the hollow loch reeds. Matching her mood and her aching heart.

"Allanna?"

"It was about Drake." She pressed her cold fingertips to her lips, the words whispering over her skin. As though saying it louder would conjure her father's ire.

Eldrin moved to stand beside her but he didn't look at her. He kept his gaze on the dark water glistening under the moon.

"What did you see?"

"Our wedding."

For an instant, she thought he stopped breathing. A long moment passed where all she could hear was the thrum of her heart, her own jagged breathing and the night noises. Then he said, very quietly, "Oh, *nethielle*."

"What am I to do, El? I have seen the future."

"Are you certain it is your future?" he asked. "And not some fanciful longing you conjured?"

No, she wasn't sure. But she didn't want him to know that. She wanted to believe it was her future. Her life. She wanted to believe she would someday marry the man she loved. Aye, she wanted it to come to pass but she also knew the difference between a daydream and a vision. Her visions were clear and always flickered quickly through her mind's eye. The one she'd had of her wedding was no different.

"No, El, it was my future. I know it as sure as I know my heart beats for no other."

"You cannot tell Father," Eldrin said.

She turned to him, forced him to look at her. "Why not?"

"Because he will never believe it is your future. You know this."

She shook her head. "It cannot be denied. It is proof Drake and I are meant to be together."

"It is not proof of anything. Only that you had a vision. The deaths of Maeve and Elyne did not come to pass as you foresaw."

"No, but I *did* see the battle. They made different choices and were able to alter the future. Save their own lives. This is different, Eldrin. This is *my* future. Those visions have never been wrong."

He glanced back to the loch, his eyes shadowed. She couldn't see his face clearly in the darkness so she couldn't read his expression. Did he think she was mad?

"I have to go to him," she whispered.

"No, you can't. I won't allow it." He turned back to her, took her by the shoulders and gave her a gentle shake. "I know you've slipped out of the Woodlands before and were locked out of the gates but things are different now."

"Different how? We are no longer at war."

"But there are still Unseelie who wander the realm. Those who would harm you. You *are* a princess, Allanna. Never forget that. Your head is worth much to Father and there are those who know that and would exploit it," he said. "Please don't do anything as rash as running away."

She blinked. How did he know? How could he read her so plainly? "But—"

"No. I forbid it."

"Are you planning to stop me then?" She put her fists on her hips, looking at him down her nose. A look Elyne had perfected and she mimicked. It always seemed to get the Fae princess what she wanted.

Eldrin's gaze narrowed at her. "Don't try that with me, dearie. I know where you got that."

She huffed out a breath, then picked up another stone and skipped it across the still water, leaving behind ripples. "Then what do you propose I do?"

"I propose you do nothing. Sir Drake is surely back to his realm by now."

"No. I don't believe that. He's still here. In the Otherworld. He must still be here."

"How can you know that? We left him at the Queen's Palace where Queen Elyne returned all the humans to their realm."

She kept her gaze on the rippling water. Something told her Drake would not have left the Otherworld. Not while she still lived and breathed. Not while there was a chance he could still find her, come to her. She imagined he would climb the trees to her balcony. He would take her in his arms and pledge his love to her forever. Together they would leave the same way he came—out her balcony. She would ride with him on his mare out of the gates of the Woodlands. *Forever.*

"Allanna?" Eldrin's voice broke the spell.

"I just know," she said.

Since leaving the Queen's Palace, she was certain his presence still lingered in the Otherworld. Mayhap that was wishful thinking.

"He will come for me," she said.

"Allanna." Eldrin said her name on a groan. "What will it take to make you forget this whimsical idea that you and the human will marry?"

"Nothing!" She clenched her fists at her sides. "Father and Andahar both told me I'm nothing but a silly girl and I should forget this 'fanciful' infatuation with the human. And now you, Eldrin? I expected more from you. I expected you to support me. To *help* me."

"How am I to help you, Allanna? I cannot bring the man here."

"Why not?" she whined.

"You know why. Navin guards the gates of the Woodlands. He will never allow a man like Sir Drake through. Even if he does come, Father will turn him away. His kind is not allowed here."

"The Fae had no problem with 'his kind', El. Why should the Elves pass judgment on the humans? I find that to be highly prejudiced."

"We are *not* the Fae." Though his voice was calm, she could see the ire rising in his face. The tips of his ears turned pink. "We are Elves." He straightened, holding his head high.

"Does that make us better than the Fae? The humans? We are no better. We are equal."

"We are *not* equal, Allanna. The Elves have lived in the Otherworld far longer than the Fae."

"And yet they rule the Otherworld." She didn't bother to hide the annoyance in her voice. "The High Queen of the Otherworld. Isn't that her true title?"

"That is an ancient title no longer used. You know that I. The Elves have our own kingdoms to tend. We do not need—"

"I am not a stupid girl, Eldrin. I know the way of things. I know Queen Maeve and my father warred against each other once. I know the Dark Elf Kieran slaughtered King Adhamh. I know of the Beforetime. The Dark Days. The Blackest Hour. Whatever you wish to call it. Our history is not so rosy, brother."

All those years of tutoring suddenly paid off as she fired back their sordid history. The Elves had once ruled most of the Otherworld. The Fae had their own domain until the death of King Adhamh when Maeve marched on the Otherworld, blaming the Elves for his murder.

Now the Otherworld was split into kingdoms, Seelie and Unseelie. Of the Seelie realm, the Elven fire king held his own kingdom in the volcanoes in the Hin'dar Rhule. Urdithane held the Woodlands for thousands of years. The Skye Elves ruled their realm in the clouds, though they rarely were seen by anyone else.

They tended to keep to themselves. Legend spoke of their ethereal beauty and they rode the moon dragons from the skies. Their strength and power were legend. It was said one Skye Elf equaled the might and muscle of ten Woodland Elves.

Eldrin pressed his lips together in a thin line. "I never said you were a stupid girl." He stepped toward her, put his hand on her arm. "Give up Sir Drake, Allanna."

"Or what?" she challenged.

"Or nothing. I implore you. Give him up. The sooner you do the sooner you can move on."

"You don't understand what it's like."

He gripped her arm and fire flashed in his eyes, something she had never seen in their long years. He actually looked angry. "I understand better than you can ever imagine."

Eldrin released her and left her by the loch. She had no idea what that meant nor could she guess and he didn't stick around to explain. She watched him walk back to his group of rangers and envied him once again. He was a man. A ranger. A warrior. He had the freedom of choice and could pick whom he wanted to love.

Could she? Nay. She was a princess. And she knew as much as she hated the thought there would come a day when her father would choose her husband. Even though he had said she was free to choose she knew different. She knew he would make a match for her and she would be forced to marry a man she did not love.

She would not allow that to happen to her. As long as she had breath in her, she would never allow that to happen. She would rather die than marry a man she did not love. A man who did not love her back.

Eldrin may have urged her not to run away, to give up her *fanciful* thoughts of Sir Drake but she would not. She would never do that.

On the morrow she would begin her plans of escape.

Chapter 3

Lord-Regent Marath already knew the Fomorian mage had arrived at his home in the Woodlands even before his servant, Aesir, announced him. He had invoked dark magic to release him from the watery prison in the Sorrow Lands and summon him to his castle. Marath believed the mage and his people would be the ones to help him on his quest to destroy the Fae once and for all.

"My lord, your guest has arrived."

The Fae had long been the bane of his existence. He harbored hate for them for as long as he could remember—since his mother had been taken from him and his father had chosen to cast him out. Aye. His hatred had been a part of him for many years. And he would at long last have his vengeance. Now was the perfect time to strike with the Treaty gone and the alliance between Fae and Elf still in its infancy. He would show his king they were still the enemy.

Even now he could feel the effects of his actions. The dark magic had taken hold inside him, rooted there and started to grow and spread. Like a sickness. He could sense the change within him. Had the cost been worth it? That was yet to be seen but he believed the mage would be able to accomplish what he wished or he would not have taken such risks.

He had watched the mage, Lorcann, approach his home following the route he had instructed him to use to avoid alerting the gatekeeper to his arrival. Lorcann made his way on foot alone. Marath steepled his fingers, well pleased. Mayhap the mage would be of use since he was able to follow his directions.

"I will receive him in my library, Aesir. Show him the way. And bring refreshments. I'm sure he is fatigued after his long journey."

"By your command, my lord."

His servant bowed before leaving Marath's private chamber. He waited a few moments before walking the short hallway to his library. It rivaled that of the king's. His bookshelves were made of solid oak and lined every wall from floor to ceiling. Well, every wall save for the east where windows displayed the breathtaking view of his home in the westernmost part of Urdithane's realm. He was but a day's ride from the palace.

Marath was liege lord to this part of the realm. When he received news of the broken Treaty of Separation, he was most displeased. How could that fool Urdithane agree to such a thing? The Fae were vile, nasty creatures. They could not be trusted. He knew Queen Maeve had stepped down and relinquished her rule to her daughter Elyne. He also knew she was but a girl. He intended to exploit her weaknesses.

He would never forgive them for what they had done to him. How they had ruined his family. It had taken years to build his name and wealth once again. Years he had spent in Urdithane's court leveraging his strengths, using his powers of persuasion. He would not allow the Fae to ruin the Elves again.

"Lorcann, my lord," Aesir announced from the doorway.

"Do come in, my good man." Marath waved him inside as Aesir closed the doors behind him.

The mage was an ugly fellow and looked far from mage-ish. His small sea-green eyes were too close together. He had jagged, yellowed teeth. His nostrils flared from a wide, flat nose. He hadn't much hair either. Thin on top showing his shiny pate through the strands. He looked tired and haggard, having traveled across the Otherworld from his deep ocean prison on foot. Marath poured two tawny ports in small, clear glasses and handed one to him.

"Welcome to the Woodlands."

Lorcann took the glass and gulped down the port in one swig. Once empty, he tossed it to the floor. It bounced on the carpet and rolled toward Marath, halting at the toe of his boot. The action sent his pulse racing and the anger to shoot through his veins. How dare he? Clearly the man did not know a fine vintage when he smelled or tasted one. But then, he wasn't truly a man, was he? More like a barbarian.

"Thank you for coming, my lord," Marath said.

Lorcann grunted an incoherent response and prowled the room. He ran long, pale fingers with sharp, pointy nails over the spines of his ancient tomes making Marath cringe. It was worse than a chair scraping across the aged wood floor.

"Please do not touch the books," Marath said. "Come, let me get you another drink and then we can discuss our alliance."

Lorcann gave him a heated glare over his shoulder and went back to prowling the room. His grimy hands touched everything. Books, statues, idols. He was nothing more than a primitive idiot. But the real insult came when the mage pushed a book off the shelf with his fingertip. The ancient tome fell to the floor with a *thwack*. And since it was so old, the covers disintegrated into pieces.

Enraged now, Marath stalked to Lorcann and shoved him away from the books.

"I will not ask again," he said.

They stared each other down, mage against Elf. An Elf who had embraced dark magic, turning him from light into a Dark Elf much like Lord Kieran had not so long ago. It had been Kieran's undoing but it would not be Marath's.

Marath looked deep into the eyes of the mage, the watery gaze that reminded him of the deep sea from which he'd come. Lorcann reached for him. Marath clamped his hand around his wrist, held him in place.

The mage's eyes narrowed and then his fingers curled into a fist and he wrenched his wrist free and dropped his arm.

Aesir opened the doors and two servant girls wheeled in a cart full of sweetmeats, pies, tarts and cakes. When the mage saw them he hurried over. He shoved one of the girls out of the way. She squealed and stumbled, falling to the floor, while Lorcann attacked the cakes with relish. Crumbs fell to the garnet rug. Icing oozed between his fingers and smeared his face.

Marath walked over and helped the girl to her feet. "Are you all right, my dear?"

She nodded though she didn't try to hide her fear as she glanced at the stranger. He patted her shoulder, trying to reassure her. Then he placed himself between her and the mage.

"That will be all, Aesir," Marath said, his lips pursed. His gaze never left the barbarian of a man.

The girls scurried out of the room. Aesir gave the mage one last look of disgust before closing the doors and leaving them alone.

Marath took another sip of port, watching the barbarian shove cake after cake into his mouth, leaving a trail of pale-yellow icing on his cheek.

"I called you here to ask for your help," Marath tried again, though he wasn't certain the mage yet understood him.

Lorcann paused in his feasting to look at him, crumbs and icing smeared over his face giving him a comical appearance. "My help?"

Finally, a response. It was more of a grunt than words. He went back to eating. This time shoving the small pies into his mouth.

"Aye, your help. With the Fae."

That stopped him cold. He stared at Marath, those eyes penetrating right through him. Marath picked up the discarded glass and refilled it.

"Fae?" Lorcann grunted.

"Aye, the Fae. The very ones who imprisoned you and your people." He handed him the glass.

Lorcann snatched it away, quaffed the liquid and again discarded the glass to the floor. This time the delicate glass cracked in a spider web when it landed, destroying one of his finest Elven crystal glasses.

"We have a common enemy," Marath continued. "I believe we can assist each other."

"Explain," he said around a mouthful of sweetmeats. Crumbs spewed. Drool drizzled down his chin.

Marath could see the question in his eyes. Mayhap there was a brain in there somewhere. Beyond the beast. Beyond the ugly.

"You want revenge. And I want something in return. If you agree to help me, I will see that your people are freed from their prison and returned to the Otherworld."

He cocked his head to the side. "How?"

"I intend to travel to speak with King Urdithane about the state of our realm. He has a daughter to which I will propose marriage. Princess Allanna will be betrothed to me."

He shrugged as if to say he didn't care.

"That is where you come in, my friend." Marath selected a pewter tankard from his collection and once again refilled it. He handed it to Lorcann "You will kidnap the fair princess from the palace. Once she's gone, I will make sure the king knows the Fae are responsible for her kidnapping and ultimately her death."

The beast of a man looked suspicious. "Why?"

"Why does not matter to you. Will you do this?"

Lorcann straightened his crooked shoulders. "What do we get in return should I agree?"

It was the first complete sentence he'd spoken that didn't sound like a grunt or a groan. Hope swelled inside Marath. Indeed the man was finally coming to the surface. Mayhap he needed to be treated as something other than a ghastly thing.

"You and your people will have freedom."

He snorted, a guttural sound that vibrated from his face. "You can give us this?"

"I know the Auld Ways. Lord Kieran was not the only one who had the ability to control the dark."

"Our leader is dead," Lorcann replied. "Lost in the underworld with the Goddess of War."

"I brought you out of your prison, did I not?" And the black magic had taken a toll on his body. Already he had begun to weaken. "You are a mage. Once the most powerful Fomorian mages who walks among us. Surely you can find a way to save your leader? Cormac's body may be gone, but his spirit still roams free."

Marath knew this when he tapped into the darkness trying to reach the Fomorians. He found Cormac's spirit roaming, wandering, searching. Confused. He hadn't understood he was dead. That his body still resided in the underworld. All he understood was the spell over him was broken and he wanted to go home.

Lorcann, though, could save him. He could bring him back. He could rescue his spirit, give it a host, and allow him to live once again. The mage cocked his head to the side, considering.

"It has not been done in thousands of years."

"But it *can* be done," Marath pressed. "I, myself, have seen the spirit of Cormac."

His beady eyes widened slightly before his face scrunched in a suspicious frown, his flat nose wrinkling. "How would you have seen him?"

Marath took a sip of port, letting the amber liquid burn his throat and tongue as he held it in his mouth before swallowing. How much should he tell him? How much should he trust him?

"I, like you, have powers."

"No Elf has powers like that," Lorcann said.

He was right. No Elf did. But because Marath had been driven by his hate and rage over the loss of the Treaty of Separation, he allowed the black power to come into him.

"No, my friend. But I do." He ran his finger around the rim of his cup. "Will you do this for me?"

"I need others."

"Of course," Marath said with a nod.

"And supplies."

"Whatever you need, I will provide."

"You give me your word?"

"By all the power I possess, I give you my word."

"Then your princess will be killed, by your command."

A slow smile spread on Marath's lips. The first step to his plan had been realized.

Lorcann shoved another sweetmeat into his mouth, chewing with his stump teeth and his mouth open. The man was seriously grotesque. But mayhap that would put the fear into the princess. And when word reached the king of her demise, Urdithane would turn to *him* for his help.

As lord-regent of one of the largest realms, he could provide the king with more Elven warriors recruited from the ranks of men to fight against the Fae. Another war, aye. But another war to take back what was rightfully the Elves—the Otherworld.

"Allow me to give you accommodations here," Marath said. "So you may rest."

"Rest, aye. And my men?"

"I will summon them for you. They will be here in the morn."

Marath ushered him out of the library. Aesir stood outside the door, awaiting his next command.

"Aesir, show this gentleman to a room."

"My lord?"

"He requires rest and will be staying with us for a time."

The revulsion was evident on Aesir's face as he led him away.

Marath waited until they were well away before heading to his own chamber. He would call upon the darkness once again. He would need to release more of the Fomorians, much as he expected. He would complete the work Lord Kieran began. He'd found the hidden prison of the Fomorians. He'd used his dark powers with the help of Cormac, a Fomorian mage, to begin his assault on the Dark Court and then Queen Maeve's kingdom. Now he had a chance to continue his work and do away with the Fae once and for all. He would see Kieran's vision to fruition.

He lit several candles and closed the tapestries to shut out the natural light. He slipped on the black cloak lined with red silk. He'd burned the ancient Elven symbol of power into the wood floor, leaving the black marks behind. It was the shape of an encircled triskelion. He knelt in the center of it and closed his eyes, invoking the power he'd so recently discovered.

He could see the watery prison deep under the ocean of the Otherworld. He connected to it, hearing the crash of waves, smelling the salty air, the caw of a sea bird. Here was where the Fae had punished and banished the Fomorians when they battled against them, the Elves and the Fir Bolg.

They had been put in stasis, sea creatures used as manacles on their legs and arms. He focused on the three he wanted to release, picking them out of the group. Gods, the Fomorians were ugly beasts. But mayhap it was due to them being underwater for so long.

Calling upon the darkness, the magic and the power, he released the bonds of the three men. One by one their bonds broke. They floated to the surface, once more alive and gasping for breath as though reborn.

I am your master. Come to me, oh lords, for I have need of you.

They trudged across the wet sand of the shoreline where each man stood. He commanded them to come to him and knew it would be done. He broke the connection with the three Fomorians. As soon as the spell was done, he fell to his hands and knees. Sweat rolled down the side of his face. His stomach cramped. The nausea came next and it took all his strength not to retch on the floor.

He heard his chamber door open.

"My lord, I have—" It was Aesir. He paused, rushed to his side. "My lord, are you well?"

Marath sat back on his heels and mopped his brow with the back of his sleeve.

"My lord, you are pale. You have performed another summoning, haven't you? Let me fetch you some water."

He was up and gone and back again, a tankard of water in his hand. He put it to Marath's lips.

"Sip, my lord."

The cool water splashed against his mouth and throat as he swallowed. He was grateful for Aesir, but he was more than his trusted servant. He was his friend, his confidant. The only one who had stood by him during his time of desperation. He had been with him since the beginning.

"You intend to go through with this? Truly?" His brows pinched together. His mouth drew down into a frown.

"Indeed," he croaked. "I must."

"Are the Fae worth such a toll on your person?" he asked. "You weaken further with every spell you do."

"Aye, I do. And aye it is worth it. The king has no idea how dangerous the Fae are."

Regaining some of this strength, he got to his feet. Aesir took him by the elbow and led him to a chair beside the cold fireplace. As Marath sat, he set about building a fire.

"How is our guest?"

"Resting, as you should be," Aesir said. With the fire going, he stood and turned to him. "Marath, I fear this plan of yours is nothing but folly. The princess—"

"Is nothing but a spoiled child," he said. "Make ready our caravan to the king's palace. I wish to leave straightaway."

"But—"

"As soon as possible, Aesir. We will ride nonstop for I must make haste to visit with the king before anything else happens. I will propose marriage to the princess and then Lorcann and his men will do what I've hired them to do."

"Forgive my ignorance, my lord, but what will killing the princess accomplish?"

"Once I frame the Fae for her death I will convince the king they are not to be trusted. An attack on the princess is an attack on the kingdom and one Urdithane will not let go unanswered."

But there was something more he wanted…needed. A dark shadow whispered in his mind, moving through it and making him see what he truly needed to do. Killing the princess wasn't enough. Reinstating the Treaty of Separation between the Fae and the Elves wasn't enough. If he could convince the king war was the answer, then he would make good on his promise to Lorcann.

Once Lorcann was satisfied with the war, Marath could make his next move. Aye, a move that whispered of control and power and glory. A move that included poisoning the king and killing the crown prince, allowing him to dominate the Woodlands.

Aye, that is what he would do. His plan was fully formed at last and rather brilliant. And once he had control of the Woodlands, he would be able to release the rest of the Fomorians from their watery prison. As their master he would be able to control them. A ready-made army to do his bidding.

Aesir merely stared at him, wide-eyed concern on his face.

"Well, what are you waiting for? Preparations are to be made at once for our travel to the king." He shooed him away with a wave of his hand.

"Aye, my lord. So it will be done."

Marath sat back in the chair as Aesir left. Despite his best efforts he tried to ignore his shaking hands. Using the darkness, he knew, would eventually catch up to him. He did not want to acknowledge the onset of the sickness crawling through him.

Nay…not a sickness. Merely the dark edging out the light. And once the light inside him was gone he would be a Dark Elf.

It would not stop him from his ultimate destiny of controlling the Woodlands.

Or the Otherworld.

Sir Drake halted his horse and stared at the large wall of foliage in front of him. It went as far as the eye could see from one direction to the other. With no end in sight. The queen had told him to ride to the Woodlands gate yet there was no gate here. Had he mistaken her directions? Did he take a wrong turn somewhere? He glanced from side to side, trying to decide what to do.

He dismounted and approached the shrubbery. Indeed it looked like nothing more than a giant bush that grew taller than he could see. He knew the Woodlands to be a magical place. It was home to the Woodland Elves, which was the princess's race, as old as time itself. According to Elyne, they built their cities in the forest among the trees and the bracken, the lochs and the water nymphs.

Not knowing what else to do he placed his hand on one of the branches. It felt like any other branch. Still not sure of where he was—though he hoped he'd made it to the Woodlands—he closed his eyes. Elven and Fae magic could deceive a human. The queen had told him to see with his heart. As he closed his eyes and imagined his princess on the other side, the branch beneath his hand began to take on a different shape. It seemed more solid under his palm.

He opened his eyes and saw the gate. Two eight-foot solid-oak doors with intricate carvings. The symbols were some sort of Elvish. One was a swirling symbol—a triskelion, Elyne had called it—that had three points. He placed his hand on it and waited. The wood warmed under his palm and then the gate swung open.

He stared, awestruck, before he snapped his jaw shut. There it was. And all he had to do was step through. He gave it a gentle nudge and the door creaked open on aged iron hinges. Elyne had told him Eldrin's brother, Lord Navin, was the gatekeeper. A shrewd gatekeeper at that. But she was certain with her letter and the token he would let Drake inside.

Taking his horse by the reins, he led her inside. As Elyne promised, Lord Navin stood on the other side. He was tall and dressed all in white with hair the color of spun gold that hung to his waist. Narrow pale-blue eyes peered out under slanted eyebrows.

"What is your business here, human?"

"I have a letter from Queen Elyne for King Urdithane." Drake rested his hand on the leather pouch that contained Elyne's script and the sapphire.

He held out his hand. "I will see that he gets it. And then you can be on your way."

It was as Elyne said. Drake shook his head. "By order of the queen, I am to personally deliver it to your king."

"*Humans* are not allowed in this kingdom," Navin said with a look of distaste. As though he'd swallowed something unsavory. "In fact it is forbidden."

"I must insist on seeing the king myself," Drake said.

"And I must insist on keeping our gates secure. I cannot allow it."

"I—"

"Ah, Sir Drake. What a pleasure to see you again." Lord Eldrin stepped out of the forest and into the clearing. "What brings you to our gates?"

Before Drake could respond, Navin jumped in. "He says he has a letter for the king."

"Then let him pass," Eldrin said.

"You know it is forbidden," Navin said.

"My brother, have you been living under a tree these least last few weeks? Sir Drake is one of the honored humans of the realm. He helped save the queen from certain death on more than one occasion, not to mention the fact he helped save the Otherworld from Dark Lord Kieran." Eldrin's voice was harsh and cold as he stared down his brother. "It would be insulting to refuse his entrance."

"But no human has ever—"

"No. Until now." He waved Drake toward him. "Come, Sir Drake. I will take you to my father. You may stay as long as you wish. We will see to the care of your horse."

Navin's fists balled. "I cannot allow it."

"I'm overruling you," Eldrin said. He had his hand on the reins of Drake's horse and pulled it along behind him. "This way, Drake."

He left without further discussion. But Drake didn't miss the look of utter distaste on the man's face as they parted ways. Elyne was right—he was not so pleasant. Drake fell in step beside the ranger as they walked through the thick, wooded area.

"You have my thanks, my lord," he said.

"No thanks necessary. My brother can be a bit stubborn. He takes his gatekeeper duties quite seriously."

"As he should. The realm is a dangerous place these days."

"Aye, but he should know you. I'll take you immediately to my father so you may deliver your letter. And then…I assume you'll want to see my sister." Eldrin kept his gaze forward.

Allanna. Aye, he'd want to see her. His heart clenched at the thought of seeing her so soon. He hadn't expected it. He didn't know if he would see her at all but now…things were falling into place.

Once he had a moment with the king, he intended to ask permission to court her.

"Aye, I would like that very much."

"As will she," he said. "I will send for her at once."

"Again, you have my thanks."

"I cannot promise you anything other than you will be able to see her," Eldrin said. "My father believes in the traditions of our people."

Drake thought he understood what Eldrin was telling him but he still didn't like it. "I want to make it perfectly clear, Lord Eldrin, I intend to court her."

"You may try, Sir Drake."

He looked at him. Drake did not see animosity there or anything unkind. What he saw was compassion and a hint of sadness. Almost as though Eldrin wanted to see the two of them together.

He knows. It was clear to Drake in that moment Eldrin knew his sister's feelings toward him. She must have confessed them to her brother at some point. And yet he didn't seem to disapprove. He seemed to want to help them see each other.

"I would never hurt her," Drake said.

"I know. But my father…he will never allow the match. She would have to give up everything to be with you. Her family, her title, her immortality. I tell you this not to be cruel but to make sure you understand the truth of it. As my father sees it, humans do not belong in our realm. Humans do not belong anywhere in the Otherworld. It will be a difficult road to travel should you decide to pursue my sister."

"I understand."

Challenge accepted.

If Eldrin was trying to warn him away from Allanna, it didn't work. It may be a difficult road, as he said, but it was a road Drake was willing to take. However, he didn't want the princess to give up everything. Mayhap there would be some way to convince the king to allow him to court her. And then over time he could win the king's favor.

They arrived at the foot of a long staircase that spiraled around the width of the tree. Drake followed Eldrin up the stairs. By the time they reached the treetop, his legs muscles burned and sweat had popped out on his forehead. He was healthy and athletic due to his jousting days but he was not accustomed to climbing hundreds of steps.

At the top, they stepped onto a rope bridge spanning the space from one tree to another. Up here, among the clouds, the air was thinner and colder. Up here, he could see beyond the treetops and in the far distance, the outline of the Queen's Palace where Elyne and Derron resided and ruled the Otherworld.

Eldrin led him across the bridge and paused at the entrance to one of the grander trees.

"I shall announce you. Wait here."

He disappeared inside, leaving Drake on the rope bridge. He turned to survey his surroundings and that's when he saw her walking down the bridge, heading for the palace. Heading right for him. He sucked in a breath and held it, watching her.

Allanna was unaware he stood there. Her hair shimmered in the light, glowing like a halo. She wore a velvet cerulean gown, the wide sleeves trimmed in the finest lace he'd ever seen. At last she lifted her head, their gazes met. She halted, blue eyes wide with surprise. He thought he heard her breath catch.

"Sir Drake."

He exhaled and bowed to her. "Your highness."

"What are you... How are you here?" She took a tentative step toward him.

"I've come with a letter from Queen Elyne."

"How did you get past the gates?"

She would know how difficult Lord Navin was to pass. He smiled. "Lord Eldrin allowed my entrance, though I daresay Lord Navin was not too happy to allow me to pass."

"Lord Eldrin," she whispered. The color was high in her cheeks. "You spoke with him?"

"Aye, I did."

"Did he—"

"Sir Drake, if you'll follow me. I will take you to the king." Eldrin stood in the doorway. "I see you've reacquainted yourself with my sister."

"I have." Drake couldn't take his eyes off her.

"Come, Sir Drake. My father waits to meet with you." He waved him toward the entrance.

Drake paused in front of Allanna, taking her hand and kissing it. "Until we meet again, fair princess."

He released her almost as quickly as he took her hand. He didn't spare her another glance—for he feared he would take her in his arms and kiss her senseless—as he followed Eldrin into the palace.

Eldrin led him through the great hall with the shiny wood floors to the throne room where a plush garnet rug led directly to the dais where the king would sit on his throne. The throne itself looked as though it were made from the ancient tree with twisted, knotted wood curved into a high back, arms and legs gnarled from the knotty wood. A garnet cloth draped the back and seat but the king was not seated there.

The king was in his private chamber. Here, too, was more of the red carpet and a small seating area with four chairs that looked inviting. Eldrin stepped inside the room, announced Sir Drake and softly closed the door.

"Sir Drake," Urdithane greeted. "Do come in. I understand you have something for me from Queen Elyne. You may approach."

"Aye, your majesty. I do. And a token of friendship." He pulled the letter and sapphire from the leather pouch and approached the king, handing over the items.

Urdithane held the sapphire up to the light, the candle flames winking off the shiny surface. "A token indeed. The queen is most generous."

Drake waited as he tore open the seal and read the letter, then dropped it in his lap. Discarded. Forgotten.

"It was kind of her to send such a heartfelt letter. Does Elyne expect a reply?" he asked.

"She did not say, your majesty."

"And you came all this way to deliver these things to me?"

"The queen asked that I personally deliver them, your majesty."

"Your pardon, Father, but it would be impolite to send Sir Drake back after such a long journey. We should at least allow him to stay for the night and recover," Eldrin said. "Mayhap offer him a seat at your table."

Drake looked at the ranger in surprise before recovering. Was he up to something?

"Aye, you are right, my son. Please see that Sir Drake has a comfortable room. Will you join us for our evening feast, Sir Drake?"

"I should be honored, your majesty." He bowed to show the king respect.

"Very good. I shall see you then."

"One more request, your majesty," Drake said. It was a leap of faith. He expected to be refused but he had to try. "I should like to ask for permission to court your daughter."

Immediately the king's open expression turned into a glower. "Is that really why you came here?"

It was the truth but Drake didn't want the king to know that. If he did, he'd throw him out this moment. And he'd come so close to staying here with a chance at seeing Allanna again. He couldn't waste it.

"Nay, your majesty. I came at the behest of Queen Elyne. I realize it seems as though I had an ulterior motive."

"Aye, it does. And this displeases me greatly." He leaned forward in his chair. "I realize the Fae have honored you humans by allowing you to stay in the Otherworld. I also realize you are a battle hero. But you are still a human. And Allanna is still a princess. She has duties and responsibilities to the realm and I expect her to carry them out. There is no room in this realm—or her life—for the likes of you."

The king's words stung deeply. He tried hard not to flinch and instead held his ground. He clenched his fist around the hilt of his sword so tight his fingers ached.

"All I'm asking for is a chance to court her." Drake knew he should keep his mouth shut. He should turn and leave before he was thrown out. But he couldn't help but plead his case. He wanted, nay, needed to see Allanna one last time. To speak to her alone. To kiss those rose-red lips.

"To court her and then marry her. I simply cannot allow that. I intend to see the princess betrothed and married to someone of our lineage. An Elf is the only suitable husband for my daughter. Therefore I'm denying your request. I will allow you to stay the night because you have been sent by Queen Elyne. But I expect you to be gone at first light. Is that clear?"

He stood ramrod straight as he stared down the king. "Abundantly, your majesty."

"Lord Eldrin, show our…guest out."

Drake had no choice but to follow the ranger from the king's private chamber.

Once outside, Eldrin turned on him. "Why did you do that? You fool!"

"I had to try," Drake said. "And now I know his true feelings for me."

"I told you my father would never allow the match yet you insist upon asking him for permission to court her anyway." He paced a short distance, spun and paced back. The rope bridge bounced with every step. "Now he will be watching you closely."

"Apologies, Lord Eldrin, but what else would you have me do?"

He reeled on him, his face mere inches from his. "I had a plan. Now it's destroyed."

"You had a plan?"

"Aye, a plan. I intended to arrange for you to see her."

"Forgive me, my lord, but it's inappropriate for me to see the young lady without a chaperone. I know what I must do and that is let her go."

He may no longer be in his human realm but he was still a knight. He still believed in duty and honor and the Code. He would never put Allanna in a position of impropriety. He would rather die than ruin her reputation.

Eldrin huffed out a heated breath of frustration. He ran his hand through his brown hair, making it spike on top. "She will not want you to let her go. This I know. My sister is stubborn to the core. However, I believe it's the best for both of you. In time, she'll come to see that was the best for her. If you leave without telling her goodbye, though, I fear she'll do something rash. So the question remains. Do you want to see my sister or not?"

"I...of course I do. But—"

"I will make the arrangements. If you follow my directions explicitly, then you will be able to see her one last time. Do we have an accord?"

"Aye, we do," Drake said.

"Good." Eldrin stomped down the rope bridge. "Come along. I will show you to your chamber for the night."

Drake followed, hurrying to catch up. "Tell me one thing, my lord. Why are you doing this? Why are you helping her? And me?"

He halted so quickly Drake nearly rammed into his back. Eldrin spun and blew out a breath. "Because she is my sister. She loves you. And because...I know all too well what it's like to love someone and not be able to be with that person. It's painful. Like a hot poker lashing through the heart. Searing it. And all you can do is hope the fire will cauterize the pain and make it disappear."

Eldrin's face took on a faraway look as he gazed into the distance. He had expressed Drake's feelings perfectly. Could it be there was a lady somewhere that had captured his heart and he, like Drake, could not be with the one he loved? Were they kindred spirits after all?

Eldrin shook out of his trance and looked back at Drake. "Do you need any other reason?"

He shook his head slowly. "Nay. No other reason."

Eldrin resumed walking and Drake followed.

She loved him. He had hoped. Now he knew for sure. How he would get past her father, he didn't know. But in time, mayhap he could find a way.

Love always found a way.

Chapter 4

Allanna stood in the shadows of the palace and listened as Sir Drake spoke to her father in his private chamber. Her heart had nearly burst through her chest when she heard him ask for permission to court her. And then shattered when her father refused. Not only did he refuse but he also made a point to tell Drake she would marry an Elf. And if she knew her father he would find someone within a fortnight to betroth to her.

She knew he would refuse. She also knew if it were up to her father, Drake would never see her again for the rest of his mortal days.

But Drake had come for her. Even though he told Urdithane he hadn't. She knew. He'd come *for her*. Every part of her tingled with sweet anticipation, with the knowledge that if he came for her then he loved her.

When Eldrin and Drake left her father's chamber, she stepped back into the shadows and hid behind one of the elaborate statues in the corridor. She watched and waited as they passed her. When it was safe, she slipped through the palace halls, her soft-soled shoes silent on the floor. She found them arguing on the bridge outside.

Eldrin. Her dear sweet older brother. How could she ever thank him for what he did for her? She'd overhead most of their conversation—snippets here and there on the wind. But what she made out clearly was Eldrin asking Drake if he wished to see her one last time. Her heart swelled again, setting her back on an emotional high. He would make it possible for her to see Drake. Because he knew her feelings.

One last time? Nay. Never. She would never allow it to be the last time. She would find a way to be with him even if that meant forsaking all that she was. She would give up her crown as sure as a candle drips wax to be with the man she loved.

It took all her strength to remain outside the palace walls as her brother took the knight to one of the guest chambers. She stood on the bridge, her hands gripping the handrail when he returned. She turned to him as he approached.

"When?" she demanded.

"When what?"

"When can I see him?"

Eldrin glanced around as though searching for listening ears and then took her by the arm and led her down the bridge as far from the palace as possible.

"You heard that?"

"Aye, I did. When can I see him?"

"How much of that conversation did you overhear?"

"Enough. So when?"

"Patience. It will be arranged after we dine this evening. I'll bring him to the loch."

All her nerve endings tingled. Excitement spread through her, creating a lightness in her chest, making her buoyant. Almost as though she could walk upon the air.

"Thank you, El," she whispered.

"It's all I can do."

"'Tis enough."

"If Father finds out—"

"He won't," she vowed. "I swear it."

"Don't do anything crazy."

Her brother knew her all too well. "I cannot promise."

"Allanna…if you run away Father will never speak to you again. You'll be disowned. None of our clan will be allowed to speak to you or help you."

"I know," she said quickly. How did he know the thought had crossed her mind?

"I know how difficult it is for you, *nethielle*, but you have to give him up."

She clenched her jaw in determination. "I can't."

"You have to." He reached for her, placed a hand on her elbow. "There are certain things we, as the children of the king, must do. Whether we like it or not. Giving up Sir Drake is one of the things you have to do. He will never be allowed to marry you."

"Please don't ask me to do that." He could not know how difficult it was for her to simply give him up.

He dropped his hand. "It's for the best. I worry about you."

"Don't worry, El." She smiled. "I'm a big girl. I can take care of myself."

"Aye and I believe Sir Drake wouldn't harm you." He paused, looking thoughtful.

"But?"

"But…are you willing to give up everything to be with him?"

"I am. I would." She said it without hesitation. She was certain she loved him enough to do that. To be with him and no other. No other would do.

Sadness crept across Eldrin's face. He pulled her into a quick hug. Almost as though it were a hug of farewell. "Be careful."

Drake joined the Elven royals for the evening feast, as he said he would. The king gave him less than a warm reception. He was quite cold. But Drake didn't care. All that mattered was getting a moment with Allanna.

The king, however, must have guessed Drake would try anything to get the girl alone. He kept her by his side all evening, never letting her out of his sight. All the two could do was exchange a glance every now and then. And even that was scrutinized by the king.

When dessert was served Allanna feigned a headache and excused herself from her father's presence. She gave Drake one last passing glance before she disappeared out of the great hall.

After she'd been long gone Eldrin leaned toward him and pushed a small piece of parchment in his hand. The ranger said nothing. Merely gave him a nod as he rose from the table and left the feast.

With his hands hidden under the table, Drake unfolded the small parchment. Written in a careful script were directions to meet Lord Eldrin in the grove by the loch at full moonrise. He said nothing of meeting the princess. But he hoped the ranger had made good on his promise to bring her to him.

Drake waited until the musicians started playing and dancers took the floor. With the king and crown prince distracted, Drake slipped out of the great hall and found his way to the long, winding staircase.

At the foot of the staircase, he paused and wondered which way to the grove with the loch. A fire pixy flittered in the darkness toward him, then buzzed around his face and circled his head. He could barely make out the little pixy's features. She had a delicate face and beckoned him after her, waiting for him to follow.

He pursued the streaming little light, heedless of his surroundings. He didn't want to lose sight of her as he stumbled along. When the glittering loch came into view, the fire pixy disappeared. He halted, looking out at the peaceful water with the moonlight reflecting upon the surface.

And there she was. His princess. Her hair was like a halo in the silvery light. Delicate shadows played upon her beautiful face. He could see the outline of her rose-red lips, the slant of her high cheekbones, the curve of her perfect, pert nose.

She smiled sweetly, fluttered her lashes down, and dipped a quick curtsey in greeting.

The small gesture sent his heart into a tailspin. His body reacted as a sensual light passed between them. And he knew he had to feel her in his arms. He hurried toward her. The smile never left her lips.

"Sir Drake, I—"

But that was as far as she got when he took her in his arms, pulling her close, feeling her small body curve against his. Enough waiting. He'd waited long enough to hold her. To feel her. To taste her. Her breath caught in her throat as his head dipped toward hers. And before their lips met, her breath shuddered out.

He paused, inhaling her sweet nectar scent. It was sultry and heady and nearly made him lose his mind. He could stand it no longer. His mouth closed over her lips, at long last sampling her taste. His tongue delved deep into the sweet recesses of her mouth. She tasted like honeysuckle wine on a warm summer night. She tasted like heaven. She tasted like forever.

To his delight, she kissed him back. Her arms slid around his neck as she pressed closer. So close he could feel every curve of her little body against him. Her small, round breasts. Her narrow waist. The curve of her hips.

Her tongue bumped against his as they savored each other, branding their first kiss in his mind. She kissed as though she'd always known how. As though she had been born to kiss him and no other. He was reluctant to break apart from her but wanted to see her face and memorize it. He wanted to store it away so he may recall it anytime he wished. Because he knew tonight would be the final night they would have together.

As he pulled away, he could see the color high in her cheeks and the pink in the tips of her pointed ears. Her lips were still damp from his onslaught and to make matters worse, she ran her tongue over them. As though remembering the last remnants of his mouth on hers. Her pulse fluttered wildly in the long column of her pale throat. She labored to breathe, as though she couldn't catch her breath.

"Forgive me," he said. "I should not have taken such liberties." He kissed her forehead and a little mewl escaped her.

Control, though. He must control his reaction. When all he wanted to truly do was tear the gown from her sweet body and make love to her until the dawn. Here on the edge of the loch amid the soft grass. Yet that would not be appropriate. He was a knight. He had honor and dignity. And he would not ruin her reputation with one selfish act. An act he could never take back. She was pure, untouched bliss. He would not destroy that. Yet he couldn't stop kissing her. His lips trailed down her face to her neck.

"Liberties, sir?" she asked. Her words were weak, soft. Her arms were still firmly planted around his neck.

"Aye." He whispered it against her skin. "But I find I could not live another day or take another breath without knowing what your lips felt like against mine."

Again her breath hitched. "Nor I."

He pulled back to look down at her flushed face. Her eyes were bright and shining with an ethereal light. And her lips still beckoned for him to sip them again. To taste that honeysuckle sweetness.

"I'd like to kiss you again, your highness."

"Allanna. My name is Allanna," she said.

"Allanna," he repeated.

Her eyes fluttered closed as he kissed her. This time gently. Taking his time to savor.

How long had they stood there kissing in the moonlight? He did not know. Nor did he care. All that mattered was that he held her. He kissed her. And she kissed him back. A warm shiver passed through him, leaving him lightheaded. And he was certainly aware of the hardening of his shaft.

When they broke at last her breath came in small, shallow pants. Reluctantly, he released her. She stepped back. Her hand fluttered to her throat. She pressed her fingers to her racing pulse. He knew what sort of effect he had on her. She had the same effect on him.

He remembered the fire pendant then. He'd stashed it in his pocket that evening before the meal.

"I have a gift for you," he said.

"A gift?" She smiled brightly, clearly delighted at the idea.

He pulled the pendant from his pocket. Holding it by the chain, he let the jewel fall so she could see it. Moonlight caught in the facets, making it sparkle. She gasped and took it in shaking fingers.

"It's beautiful!" She turned it over in her delicate hands. "A fire crystal. This is Elvish. Where did you get it?"

"Does it matter? It is a gift for you, my sweet princess. Will you wear it?"

But she was already slipping it over her neck. The length of the chain was long enough to allow the jewel to hang between her perfect breasts. He stifled a groan.

"Always. Forever. Until I take my last breath." Her gaze meet his, those blue eyes sparkling with admiration. "Thank you, my lord."

"Drake." He took her hand in his, his lips grazing her knuckles. "If I'm to have your name, then you must call me Drake."

"Aye, Drake. As you wish."

She opened her palm and flattened it against his bearded cheek. He closed his eyes, relishing the feel of her soft skin.

"I will cherish it, always," she said.

"As I know you will."

He planted a soft kiss in her palm. "I spoke with your father today."

"Aye?" She sounded wary.

"I asked for permission to court you."

A heartbeat passed before she responded. "What did he say?"

"What we knew he would say."

She dropped her hand, not hiding her disappointment. "I knew he would refuse you."

He took her hands in his, holding them close to his chest. "But I had to try."

"Then there is one thing left for me to do," she said, her voice strong with resolve. "Take me with you."

His heart lurched. Oh, how he would love to do that. He would love to take her away from here. To sweep her into his arms, climb into the saddle and ride away. Never to look back.

But Eldrin's warning rang in his head. She would lose everything—her crown, her family, her life here. She would be considered dead to the Elven people. He couldn't allow that to happen to her.

"Nay, my princess." He kissed her fingers. "I cannot."

"Why not?"

"You will lose all that you have."

"I'm willing to risk it to be with you, Drake. I want to come with you. Don't you want to go back to your home? Your family?"

He loved her determination as much as he loved her. "There is nothing for me there. I have no family. No one to return to."

"Yet you're going back anyway? Without me?"

"It's what I must do. If I take you from your kingdom, you father will never forgive me. And he will never allow you to come back here."

"I don't care."

"Aye, you do." He pulled her to him, holding her close. He stroked the length of her hair. "You care. It would hurt you and your family if you left with me. And I care what happens to you. I want you to be happy."

He hated saying it to her, but it was the truth of it. Eventually, she would forget him and find an Elven prince to marry and love. She would live forever. He would die alone. An old man.

"I won't be happy without you," she said. "I will never be happy without you."

"You will. Someday you will forget me when you've been married for a long while and have children of your own."

She flattened her hand on his chest. "The children I want are yours."

He smiled. He rather liked the thought of that. He could imagine her belly round with his child. Would they look like their mother? With the pale hair and blue eyes? Would they have her pointed ears and her milky-white skin? He could easily see a smaller version of her.

"Even if they were half human?"

"Halflings," she said. "'Tis what they're called. Halfling or not I would love them. Especially if they were yours."

By Saint Mary, she was killing him. Did she know what she was doing to him? The thought of living the rest of his days without her was like a knife shoved through his heart, twisting painfully.

"I don't want you to go," she said.

"Nor I. But there is no place for me here. Your father made that clear."

"Mayhap we can change my father's mind. Together. We could go to him. Talk to him. I'll request a private audience."

"Nay, Allanna. He's made up his mind. I don't think there is any use trying to change it."

She pulled away, stepping back from him. Her cheeks were flushed with her emotions. "Then what will you do? Will you return to the human realm?"

"Aye."

"You're leaving me?"

"It is for the best."

"No." She shook her head and grasped his hand, pulling him to her. "I will speak to my father."

"I don't think it will help. He is against the match. You are a princess. An *Elven* princess and I am…"

"A knight. Brave. Honorable."

"Human," he reminded her.

"That has never mattered to me."

"Because you can look past it. But your father cannot. Allanna, if I stay it will make things difficult for you. I don't wish to cause you heartache. 'Tis better for me to return to the human realm."

"When do you plan to leave?"

"At first light."

"Then we have tonight."

"Aye, we do."

"Stay with me, Drake."

He could not refuse her though he knew he should. He should leave her here on the edge of the loch and return to his chamber.

But he would never see her again after tonight. And he wanted these last moments with her. Would he give in to his carnal desires? Nay, he would not. He would treat her as the lady, the princess, she was.

She edged close to him. Her soft scent went over him and he closed his eyes, inhaling the heady aroma. Honeysuckle and a hint of bergamot drifted into his nose, teasing him. Tempting him. Her hands slid up his chest as she stepped toward him. Closer. So close.

When he opened his eyes, her Elven face was upturned to his. Moonlight danced in her golden hair and sparkled in her eyes. Her lips parted.

He could not deny her. He kissed her again, their mouths melting together as hot wax melted over the edge of a candlestick. She pulled him downward until they both fell to the ground. Then she rolled, tugging him on top of her.

His heart rammed so hard in his chest he thought it would break through skin. His body responded to her invitation as she opened her legs. His shaft hardened against her thigh, the blood boiling in his veins. Her instincts took over and she moved against him, pressing her core to him and lifting her hips.

Drake severed the kiss and pushed off her. He rolled to his side but pulled her into his arms, cradling her against his chest.

"Why did you stop?"

He stroked her silken hair. "I will not take you this way."

"Why not?" She didn't hide the frustration in her voice.

He knew he disappointed her but he was not a man who took advantage of a woman. Even if he was completely in love with her. He would not take her innocence this way. She was a princess. She deserved better. She deserved being made love to in a bed surrounded by candlelight, not on the hard, cold ground in damp grass.

"You are innocent, aye?"

She rose up to face him, her eyes held a hard, determined glint. "I am but I want to be with you, Drake. You and no other."

He brushed hair from her face. "And I with you. But not like this. Not here. I will not allow your first time to be here on the edge of the loch."

"But this is what I want," she said. "Here. Now. With you." She sat up straight, looking down at him, straddling his waist. "Do you not want me?"

Was she mad? Didn't she feel how much he wanted her by the bulge in his trousers? Did she not know what she sat upon? Having her sitting there nearly killed him. He could quite clearly imagine how she would look naked. Her skin rosy and flushed. Her hair spilling over her shoulders. He stifled the groan that wanted to erupt and instead sat up, pulling her into his lap.

"Oh, aye. I want you. But 'tis not the time or place."

"If you're worried about my brother finding us, he won't. Nor will my father." She paused, a heartbeat passing between them before adding, "I wouldn't care if they did."

He wondered then. Did she do this as vengeance? Did she hope to get caught? He saw nothing good coming of that scenario. He would lose his head if he were to be found in a compromising position with the princess.

"But I care," he said. "We must respect your father's wishes, Allanna."

"I don't want to."

"It's the right thing to do. The way of things. I will stay with you tonight and hold you while you sleep, if you wish. For now, it's all I can offer you."

He watched her face intently and the light diminished a little in her eyes. As though she were resigned to accept their fate. And his heart broke even more for her. For him. For their future, which could never be what they wanted.

Her small hand flattened on his chest over his heart. "I wish things could be different."

"As do I."

They listened to the chirping of the night creatures and the breeze toying with the treetops. He couldn't think of a better way to spend his last night in the Otherworld than by holding her in his arms, stoking her hair and inhaling her scent.

"You are a true knight, Sir Drake," she whispered.

Her body went limp and heavy in his arms and he knew she slept.

Drake watched as the sun broke the horizon, peeking over the edge and reflecting golden light on the loch. Somehow he'd managed to stay awake all night, listening to her deep breathing as she slept. The land came awake and he knew their time together had finally come to an end. He kissed the top of her head and gave her a gentle shake.

"Allanna, time to wake, my princess."

She stirred. "Morning already?"

"I'm afraid so," he said. "We must get you back to the palace straightaway before you're missed."

"She's already missed."

Allanna bolted upright and scrambled out of Drake's arms. She tugged her fingers through her tangled locks. "Eldrin, what are you doing here?"

By her reaction, Drake knew she really did care about who found them. Deep down, he knew she didn't want to lose her family. Especially Eldrin—he was clearly her favorite brother. She loved her family too much to let them go. He was right to refuse her, though he hadn't wanted to.

"Looking for you," he said. "Come quickly. I've managed to stall Father by telling him you were out early this morning. That will not appease him for long." His gaze landed on Drake then. "He's also looking for you."

"God's teeth," he swore.

"I told him you'd already left and were heading back to the Queen's Palace to return home," Eldrin said. "Otherwise, he'd be sending the dogs out for you. You must return to the palace, Allanna. We have guests arriving today."

"Guests?" she asked.

"Lord-Regent Marath and his men," Eldrin said.

She scrunched her nose. "That bore? What do I care about him?"

"Father wants you in attendance when he arrives and is announced. So you better care. Off you go now. I want a word with Sir Drake alone."

"Eldrin—"

"Go," he said. There was no room for argument by the sound of the hard edge of his voice.

But Allanna was not to be bullied by her brother. She stepped toward him. "I want a moment in private."

"Allanna—"

"One last moment, El," she insisted.

He glanced between the two of them then nodded. "Very well. But only a moment."

When he was out of sight, she turned to Drake and fell into his arms. His hands were in her hair a second later. Their mouths were on each other, their tongues colliding in a mad, passionate final farewell. She emitted a tiny mewl as they kissed, sending his heart into his boots and turning his shaft into stone. Her body pressed against him, making him aware of her every curve.

God's teeth. He loved her.

And it pained him to think he would never see her again after this one perfect moment.

Eldrin cleared his throat loudly but Allanna took her time stepping away from Drake. When she finally did, he saw the shimmer of tears on her cheeks. He brushed one away with the pad of his thumb.

"I'll not say goodbye," she whispered. "Not yet."

"We have to," he said.

"I will see you again someday, my knight."

With one more brush of her lips, she stepped away, picked up her skirts and ran back to the palace. Drake turned his attention to her brother who gave him a scorching look.

"Did you and my sister…"

"Nothing inappropriate happened, my lord. I assure you," Drake said. "You have my word as a knight. The princess's reputation is still safely intact."

Eldrin blew out a breath. "I didn't think you would do such a thing. I feared the worst when I saw you together. When I saw you…holding her that way." He flushed.

"She slept. I did not." He would never forget the way she curled against him. Or how soft she was in his arms. "I would never take advantage of her."

"Sometimes my sister can be reckless. I feared she talked you into her hasty ways." He clapped him on the shoulder. "Thank you for taking care of her."

"I would give my life for hers if you asked."

"I believe you," Eldrin said. "You must go. I have your horse saddled and ready. The gates are clear. Lord Navin will not interfere with your departure."

"Thank you, Lord Eldrin, for giving me one last moment with her."

"It was all I could offer." He held out his hand. "This is goodbye then?"

"I'm afraid so."

"Good luck to you, Sir Drake."

With nothing left to say, Drake headed for his horse.

Chapter 5

Allanna ran up the winding staircase, blinking away tears. Once she reached the top, she paused only a moment to catch her breath before trudging back to her chamber, her heart heavy. Why should she stop the tears? She lost the love of her life. The only man she wanted to give her heart to. He would leave and return to his home. Her last hope now was finding a way to get out of the palace without her father seeing her and head for Queen Elyne. She was her last hope. She could sift her to Drake.

She knew today would be the last day she would spend here with her family. Her decision was made.

The hours she'd spent sleeping in Drake's arms were some of the best hours of her life. She would never forget that. Nor how he stroked her hair and held her close. How he kissed her and made all her senses come alive. As though she'd been waiting for him her entire life.

She knew he wanted to love her by the way he kissed her and the words he'd said. He had freely admitted he wanted to be with her. She'd offered herself to him and he'd refused. Humiliation had burned her cheeks and she'd been thankful for the darkness to cover it. She didn't want him to see how hurt she was by his rejection.

Allanna didn't wish to dress for Lord-Regent Marath. Noble or not, she had no interest in hearing what politics he would bring with him to her father's court. For he always brought politics and controversy.

He was the sort of man who gave her an odd feeling when he looked at her. He made her feel as though he could see right through her. As though the thoughts in his head were far from proper. She disliked his dark, assessing gaze that seemed to follow her everywhere, his hawkish nose and pointed chin, his brutish looks. What he lacked in looks, he made up for with his disarming character. A trait she disliked even more. He had often come to court as one of the highest-ranking lords in the Woodlands. And every time he came, he'd bring some trinket for her. Pearls from the Water Elves. A vial of raindrops from the Skye Elves, though she couldn't fathom how he acquired such a thing. What would it be this time?

She entered her chamber and saw her handmaiden and the copper tub waiting for her by the fire. She didn't want to be tended. She wanted to be left alone. So she could sulk in private. Emptiness pressed her heart. While she understood why he had to return, she didn't have to like it.

"Good morrow, your highness." Igraen dipped a curtsey. "Your bath is prepared."

She could tell no one of her plan to leave. Not even Igraen or Eldrin. She could trust no one with her secret. As the girl helped her bathe and dress, she glanced around her chamber as though seeing it for the last time. Already her mind was preparing a list of items she would need to leave this place. She'd dress in her brother's old riding clothes. Hide her hair under a hooded cloak. She'd steal a wheel of cheese and loaf of bread from the kitchens and then ride Moonshadow to the Fae queen.

Igraen brushed Allanna's hair to a high shine. She dressed in a pale-pink gown with a scooped neckline and lace at the hem and edge of the sleeves. Taking a deep breath, she made the long walk from her chamber to the throne room where her father and Andahar waited. When she entered, she didn't miss her father's scrutiny.

"Where were you this morning? Have you been outside the gates again, Allanna?" he asked.

"No, Father." That, at least, was the truth. But later she would be leaving forever.

"Where were you then? You were not in your chamber early this morning." His gaze narrowed as he looked at her.

Allanna resisted the urge to squirm. She forced herself to remain calm as she took the seat at her father's left. Prince Andahar sat on his right, also giving her an intense glare.

"I got up early to practice my shooting," she said.

"Hmm," was Urdithane's response.

"Lord-Regent Marath, your majesty," the herald announced.

Allanna was grateful for the arrival of the noble so she would avoid further inquiry. Her gaze landed on him as he entered the throne room, his servant trailing behind him. He was tall and lithe and strolled forward as he carried himself neatly erect. His steps were as graceful as a cat as he prowled into the room. He held his head high to keep the attention off that awful nose. His long black hair was plaited on either side of his face, the rest hanging down his back. His assessing gaze flickered from the prince to the king to the princess and back again. As though he took stock of each of them.

Allanna didn't trust the man. She never had. He may be the ruler over his own lands, but she never liked him and always thought he had a hidden agenda all his own. The very sight of him made the tiny hairs on the back of her neck stand at attention.

She stole a glance at her father, who seemed unconcerned with the arrival of the lord. He sat on the edge of his chair, leaning his elbow on his knee as he watched the man walk toward them.

"Welcome, Lord-Regent," Urdithane said.

"Greetings, your majesty. Thank you for seeing me on such short notice." He bowed low at the waist, showing reverence for his king.

His fake and forced admiration made her mistrust him all the more.

"What brings you here, my lord?"

He glanced around the throne room where others had requested an audience with their ruler. As lord-regent, Marath took precedence.

"I come to speak my concerns over the recent dissolution of the Treaty of Separation," Marath said. "I had hoped we could convene in your private chamber."

"What you have to say can be said here. My time is limited. What are your concerns?"

He cleared his throat. "I'm sure you realize how dangerous the Fae are and continue to be, my king. I do not wish to have another incident as we did so long ago."

"That was six thousand years ago, Marath. And Maeve no longer rules the Otherworld or the Fae."

"And this new queen…you believe she will not try to cause the Elven race harm?"

"Queen Elyne is honorable and trustworthy, as is her husband. What troubles you, my lord?"

"I believe the Fae still pose a threat to us."

Murmurs went throughout the room. The king narrowed his gaze at Marath. "On what grounds?"

"They are a dangerous lot, my king. Their magic is powerful. More so than the Elves could ever be. This new queen has the ability to alter time. How do you know they are not intending to take over the entire Otherworld? Or change our history?"

"Nonsense," Urdithane said. "Elyne would never do such a thing to harm us. I trust her as I trusted her father. Our alliance is quite solid."

Marath paused long enough to tell Allanna the man wasn't speaking the truth. "Mayhap you should reconsider when I present my proof. I have heard they are planning to attack your kingdom. And steal your daughter."

Gasps this time. Allanna straightened a little in her chair and fixed her gaze on the Elven lord.

"What is your proof?"

"May I approach, sire?"

He waved him forward. Looking intently at Allanna, Marath walked with fluid steps, removing a parchment from a leather pouch as he did so. He handed it over to the king who read it quickly then looked back to the lord.

"Are your spies reliable?"

"Aye, sire, they are. Your rule is not safe from the Fae."

Urdithane sat back in his chair and ran his hand over his chin. "I fail to understand. Why would Queen Elyne launch an attack against us after all we've done for them? Have you heard such information, Andahar?"

"No, Father."

Urdithane turned his attention back to Marath. "And you're certain your sources are reliable, my lord?"

"Quite certain."

"It doesn't seem like Queen Elyne to do such a thing. Nor would she want to kidnap the princess."

"Mayhap she's had a change of heart," Andahar suggested. "We could send a messenger to the Fae queen asking her to attend us here at court."

"With all due respect, your majesty, I don't think that's such a good idea. She will be expecting such a thing."

"Seems unlikely," Urdithane said. "Several of our Elven warriors were acting Guardians after the war. The queen trusted them with their treasures. I don't understand why she would have had a change of heart now."

Marath shifted from one foot to the other. "There is also word that she's quite ill, your majesty."

"Ill?" The king looked at Andahar again. "Have you heard such news?"

"No, my father."

Allanna knew Marath lied. Elyne was in perfect health when they left the Fae palace. She was looking forward to her coronation. She had stood with Drake as they rode away from there and that was only days ago. Marath wouldn't have that information even if he employed the best spies in the Otherworld.

"This is preposterous, my lord," Urdithane said. "I've heard nothing of the sort about the Fae queen. Nor have I heard she intends to attack the Elves. I'm not so inclined to believe you, Marath."

Allanna suppressed the smile that wanted to erupt. Her father was no fool. And anyone could see Marath was trying to sabotage their relationship with the Fae. Her father was right—Queen Elyne would not do such a thing. She had no interest in taking over the Otherworld. Her primary concern was rebuilding the Queen's Palace after Morrigan's attack. It had nothing to do with the Elves.

In fact, they had been honored in her court. Clearly, Lord-Regent Marath had no idea what had been happening at the front lines. The fool.

"Believe what you will, my king," he said. "I came to warn you. If you will not listen, then I cannot help you."

Urdithane raised one brow. "Is that so? Are you saying should there be a call to arms, your people will not be available to assist?"

He cleared his throat. "Of course not, my king."

"Then what is it?" he asked.

"I simply meant, my king, it is out of my hands. I've done my part to help you."

"I'll certainly keep your concerns in mind."

And send his own spies, no doubt. Allanna knew her father was cautious and she trusted he would make sure Marath's allegations against the Fae were true before he acted.

"What other business have you come about? Surely that isn't all."

"No, your majesty. There is one other thing."

His dark gaze landed on Allanna again and something about it sent her heart into a tizzy. She suddenly had a sinking feeling in the pit of her stomach as though she knew what he intended to say next. Her fingers clenched around the arms of the chair, her knuckles leaching of color. Her nails digging into the soft wood. He wouldn't be as bold as to suggest such a thing, would he?

"In light of the current situation, I believe it would be best if the princess was guarded daily. She is quite lovely, your majesty."

Oh, he would. The blood drained from her head, leaving her dizzy. Black dots prickled her vision. She blinked them away and inhaled a deep breath to keep steady her thoughts.

"Aye, that she is."

"She is not yet promised to anyone, is she?" Again that lingering gaze.

Her skin crawled with disgust. No. Her father couldn't— wouldn't—agree to anything this vile creature said, would he?

"That is correct. She is not spoken for."

"Father…"

Urdithane held up a hand to hush her.

"It would be my honor then, you majesty, to ask for her hand. To bring her under my protection to make sure nothing nefarious happens to her."

"Father, no," she said, unable to keep silent.

"Do you propose a proper betrothal?" Urdithane asked.

"I do with the stipulation she travels with me back to my home. Removing her from the kingdom is the only way to keep her safe."

"No!" Allanna shot to her feet.

"Sit, my daughter," Urdithane commanded. "And remain silent. I will not tolerate any more outbursts in front of our guest."

She sank to her chair and clutched the arms again. This couldn't be happening. This was a dream. Nay, a nightmare. A proper betrothal would last a year. A proper betrothal under Marath's roof would be unbearable. And even if her father were to allow her to stay in the palace, Marath would have free rein in court. He could come and go as he pleased. He would be there hovering. Always. He would keep that dark, calculating gaze on her at all times. She would never be able to escape.

"It's high time my daughter found a suitable husband," Urdithane said. "Since you seem to be the best suitor—"

"He's the only suitor!"

Urdithane shot her a look that told her to be silent before he continued. "Then I grant your request for her hand. I'll have the High Druid draw up the necessary papers for the betrothal."

"Thank you, your majesty. It honors me that you have accepted my request. I eagerly await the day we can take our marriage vows."

Allanna wanted to gag. Could her father not hear the sickly sweetness dripping off every one of his words as he spoke? The man was vile as vile comes. The last thing she wanted to do was marry him. And when she thought of the marriage bed, she blanched. Her stomach clenched and her heart did a wicked dance in her chest. She wanted to retch all over the man's boots.

"However, I must deny your request to remove her from the palace. My royal guards will be able to keep my daughter safe from anyone who intends to do her harm." He punctuated that last by leaning forward with a pointed gaze. "As long as she remains here, she is under my protection."

How could her father give her away like that? Marath wasn't the best suitor and her father knew that. Marath was the *only* one who had come forward. Nay, even that wasn't true. Sir Drake had asked and been refused. There was a sudden stabbing pain in her heart. Was her father doing this to punish her? To prove to her he was still in control of her world? How could he *do* this to her?

"You are welcome to stay, of course," the king said. "For as long as necessary."

Oh, *gods*. He was allowing the vile man to stay in the palace? Where he would have unlimited access to her?

"You have my thanks, sire. May I approach the princess?"

"By all means," the king said.

Allanna watched in horrified silence as he walked toward her. She tensed, her stomach threatening to heave. Bile clotted the back of her throat. And all the while Marath keep that evil stare on her. He knelt at her feet and took her hands in his. His cold, wet lips touched the back of her hand. Cold lips that reminded her of a dead fish.

"It is my honor to make you my wife, princess," he said. "I look forward to spending time with you, getting to know you and marrying you."

She didn't look forward to it. She didn't want anything to do with the man. She wanted to jerk her hand back and wipe away the remnants of his kiss. Instead she forced a faint smile. "Indeed, my lord."

Urdithane cleared his throat loudly. "The princess is clearly taken aback by your sudden proposal. Aren't you, Allanna?"

"Clearly, Father." She forced the icy, whispered words out of her mouth. She would rather fall on a sword than marry this man.

As Marath released her hand and rose, the light went out of Allanna. In one instant, she had died inside.

King Urdithane stood. "Come, then. Let us summon the High Druid and speak to him at once to expedite this arrangement and make it official. Prince Andahar, please continue meeting with our other honored guests and assist them as you see fit."

Allanna refused to move and watched as her father and Marath walked away from the throne room. As he led the lord-regent away, he turned and gave the princess one last hard look. As though giving her a silent warning that if she crossed him, he would make sure she suffered.

Well, she wouldn't suffer. Nor would she suffer the indignity of a betrothal with that man. Her last hope was getting out of the palace and finding Drake before he made it back to the Queen's Palace. She would ride Moonshadow hard and fast back to the Fae. She would find him and beg him to take her back to the human realm.

It was the only way she could escape this hell in which she had suddenly been thrust. She rose to her full height and excused herself from the throne room. Andahar hardly noticed. He was busy discussing one of the noble's crops for the year. And who cared about that when her life was falling apart?

She hurried out onto the rope bridge where the vision exploded so suddenly into her mind, she doubled over and fell to her knees. To steady herself, she put out her hands and stared down at the aging wood planks. After several gulps of air, she managed to grip the frayed handrail with one hand while clutching her stomach with the other.

In her vision, she saw her father laying on his deathbed. His face ashen. His lips blue. His eyes had sunk and he had dark shadows under the bottom lashes. He looked frail and old. Not at all like the vibrant man who had walked out of the throne room moments ago. She knew he was dying.

Andahar stood beside the bed talking to the royal healer, Brom. "Tis poison, your highness," the healer said.

"Poison? Who could have done this?"

"I know not."

And as quickly as it came the vision was over. Allanna gasped. Her stomach clenched into a knot. Someone was going to kill her father. He had no enemies so who would be so bold as to try to kill him under the palace roof?

She gulped in a deep, cleansing breath and sat back on her heels. But as her heart slowed from the rapid beat, another vision slammed into her. This one of Andahar fighting a battle. She could hear the clank of swords all around her. She could see her brother fighting someone but his face was in shadow. She couldn't make it out. Until he turned and revealed his identity. Marath plunged the sword right through Andahar, killing him.

And again the vision disappeared as quickly as it had come. Her heart throbbed with pain from the two successive visions. She pressed cold fingertips against her temples.

Lord-Regent Marath was a traitor and intended to kill her father and Andahar. He was the enemy and now he had her hand in marriage. She had to warn them, even if they didn't believe her.

What could he want, though? The throne? But that was impossible. Andahar was next in line followed by her ranger brother, Eldrin. Navin was next, though he wasn't fit to rule. He was nothing but a guardsman. She was last in line to the throne.

Was he planning to take out all her brothers to rule the kingdom? If her father fell ill, then Andahar would assume duties as king regent.

"Allanna, can you hear me?"

Eldrin's voice broke through to her. She blinked and looked up at him. His face was pinched with worry. He towered over her, held out his hand to help her to her feet.

"I've been calling your name. What happened? Another vision?"

She accepted his hand and got to her feet. "Aye. Two this time."

"You're pale. I'll fetch some water."

She leaned against the handrail, the rope creaking with her weight. Eldrin disappeared inside and returned a moment later with a tankard of cool water. He placed it in her hands.

"Sip. Then tell me what you saw."

She took a swallow of the cold liquid. "Father was ill. Dying. Poisoned. And then Andahar. He was…killed during a battle."

"What kind of battle?"

"I…don't know. It wasn't clear. El…it was Marath. He killed Andahar. I think he also might be the one responsible for poisoning Father."

"Marath?" Eldrin repeated. "That's impossible. He's loyal to the crown. He is liege lord of his own area. He would never do such a thing."

"It was him, El. I know it," she said. "Father has agreed to a betrothal."

Eldrin blinked his surprise. "A betrothal. With you? And him?"

"Aye. He asked for my hand. Father agreed."

"You think your visions tell of the future? That he's up to no good?"

"Why else would he want to ask for my hand? Father only agreed because he's an Elf."

Eldrin grimaced. "I'm sorry."

"So am I."

She knew what she had to do.

Allanna had no choice but to attend the banquet that evening. Andahar was sent to make sure she was properly dressed in one of her finest gowns. He escorted her to the dining hall where the king would announce the betrothal of Princess Allanna and Lord-Regent Marath.

"There's no sense sulking about it, Allanna," Andahar said as they walked.

"Then you marry him," she snipped.

"He's not so bad," Andahar said.

"Why are you defending him? The man is despicable. And I don't trust him. Why is he trying to say Queen Elyne is going to attack the Elves and kidnap me? It's unbelievable. Elyne and I are friends."

Why else would she send Sir Drake to the Woodlands?

"I've no idea."

"You don't believe it, do you, Andahar?"

After hesitating, he said, "No."

"Why would Father allow him to stay? Why would he allow him to court me? I don't understand any of this."

"Mayhap Father has an agenda all his own," Andahar suggested. "One he has not shared with me."

"I do not wish to marry that man."

"It would behoove you to make the best of your situation," Andahar said.

"Or what, brother?"

"Marath is one of our biggest land holders. He's a noble."

"Aye, but he bought that title. He swindled Father into giving it to him."

"How do you know that?"

"I know lots of things."

"Well, at any rate, he should be treated with respect as a noble."

"Bollocks." Allanna tried out the curse she'd heard Elyne use. She liked it.

"Watch your language."

"I'll not, Andahar, as long as that man lives and breathes. I don't like him."

"Why this sudden hatred against the man?" Andahar asked.

"He's going to... I don't trust him, that's all."

His eyes narrowed into slits. "Did you have a vision?"

"If I did, what of it? Neither you nor Father believe them."

He halted in the corridor, took her by the arm and spun her toward him. "Tell me."

"No." She could be as stubborn as her brother.

He huffed out a heated breath. "Tell me, Allanna. If there's something you saw...something you know...I need to know."

"And then what will you do? You'll break the betrothal? You'll keep me away from him?" She shook her head. "Once the official papers are drawn and signed by the king's hand, there is nothing that can be done unless he decides to break it."

"But if there is some danger—"

"If there is some danger there is naught to be done about it. It has not come to pass."

"'Tis the future you saw."

"Aye. I saw the future."

"Tell me, please." His fingers dug into her arm to press his point.

"Why this sudden interest in my visions, Andahar? You never cared before."

"I care now."

She glared at him. "You've never believed me. Only Eldrin has. Why should I tell you?"

"If Eldrin knows, then I'll ask him." He released her arm.

"Eldrin is the only one who has treated me like a sister. You treat me as though I were royal property."

"Allanna, that isn't true and you know it. I treat you as a princess."

"Aye, you treat me as a *princess* but not a *sister.*"

He pressed his lips together. "You have duties and responsibilities. Yet you continue to shirk them. You've refused to show up for your dancing lessons, your lute lessons, or any of your tutors. Instead you don boy's clothing to climb trees and shoot arrows. It's disgraceful."

"Disgraceful, am I?"

Aye, it was all true. She hated those classes. What good was learning to dance or play the lute? A lute wouldn't protect her like a bow and arrow would. A lute was nothing but a worthless instrument. A bow, though, was not.

"Not *you*. What you do."

She huffed out a breath and folded her arms. "You were killed by Marath's sword."

He stared at her and then shook his head. "Preposterous."

"See? I knew you wouldn't believe me." She stalked down the corridor.

"Why would Marath kill me?" Andahar asked, following her.

"I don't know. Why don't you ask him?" she retorted.

He pulled her to a stop. "All right, then. I'll have the man watched while he's here. Mayhap there is something to these visions of yours."

She decided now was not the time to tell him she'd also had a vision of marrying Sir Drake. "Thank you, my brother. I would feel more at ease knowing he is being watched closely."

"Come along. Let's get to the banquet before the king wonders where we've gone off to."

He led her into the banquet hall. Toward her doom.

When they entered, she pulled him to a halt and pressed her hand against her roiling stomach. Lord-Regent Marath was already there sitting with her father and Eldrin at the high table. Several long tables lined one side. The other side was for dancing and the small group of musicians already playing music.

Most of the nobility were in attendance, clearly expecting the great announcement their princess was to be married. Servants walked briskly through the room, setting out trenchers and filling goblets with mead or wine. Everyone seemed to be dressed in their finest attire.

"I can't do this, Andahar," she said.

"Aye, you can. You will."

"Can you not tell everyone I suddenly fell ill?"

"Nay, I cannot. Come along." He gave her a gentle tug and walked toward the high table.

Marath's dark, glittering gaze latched on to her immediately. Ogling her as though she were some prize. Her stomach clenched. The men rose as they approached. Marath gave her a halfhearted bow as Andahar delivered her to her seat between the lord and the king.

She was not pleased she would have to endure sitting next to him all evening.

Before the king took his seat again, he called for the attention of all those in the hall. He held his silver goblet.

"Thank you all for coming. It is with great joy I make this long-awaited announcement. Lord-Regent Marath has asked for the princess's hand in marriage and I have agreed."

Silence descended. Was it shocked silence? Or merely Allanna's imagination? She glanced around the surprised faces of the nobles. Finally one brave soul clapped and others quickly followed. It was nothing more than polite applause, though, and everyone in the room knew it.

Urdithane raised his goblet. "A toast to the happy couple."

He lifted his goblet and sipped. The nobles in the room responded with, "To the couple," before sipping their own wine.

Allanna caught Eldrin's sorrowful gaze, as though apologizing for her betrothal. But what could he do? Could he help her? Their father was their king and they too must abide by his rule.

Well, she wouldn't. She wasn't going to do anything of the sort. Already her mind worked on an escape plan.

"Princess, do me the honor of a dance," Marath said.

It was the last thing she wanted to do. But Marath was on his feet holding his hand down to her. Some of the nobles gave her expectant looks. She hesitated and her father gave her a nudge.

"Go on, princess. Dance with your betrothed."

Reluctantly, she reached for his hand. His cold fingers closed over hers. He was nothing like Drake. Not warm and charming. Not handsome and dashing. He was cold with cold eyes.

He led her to the floor where the musicians played a cheerful tune. A lively reel in which she would be able to switch partners throughout the dance. Thank the gods. She would not have to endure his closeness for the entire dance.

"I'm quite honored the king has agreed to our marriage, princess," Marath said.

"Are you?" She wanted to tell him how unhappy she was but instead clenched her teeth to keep from speaking.

"Your surpassing beauty is one of legend."

Was that his roundabout way of giving her a compliment? The hair on the back of her neck rose, standing at rigid attention. What did that mean? She granted him a faint smile as he spun her on the dance floor.

"I thank you," she said. "At least it seems appropriate to thank you if you intended that to be flattering."

"Indeed. Though I confess I hope we can accelerate the amount of time we must be betrothed," he said.

"Oh? And why is that?" Less time to be engaged? She hated the thought of accelerating the time before she must take her marriage vows.

"Aye. A year seems much too long to wait for you." His lecherous gaze went over her before coming back to her face.

Her skin crawled with icy pinpricks sending cold fear into the center of her heart. This was not a man to whom she wanted to give herself.

"I do hope you feel the same way," he said.

"About you, my lord?" she asked, cocking her head to the side in innocence. Was he insane? "I much prefer you to court me for the allotted time. It would give me ample time to get to know you."

And ample time for her to run away.

"Mayhap you will allow some time together in the near future," he suggested.

"Aren't we having time together now, my lord?"

"I meant time *alone*, princess."

Her stomach clenched. No, no, no. She had no intention of ever being alone with him.

It was then she realized Marath had been ignoring the dance rules and not allowed her to go with the other partners as she should have. In fact, he'd managed to spin her away from most of those in the crowd. A few were nearby but those seemed to turn a blind eye to her predicament.

But she wouldn't panic. Not yet. Despite the jolt her heart made followed by the wild pumping. She must maintain her cool. The last thing she needed to do was make him angry. Even so, she didn't like the way things were going.

He stopped dancing and pulled her to him, holding her hands in his, close to his lips. His rancid breath wafted over her face. She clenched her mouth and held her breath, determined not to flinch or show him any sign of weakness. She didn't want him to know he was getting to her.

"Time alone, my lord?" Her voice shook and her mouth went dry. She hated he could hear her fear. She clamped down on that fear and tried to push it away.

"Walk with me."

His hand clamped around her wrist as he led her from the great hall down the corridor. He'd been in the palace enough to know the layout and she suspected he took her toward the hanging gardens. Her people had cultivated the gardens to live among the branches of the trees. The flowers were colorful and fragrant and found nowhere else in the realm.

She thought for certain that's where he headed. Instead, he took the turn toward the palace exit and started for the rope bridge that connected it to the winding staircase leading down to the ground. Fear clawed through her at breakneck speed. Where was he taking her? Had anyone seen them leave together?

"Where are we going?" she asked. She had to do something to keep her mind distracted from being alone with the man.

"To get to know each other." His leering smile made the panic swell inside her. "I look forward to our marriage."

"Do you?" She didn't. Anything would be better than marrying that man. Anything including a hot poker in the eye. "Why is that, my lord?"

"You are a princess, are you not?"

"Is that why you want to marry me? I find that rather off-putting if you want me solely for my title."

"Not merely for your title."

Those dark and devious eyes glinted with a malevolent light as he looked her over. As though he stripped her bare. As though he knew what she looked like under her shift. As though he knew what he wanted to do to her body with his mouth. That dark-pink tongue darted out over his lips to moisten them.

Acid churned in the pit of her stomach.

Allanna had the urge to cover herself with her hands. But it was too late. He'd already surveyed her body in an intimate way that made her shiver with fear. There was *nothing* attractive about this man. Nothing she wanted in a husband. No characteristic she could overlook to at least *want* to consummate their marriage.

She knew exactly what he meant by saying that. She could read between the lines. She understood his innuendo and it disgusted her to the core. He was truly someone of whom to be terrified.

"Come. I want to introduce you to some friends of mine."

"Friends? I thought we were going to get to know each other."

"Oh, aye, friends. They want to know you too." He gave her a sidelong glance that did nothing to stave off the dread. "They will take good care of you."

A scream clotted in her throat as her hand flew up and pressed against her neck. "They?" She whispered it and she hated how it made her sound weak and afraid. She didn't want him to have that kind of control over her.

"Don't be afraid, princess." His tone was mocking, his smile so dark it didn't meet his eyes. Those dark, despicable, devious eyes.

"Let me go." Allanna tried to tug her wrist free of his hand but he held firm. Like a manacle clamped around her wrist.

"My friends are really quite lovely," he continued as though she hadn't spoken. "They'll enjoy having you in their presence."

Her stomach clenched tight and a cold heat broke out over her skin. "Let me go or I'll scream."

"Go ahead and try, princess," he said. "Scream."

His eyes had darkened so much she could no longer see the pupils. His skin had turned a white, sickly pallor. Sweat beaded his top lip and the angry crease in his forehead. He leaned in closer and that's when she released the scream that had lodged in her throat. When she stopped, he laughed.

"No one can hear you or see you, highness. I have placed a concealment spell over us. You and I are hidden from prying eyes."

He wrapped an arm around her shoulders and pulled her tight against him. His body heat penetrated through her gown and she fought the bile rising in her throat.

"Allanna?" Eldrin called.

She gasped and wiggled against Marath. "Eldrin, here!"

"He can't hear you, highness."

Holding her against, him he dragged her down the rope bridge and toward the stairs. She had to get away from him before he got there. But first she had to release her fear. Years of training with her brother kicked in and she dug her heels in, halting them. Marath loosened his grip on her enough for her to wrench around in front of him.

She lifted her knee and embedded it in his groin as hard as she could. He grunted and doubled over. While he was incapacitated, she kicked him in the shin with the toe of her slipper.

She spotted her brother then as he charged toward them. Mayhap kicking him broke his concentration enough to release the spell. She didn't know but she was relieved to see Eldrin, his face pinched in fury and his sword drawn.

"What's going on here?" he asked.

Marath had recovered enough to stand straight. Sweat beaded his entire face now.

"Your sister and I were getting acquainted. That's all. She offered herself to me."

"You filthy liar! He was taking me to his 'friends'."

"Your friends, my lord?" Eldrin moved to stand between her and the lord-regent. "Stay away from her."

"Would that I could, my lord, but she and I are betrothed. I have every right to her."

"Not if I have anything to do with it. I'm no fool. I saw you drag her away." Eldrin stepped closer and lifted his sword, putting the point in the Elf's face. "If you lay another hand on her, I'll kill you."

Marath snickered, clearly unflustered by Eldrin's threat. He swept a hand through his hair and then stepped around them, walking down the staircase to the ground. Allanna blew out a breath. Her hands shook and she thought she might retch. Eldrin turned to her.

"Are you all right?"

"Aye, I'm fine. But he scared me. He said he put a concealment spell over us. I tried to scream."

"That explains why I couldn't see you at first. Then suddenly I could."

"I kicked him in the groin," she said. "I think he must have lost his concentration."

He snickered. "Good. I'm glad you're okay."

"I don't trust him."

"Nor I. I will speak to Father."

"The sooner the better," she said. "I don't want to marry that man."

"I don't want you to either. Come. I'll walk you to your chamber."

Chapter 6

Drake kept the gates of the Woodlands under close surveillance. The Elf who'd entered earlier had made the hairs on the back of his neck stand on end.

Instead of riding back toward the Queen's Palace as he promised, he'd taken up residence in the thicket not far from the egress. The shadows from the trees kept him concealed enough to keep a close watch. He'd waited until sundown but nothing happened. No one had emerged. His horse stomped one hoof, as restless as he.

He patted her neck.

"Easy, old girl. If nothing happens by sunup, we'll be on our way."

The mare snorted in response.

He doubted the horse could understand him, but it gave him comfort to hear his own voice in the silence.

"I don't trust him, either," he said.

When Drake had ridden out of the Woodlands, his heart had been heavy. At least he'd had one last chance to spend with the princess. One last moment of farewell. Her sweet face would linger with him always so he could call upon it during the lonely nights. The nights he ached for the want of her. Nights like this.

He knew the best place for him was back in his realm. Where he would joust once more and become a hero again. And he would do his best to forget the aching hole in his chest.

But he didn't want to forget the aching hole in his chest. Or the princess. It was what drove him to remain in the shadows of the night, watching, waiting.

The Elf he'd seen enter the gates was dressed in fine clothes, which indicated he was someone of importance. A small entourage followed him. He assumed this was Lord-Regent Marath that Eldrin had mentioned was on his way to see the king. His slender form sat tall in the saddle with his head held high and his hawkish nose firmly planted in the air. As he trotted by Drake, his black gaze landed on him. His black, depthless gaze that seemed to speak of evil and darkness.

Something about the look sent a coldness piercing through him. Drake watched, kept his gaze trained on him as they passed through the entrance and into the Woodlands. Who was he? What did he want from the king? If Allanna was ordered to be in attendance, then did this lord-regent intend to propose marriage?

The thought sickened him.

So he waited.

And his waiting paid off. Shadowy movement caught his eye and he turned his head to see four robed figures skulking through the gloom. He patted the horse again and slid out of the saddle.

"I'm going to get closer and see what they're about."

The horse softly whickered, as though she understood what he said.

He unsheathed his sword, gripping it as he skirted from shadow to shadow, trying to get closer to the figures.

The gate opened and the tall, slender Lord-Regent Marath slipped out. When he spotted the men, he met them outside. Drake was too far away to hear what they were saying. But he could clearly see him pass a coin bag to what appeared to be the leader. Then he turned and went back inside.

How had Marath managed to get past Lord Navin? The Elf was a fierce guard. Unless Navin was somehow incapacitated.

Drake watched as the four men turned and walked back the way they'd come. They seemed to meld with the darkness, disappearing almost as quickly as they appeared.

Something wasn't right. His instincts told him so and he needed to get back inside the Woodlands. He needed to get back to Allanna. No one was about now that the four men had disappeared. He took a look left and right and then bolted. Panting hard to catch his breath, he noticed the gate was cracked open as he approached.

That was certainly not like Lord Navin either. He would never leave it open. Another warning sign. With the tip of his sword, he pushed it open. On the other side was nothing but shadows and darkness. And an unconscious Lord Navin.

He stepped inside and knelt at his side to check his pulse. The lord was still alive but he had a bleeding gash on his head. He would need medical attention and soon. Drake glanced around but saw no one. How could he get back into the palace to find Lord Eldrin? The ranger could help him. The one Elf he considered friend.

As he rose to his full height, an arrow flew past him, missing the side of his head. He stepped back, cowering into the darkness.

Lord Marath came into the clearing, a bow and arrow at the ready. "Show yourself."

Drake pressed his back into a tree, still holding his sword and weighing his options. Should he attack? He was fast but was he fast enough to avoid the next flying arrow? How good of a shot was this Marath? As he prepared to step out of hiding, Lord Eldrin arrived. When he saw his brother on the ground, he hurried to him.

"Marath, what happened here?"

"There's a man hiding in the shadows there. I think he must have attacked Navin."

Bastard.

Eldrin looked up, his gaze landing on Drake. He knew he could do nothing but surrender. Sheathing his sword, he held up his hands and stepped into view.

"Sir Drake?" Eldrin didn't hide the surprise in his voice. Even in the darkness Drake could see his raised eyebrows. "What are you doing here?"

"I was outside the gates when I saw Marath exit. He spoke to four men and then returned. He left the gate open. I found Lord Navin." Drake nodded to the unconscious Elf lord.

"That's a falsehood. I'm the one who found Lord Navin," Marath said.

Eldrin glanced from Drake to Marath and back again. "You saw him outside the gate?"

"Aye, I did," Drake said.

Eldrin's gaze swung back to the lord-regent. "Tell me, my lord, what you were doing outside the gate."

"You believe this…this…human over me?" He spat out the word *human* as though it were something vile and tasteless. "I am a lord. A noble."

"Aye, I know who you are. I also know what you're capable of," Eldrin said. "And now is not the time to discuss this. Lord Navin requires the healer. Sir Drake, will you help me?"

"How can you request the assistance of him?" Marath asked.

"I know Sir Drake," Eldrin said. "He fought for us against the Unseelie. I trust him with my life."

Marath's eyes narrowed to nothing more than slits. "Do you."

It was not a question. It was nothing more than a statement, as though Marath couldn't believe Eldrin would agree with the human.

"Aye, I do," the ranger said. Drake shouldered one side of Navin while Eldrin took his other. "Come. Let's get him to the healer."

Together, they carried Navin from the clearing, leaving Marath behind.

"Is he telling the truth?" Eldrin whispered.

"No," Drake said.

"As I suspected."

"He gave the men a pouch filled with, I assume, gold."

"Are you certain?"

"Aye, I am. I daresay I don't trust this man, Lord Eldrin."

"Nor I."

After Eldrin had taken her back to her room, Allanna had immediately dismissed her maid, wishing to be alone. To think. She paced the length of her chamber, biting her thumbnail.

How long had she paced? Her feet ached. Her head pounded with all her emotions. The banquet must be over by now. Had Eldrin returned? Did her father know what Marath tried to do? And what of the lord-regent? Had he returned as though nothing were amiss?

If Eldrin hadn't come along…she couldn't think about that now. She put her hand to her throat, aware of the fluttering pulse. She couldn't allow him near her again. Therefore, her mind was made up. She'd come to a final decision.

Drake was her heart. The man she wanted. The man she loved. Not Marath. She came to an abrupt halt as she glanced around her room, a sadness taking root. Aye, she would be leaving here forever. Her father and brothers would never speak to her again. She would be cast out. Disowned. Forgotten. She would never be allowed back into the palace. She would forsake all that she was to be with Drake.

He was worth it.

She needed a horse. She would leave *tonight*. She would not wait another minute. Nor would she stay here and suffer the indignity of being betrothed to that monster. She quickly changed into trousers and a tunic—some of Eldrin's old clothes she'd managed to confiscate years ago. She'd traipsed all over the Otherworld in them as she fought alongside Derron, Elyne and her brother. She could do this.

She *would* do this.

Determination set up in her bones as she pulled on her riding boots and grabbed her quiver of arrows, then slung her bow over her shoulder. She would not go unarmed because, as much as she hated to admit it, the forest was still a dangerous place to travel. There were still Unseelie scavenging the post-war land.

She crept to her chamber door and pressed her ear against the wood. She heard nothing but then she wouldn't. Damned Elven oak. She could hardly hear through it. She cracked open the door and peered into the hallway. She could see no one about. It seemed to be deserted.

Allanna swung wide the door and stepped into the light. Her heart rammed hard and fast as she stood there, scanning her surroundings. She heard a commotion below and stepped toward the edge of the railing to look over into the great hall. Eldrin and Sir Drake carried Lord Navin between them, Marath trailing behind.

Sir Drake!

She blinked, making sure her eyes didn't deceive her. Why was he still here? And what had happened to Navin? When Marath's gaze lifted to her, she jumped back, pressing into the cold stone wall. She turned and deposited her bow and arrows back into her chamber and bolted for the stairs. She ran down, skidding to a halt near her brother.

"What happened?"

"Someone attacked him," Eldrin said. "Fetch the healer. Marath, clear off that table."

"I will do no such thing." Marath folded his arms over his chest and turned up his nose.

What a knave. Allanna shot him a heated glare, her fists clenched at her side.

"Allanna, please, fetch the healer." Then to Marath, "You *will* do it. And now."

He gave one last glare at Eldrin before he swept his arm over the table. Cups scattered, clattering to the wood floor. Drake and Eldrin gently laid Navin on the table.

"I will escort the princess," Drake said.

Allanna didn't miss the narrow gaze of Marath as she and Drake took off for the healer's chamber. She walked at a fast clip, but Drake's long legs easily kept up with her.

"I thought you were gone." She tried desperately not to look at him.

Looking at him would be her undoing. Looking at him would make her weak in the knees. It would make her want to kiss him.

"I was," he said, his voice low. His eyes averted. "I'd left the gates when I saw Marath and his men enter. Something about him didn't feel right so I stayed. I hid in the copse of trees and watched and waited."

He halted then, taking her arm and pulling her to a stop. He stepped close enough to her she could smell leather and horse. Scents she would always associate with the towering knight. Her heart skipped a beat.

"He spoke to four men outside the gates and then returned. He left it open. I followed him straightaway and found Navin. Allanna, that man is dangerous. I don't want you anywhere near him."

"I agree. But we...we are betrothed." She didn't want to tell him but she didn't want to hide the truth either. As soon as she said the words, pain flashed through his gaze and then he straightened, his face taking on the hard edge of determination.

"Betrothed?"

"Aye but not because I wish it." She clutched his sleeve, her nails digging into his wrist. "You must understand my father agreed to the arrangement, I believe, to make me forget you. And because he is Elven."

He said nothing as he looked at her, considering. Then, "Have you? Forgotten me?"

"Gods, no. Never."

"Good. Then let's see what we can do to get you away from him. But first, to the healer."

Minutes later, they woke Brom and dragged him from his bed. They led him back to where Eldrin waited. Lord Marath was nowhere in sight. She was glad. She detested that man.

The healer checked Navin's head. "He will live. Though he will need much rest in the coming days. Eldrin, help me take him to his chamber."

Allanna watched as the two lifted Navin from the table and carried him away. That left her alone with Sir Drake. He stood behind her. Before he could say a word, she spun and put her hands on his chest. She glanced around, checking to make sure they were alone. She felt certain there were no prying eyes—or ears.

"I'm coming with you," she said.

"Shh. Do not speak of that here."

"We are alone." Yet she cast another cursory glance. "There is no one to hear. I'm coming."

"No." He gave a quick shake of his head. "I cannot allow you to do that."

"It is my choice to make. I choose you."

Indecision flashed through his eyes. He took her hands in his, kissed her fingertips. "Are you certain? You risk—"

"I know what I risk. Am I to stay and marry a man I do not love?"

"You would forsake all that you are, Allanna. I cannot allow you to do that. I would never forgive myself for allowing you to do that."

"*You* are worth it, Drake. I cannot walk through the rest of eternity without you. You have nothing to forgive if I make the decision."

"But you are immortal. And I will age and die." Even as he said it, he pulled her into his arms, held her to him and brushed his hand down the length of her hair.

"Queen Maeve gave up her immortality for Henry. I can do the same. We will visit Elyne for she knows the spell."

As she rested her head against his chest, she could hear the distinctive *thump thump* of his heart. "Ah, princess. You would give all that up for me?"

"I would give everything up for you." She tilted her head back to look at him.

The tenderness in his gaze nearly rent her heart in two. She placed her hands on either side of his face and stood on tiptoe.

"I swear it."

"And your family? What of them?"

Sorrow slashed through. She would miss Eldrin most of all. "I love you, Drake. I've always loved you. I will always love you," she whispered and then touched her lips to his.

But Drake was not so content with a gentle kiss. He cupped the back of her head and dragged her to him, kissing her thoroughly, madly, passionately. His tongue dove into the recesses of her mouth, tasting, sipping. For that breath of time, their mouths devoured each other, their souls touched, and she knew she would never regret her decision to love this man.

He broke and kissed her forehead. "And you're certain?"

"Aye."

"Then follow my directions and we will escape this place."

"I will do whatever you say."

"I will ride out past the gate and wait for you in the copse of trees. Wait as long as you can and then come to me there. Make sure no one sees you. Can you do that?"

"Aye, I can. I will."

"Good." He kissed her forehead once more. "Stay safe, my princess."

Before she could respond he released her and hurried toward the door. He was gone in an instant, leaving her standing there with kiss-bruised lips and her heart pumping madly.

He was hers. And she was his. And that was all that mattered.

Lord-Regent Marath stood in the shadows at the top of the stairs and watched the romance play out in the great hall below. He had intended to return to convince the princess to come with him so he could deliver her to Lorcann himself. However, when he saw the two standing together speaking in low tones, he pressed into the shadows and cast his concealment spell to hide his form. He overheard everything.

So the princess was in love with a human. Heated anger spilled through his blood, igniting the dark magic there. Fueling it. He would not let her get away. Not like this. She was his to do with as he pleased. And he was pleased to kill her.

They planned to run away together? He thought not. He would do everything within his power to make sure the couple never saw each other again. Even if he had to kill the man.

His fists clenched then he relaxed his muscles. It would not do to be angry. Mayhap he could use this situation to his advantage. He needed to remove the man from Allanna's thoughts and the only way to do that was ridding the Otherworld of him.

Smiling, he steepled his fingers as he watched the knight leave.

Allanna took the stairs two at a time. He waited until she was at the top before he stepped out in front of her. She gasped in her fright and stumbled backward, her heel slipping off the top step. Her arms flailed as she tried to keep her balance, her eyes wide with fear.

He didn't want his prize damaged. Not yet. He dragged her to him, holding her close. He could see the flutter of her pulse in the long column of her neck. Her eyes were wide and wild as she looked at him.

"Do I frighten you, princess?"

"You startled me. That's all."

She wrenched free and stepped around him, as far as she could get. Inching down the length of the hallway toward her door. He moved with lightning speed. So fast he hadn't realized he'd done it. Was this a new ability he'd somehow developed? If so, it was something he could certainly use to his advantage. He crowded her against the wall, placing a hand on either side of her head to pin her there. Her owlish blue eyes, glassy with fear, blinked back at him.

He could feel the tingle of darkness in his blood surging forward. Stoking the fire of his anger and hatred.

"Did I? Does that explain the rosy color in your cheeks then? Or is that from something else?"

She dragged her lower lip through her teeth. "Let me go or I'll scream."

"Scream all you wish, highness. There is no one to hear you."

He'd invoked his concealment spell again. No one would see them. She pressed against the wall, trying to get farther away from him. He pressed toward her, closing the small gap between them. She turned her head away, her eyes squeezing shut. He could hear her labored breathing.

"Please," she whispered.

A fire pendant nestled between her small breasts. The orange crystal reflected the candlelight in the corridor.

"Lovely pendant. Where did you get it?"

She didn't answer. He ran his finger down the chain to the jewel in the center. As soon as his flesh met the gem, his skin sizzled. He jerked his hand back with a curse. Allanna's eyes flew open in surprise.

"How did you do that?" he demanded.

"Do what?"

"You invoked the crystal."

"I didn't. I swear. Please, Marath. Let me go."

Touching the gemstone had killed his concealment spell. It would do no good to have her damaged now, even if he did want to take her against the wall. Even if she did have this shield of protection around her. He smiled slowly.

"Your brother will not be able to protect you forever, princess."

Allanna skittered away from him and hurried to her chamber. She pushed open the door and slammed it without a backward glance.

There was still the human to contend with. Once he was taken care of, Marath would return for the princess and deliver her to Lorcann himself.

Marath hurried down the stairs and out the door. He still had time to catch the human knight. The magic stirred again in his blood as he stepped through the doorway. He'd flashed to the princess earlier. He wondered if he could do it again. If he could find the knight. The Fae called it sifting. Flashing was not so different yet it was something Elves could not do. This new skill must be something he'd acquired as a side effect of the dark magic he'd invoked.

Once outside the palace, he slipped the glass-blade dirk from his belt and closed his eyes. He had but to imagine the man. Seconds later he flashed to the knight's location.

He appeared next to Drake as he was leading his horse out of the stable. His eyes widened when he saw Marath's sudden appearance. He fumbled as he tried to draw his sword but Marath was quicker. He lunged and struck. He buried the dirk in the human's side under his ribs. Marath twisted the blade as Drake wrenched to the side. He stumbled away, gasping as his hand closed around the hilt of his sword.

He unsheathed his blade with one hand and pressed his other against the wound. Blood seeped through his fingers. Marath held the dirk and lifted it but noticed the tip was curiously missing. He concealed his smile, knowing the Elven glass had broken off inside the human. He had not intended to break the tip off but now he was glad. The man would experience a slow, painful death and that made Marath happy. The obstacle between him and Allanna would be permanently removed.

The knight swung his sword in a wide arc but Marath anticipated that. He put up a hand, knocking away the sword with a flash of light. The magic came all too easily to him now. He could invoke it at will. And he did not need to stand in the middle of the circle of power. All he needed to do was think about what he wanted.

Drake lost his hold on the sword. It tumbled to the ground with a muffled *thunk*. Marath waved the bloodied dirk with the missing tip at him.

"I assume we need no exchange of threats, sir knight," Marath said. "The princess is mine."

"She belongs to no man."

"Even you?" He arched a brow. "If you take her from the palace, I will hunt you both down."

"Stay away from her," Drake warned.

"Or what? You'll kill me? You'll soon be dead and the princess will have no one to protect her."

"I'm not afraid of you," the knight said. He pressed his hand against his side to stanch the bleeding but it was really no use. He'd already lost color in his face. "I *will* kill you."

Marath had more important things to do than waste time with this useless human. He had one more stop to make before he returned to the princess.

"I look forward to it." With a flourish, he bowed and flashed away.

Allanna slid the bar into place on the back of her door and pressed against it. Sickly fear crept through her. Had Marath seen them in the hall? Did he know the truth? She pressed her hand against her mouth as bile rose to the back of her throat.

That look he gave her was evil. Pure and simple. She had never seen his eyes so black and depthless. And for a moment she thought she could see something spark there. Something not of this world.

Now more than ever she had to get out of here. She snatched her bow and arrows and turned back to the door. She pressed her ear against the wood to listen but, again, heard nothing. She was about to slide the bar out of place when something or someone banged against the door, trying to open it.

Her heart jumped as she leapt back with a squeak.

Bang. Bang. Bang.

"Let me in, princess."

Marath. By the gods, she would never let him inside her chamber. She swung around to the balcony and charged outside. It was too far to jump. Hot tears stung her eyes. How was she going to get to Drake? Would he wait for her?

Another bang on her door and she gripped the railing. She had no choice. She had to find another way out of her chamber. She turned back to her room, scanning it. She had lots of gowns she could rip into shreds and use. But she didn't have time. Marath was determined to get through. The wood had started to splinter.

Where was Eldrin? And her father? And Andahar? Would they hear the noise coming from her room? Unless that devil Marath used another concealment spell. By the gods!

She ran back to the balcony and peered over the edge. There seemed to be plenty of handholds and footholds. Maybe she could climb down most of the way. Or over to another balcony. With her heart in her throat, she stepped over the railing as her door splintered into a thousand pieces. Wood shards rained down and scattered on the floor. With a gasp, she ducked down, perching on the narrow ledge and plastered her body against the balcony.

She prayed the cover of darkness would hide her from Marath. She heard his footsteps in her chamber as he walked out onto the balcony. He stopped, his boots scuffing on the floor as she held her breath. She wasn't sure how much longer she could hang on. Her muscles ached and sweat popped out on her brow. Her legs cramped and it took all her concentration to keep still.

Then she heard him walk back into her chamber. He banged open her wardrobe. She pulled up to peer over the edge. He flung gowns, cloaks and shoes out, leaving a mess behind. Then he turned to the bed, yanked all the blankets off and peered underneath.

Standing to his full height, his hands fisted at his sides, he let out a blood-curdling scream of frustration. Fear jolted through her as she ducked down again. Why was he so desperate to find her? What did he want with her?

It couldn't be anything good.

She heard receding footsteps and waited several heartbeats before she stood again. Her muscles stiffened. She nearly lost her balance. One foot slipped off the tiny ledge as she grabbed the balcony railing. Then she hoisted over it and landed on the floor. She huddled there, trying to slow her heart and catch her breath. She didn't want to linger too long. He could come back to do a more thorough search.

With a surge of adrenaline, she shoved to her feet and ran out of her chamber, grabbing her bow and arrows as she went.

Chapter 7

When Marath disappeared in a flash, Drake blinked, the bright light still bobbing in his vision. He fumbled for his sword and snatched it up. He glanced around the stables looking for something—anything—he could use to stop the bleeding. He found old rags. Dirty but usable. He wadded one up and stuck it under his tunic, pressing against the wound. Then he found a tattered black cloak and snatched it off the hook, slipping it on. It would conceal the blood soaking his tunic.

He would deal with his injury when he and Allanna were safely away from the palace.

It took some effort to get on his horse, but he was able to climb into the saddle. Grabbing the reins, he trotted out of the stables and toward the gate. Toward freedom. He knew he'd lost a lot of blood but couldn't think about that right now. Nor could he think about the pain burning through his side. Whatever the man stabbed him with, it left a fire burning there. He had to get to the copse of trees where he'd promised the princess he would be waiting for her.

The gate was unmanned and still ajar. With a groan, he slid out of the saddle and threw the gate wide enough to lead his horse out, limping every step of the way. Once on the other side, he pulled the gate closed then remounted and trotted to the trees. With every jarring trot, heated pain lanced through him. The ground tilted. It took all he had to remain seated. He gripped the reins tighter to stay in the saddle and clenched his teeth to tamp down the pain.

Moments after settling into place, he saw four hooded men. They jogged down the length of the wall toward the gate. They must be the same ones he'd seen earlier with Marath. He sat straighter in his saddle, giving a valiant effort to ignore the fiery pain in his side. His hands had started to shake. He saw pinpricks of light in his vision—and not from Marath's flash. He'd been injured enough in the past to know he would pass out any moment.

But he had to stay conscious for her. He could not fail her.

They paused beside the gate, pressing against the wall and blending with the shadows. He would have never known they were there if he hadn't seen them. Who were these men? What did they want? The only thing Drake knew for certain was they worked for Marath, which was not a good sign at all.

Moments later the gate swung open and a second after that, Allanna burst through on foot. She'd run all the way to him? Mayhap she hadn't wanted to take the time to saddle a horse, thinking only of getting to him.

As soon as she burst through the gate into the night, the men leapt into action. Two were on her before she even knew what had happened. She emitted a startled scream before one of them got behind her and clamped a hand over her mouth. She struggled against him and kicked at the others coming at her.

Drake wielded his sword and kicked his mare into a gallop. He would reach her in moments. Moonlight glinted off his sword as he held it high enough for them to see.

But none of them seemed to be threatened by his sudden appearance. He couldn't make out any of their faces, as their hoods concealed their features. One turned toward him, his hands up as though in surrender. But the man was not surrendering. A yellow flash streamed from his palms.

The light hit him square in the chest, making him lose his grip on his sword. It slid out of his hand and fell to the ground next to him. He gripped the reins so tight, his mare screeched and reared back, threatening to dump him off her back. He'd been hit with a lance harder than that. Granted he'd been wearing armor at the time, but he still managed to stay astride even then. His chest smoked from the impact, leaving his tunic singed and more pain erupting through him. The bastard would pay for that.

He crooned to his mare, trying to calm her even as he kicked her into action again. Another flash of light came from the man but this time Drake veered to the side and it missed him.

By now, the other three had managed to tie Allanna's wrists together. They hoisted her between them as though she were a fresh kill and started trotting away. She struggled against them, looking like a fish out of water.

No. He wouldn't let them take her. Not while he still breathed.

The leader still held his ground, ready to send another strike. As he neared, he jerked up on the reins, making his mare rear back again. This time, she kicked at the man. Drake would have thought deadly hooves and two thousand pounds of muscle would be intimidating. But it wasn't. He merely took a step back, the mare barely missing him.

Bloody hell.

The moment of distraction cost him. Another bolt of light hit him in the shoulder. It was so powerful it knocked him out of the saddle. He tumbled to the ground, landed with a grunt. Heat lanced through the stab wound in his side and he thought he might retch. His stomach roiled. All his limbs felt as though they were encased in fire.

How could he fight magic unarmed?

And then he spotted Allanna's bow and quiver of arrows discarded on the ground. He scrambled through the dirt to get to them. It'd been a while since he'd used the weapon but he knew it would come back to him with ease. He snatched up the bow and nocked the arrow. In one fluid motion, he spun and released the arrow at the same time.

He hadn't really aimed, nor could he see all that well in the dark. He was as surprised as the leader when the arrow lodged in his shoulder. The enemy emitted a low growl as he looked down then broke it off and flung it to the ground. The small distraction gave Drake enough time to release arrow after arrow, his aim true. He would not allow the others to get away with his woman. He hit every one of Allanna's captors. They dropped to the ground. Drake cringed when Allanna hit with a thud.

But the leader wasn't done with him yet. He sent another flash of light toward him. It hit him in the chest again and he stumbled backward. Unable to keep his footing, he dropped to the ground. Luckily, he landed near his felled sword. His hand closed over the hilt. As he snatched it and climbed to his feet, he turned toward the leader.

Allanna had managed to get out of her bonds. He saw her rushing toward them. He wanted to cry out for her to stop but he couldn't. The words froze in his throat. And then he saw the flash of a small blade in her hand. The leader spun to face her, his hands raised in the air, ready to strike. When she lunged toward the man, though, he flashed away. She sliced through air.

She stumbled forward a few steps before she regained her footing. Even in the dim shadows, he could see her momentarily disoriented as she blinked her eyes and then recovered. She sheathed the dagger and ran to him.

"Drake!" When she fell to her knees at his side, her gaze met his and he could see the relief evident in her face. "Gods, are you all right?"

"How did you get away?"

"They didn't tie very secure knots," she said.

"Come. Let's get you out of here."

Fighting through the pain that had erupted all over him, he climbed to his feet, hiding his wound from her as best he could. She retrieved her bow and arrows. Then he took her by the hand and hobbled back to his mare.

"You're limping. Are you all right? Did he hurt you? Gods, I thought he'd killed you. Let me see your chest."

She shoved him aside to get a look but he turned away.

"I will be all right," he ground out through gritted teeth, though he felt as though he would pass out any minute. "Up you go now."

He helped her into the saddle then mounted behind her. Taking the reins in his hands, he kicked the horse into a gallop and rode away from the Woodlands.

Lorcann flashed away before the princess could attack him. The bloody girl. He paused inside the gate long enough to use his senses to find Marath. When he discovered him in one of the palace chambers, he flashed there. The Elven lord rose to greet him.

"What news?"

"The princess was taken, my lord."

"Taken? By whom?" Marath demanded. He clenched his fists and charged forward, stopping a breath away from Lorcann. "And what happened to you?"

"I was attacked by a man."

"A man?" Marath's gaze narrowed. "That bloody human knight. He must have survived and waited outside the gate. And what of the girl?"

"Escaped with his help."

"Why are you here? Go find them!"

"He killed my men," Lorcann growled. Already he grew tired of Marath and his demands. Was making an alliance with him truly worth it? It was time to make some of his own. "We have been slighted. My prize has been robbed from me. The princess is gone. Using so much of my power has drained me, therefore, I demand you release more of my people. So that I may serve you, my lord."

Serve him, aye. He would serve the lord-regent for as long as it was advantageous.

Marath stared at him a long moment. "That will take more magic than I possess."

"Then mayhap I will give you some of mine. Just enough to give you the power you need to free my men."

Lorcann snatched the dagger from Marath's belt. He swiped it down his palm and clenched his fist closed. Black blood seeped through his fingers and dripped to the floor. He held the dagger out to Marath.

"Your hand, my lord."

He could see the indecision and hesitation in his eyes. "You promised me my own land to rule. You promised me a title. You promised me a war. Are you now going back on that, Lord Marath?"

"Nay. I am not." Marath stretched out his hand.

Before Marath could change his mind, Lorcann sliced open his palm. Then he opened his and put them together. He could feel the magic in his blood seeping into Marath's. He tried to pull away but Lorcann closed his fingers around his palm and held him steady.

Marath shuddered. His eyes rolled back in his head. Lorcann could feel the darkness moving into him, tainting his blood. Sweat beaded his brow and the mage knew their blood was melding. Then Marath released a guttural cry before the flash of light enveloped the two of them. Their hands released and Marath drew back, holding the wrist of his injured hand and stumbling a few steps backward.

"The transfer is complete," Lorcann said. "Now...call my people. Bring them to me."

A ragged breath shuddered out of the man. "Aye. I will call your people."

"On your knees then."

"Now?"

"You wish me to wait? Is there no other suitable time than now? Call my people. You are quite adept at releasing their bonds so do it."

Marath fell to his knees. He braced his hands on the floor as he knelt. He closed his eyes and chanted the words. Hearing them after eons of being imprisoned put a smile on Lorcann's face. He too closed his eyes. Saying the words with the Elven lord in his head.

At last, his people would be freed from their prison. They would breathe and walk the land once again. But getting them here would take power and he had yet to recover from the attack by the human.

When Marath completed the chant, he sat back on his heels. His hand had left a bloody imprint on the floor.

"They are free," Marath said.

Lorcann smiled. But there was one more thing he needed the lord to do for him. "I thank you, my lord. Now flash three of my men here."

He pushed to his feet, the color drained from his face. "Flash them here? I do not have such an ability."

But Lorcann was already slashing his other hand with the dagger. He held it out to him, blood dripping to the floor, and extended the bloodied knife to him. "You will."

Marath stared wide-eyed at him a long moment before he finally took the knife and sliced his other palm. They joined hands again, Lorcann closing his eyes. More darkness poured out of him and into Marath. There was an exchange of power—his seeping into the lord's blood while Lorcann took Marath's health and strength to regenerate himself. He gripped his hand hard before releasing and shoving him away. Marath fell to the floor, falling into the small pool of blood.

"Flash them," Lorcann commanded.

Still he hesitated.

"Do you want your princess or not?" Agitation crawled through his veins. "Did you hire me or not?"

"How do I do it?"

"Use your senses. As you do to flash yourself. You released them from their prison. Now bring them to me."

Marath hovered closer to the floor, his eyes closed as he concentrated. A flash of light and one arrived. Another flash of light and there was a second. Yet another and a third arrived. They were clearly disoriented at first and then quickly got their bearings.

"Welcome, my friends," Lorcann greeted, bloodied palms outward.

The three of them fell to the floor next to Marath and bowed. Marath sat back and surveyed the small group.

"You have your men," he said, his voice weak. "Now go find my princess."

"As you command, my lord." He turned to his men and they all clasped arms. "Shall we?"

With their help, Lorcann flashed away with them.

Drake and Allanna hadn't ridden long when it started to rain. It wasn't a light mist either. It was more of a torrential downpour. And with every jostling bounce, Drake knew he lost more blood. A quick glance down and he could see the dark stain seeping through his tunic and onto his leg. Blood had soaked the rag. It wouldn't be long before he passed out completely. He needed to find shelter and get somewhere safe. Somewhere he could recover.

He spotted a crofter's cabin ahead. It appeared to be dark inside. No telltale smoke curling from the chimney. No glowing candlelight in the windows. There was even a stable for the horse. He headed for it, slowing when they made it to the stable.

He all but fell out of the saddle.

"Drake!"

Allanna was at his side in an instant. She pulled away the cloak and saw his blood-stained tunic and trousers and blanched. "By the gods, Drake, you're wounded. Why did you not tell me?"

"Had to…get you to safety."

"Can you stand?"

Even as she said it she was trying to lift him. The charming girl. She couldn't lift him. He was too big and too heavy for her. Even so, he knew he had to try for her. He had to make it seem as though she were helping him. He struggled to stand and then stumbled toward the open stable door.

The ground wavered in front of him as rain pelted him in the face. He'd lost sight of the mare. Where had she gone? Allanna grunted as she led him into the stable and eased him down to the ground in a pile of hay.

"The horse?"

"I'll get her," she said and bolted before he could object.

A moment later she returned, leading the mare. She put her in one of the stalls as the mare whickered softly. Apparently even the horse was happy to be out of the weather. Allanna was back at his side, hovering over him.

"Let me see that." She shoved his tunic up and pulled the rag out of the way. "Gods…"

"That bad, eh?" he asked. "I daresay…it's…a mess." His teeth chattered. He'd never been so cold.

She stood and glanced around. He had no idea what she was looking for but then she disappeared from his side and returned a moment later with horse blankets. She tucked them around him.

"I need something to cleanse that wound and sew you up," she said.

"You…can…do that?"

"Never tried." She flashed a confident smile. "I'll be back."

Before she could go, he caught her wrist. "No, princess. It's too dangerous."

"I'll be fine," she whispered.

Her kiss was the last thing he remembered before surrendering to the pain.

Drake had lost a lot of blood and it scared Allanna. The gaping stab wound had already started to fester. Truthfully she hadn't a clue as to what to do for him. She needed a healer. But she hoped she could find clean bandages in the cabin. Who had stabbed him? Was it Marath? She couldn't understand how Marath could have stabbed him when he was making a valiant effort to break into her chamber. But then the man had changed since his arrival to the Woodlands. There was something darker and more dangerous about him.

She stepped to the doorway of the stables and peered across at the darkened cabin. Drenched to the bone, she had no other choice but to go there to see what medical supplies she could find. She had to save Drake. He couldn't die.

Taking a deep breath, she bolted for the back door. She saw the flashes of light behind her but assumed it was nothing more than lightning. She realized she was wrong when someone grabbed her from behind.

The mage that had tried to capture her before now appeared in front of her in a spark of light. She kicked at him but it did no good. He held up his hand, stained with blood. The beam hit her in the shoulder and she flew backward. She landed on her rump in the mud and slid before she managed to stop.

She glanced at the barn, wondering if she could get to Drake's sword or her bow and arrows. Like a fool, she'd left them behind and getting to them could be her only chance. She climbed to her hands and knees, keeping an eye on the mage.

"Do not attempt to run," he said. "It will make things worse for you, my pet."

She was no one's pet. The fire pendant Drake had given her swung back and forth as she hovered there. She knew he would try to attack her again but she had no choice. Mayhap she could outrun the man before he sent another bolt of light flying toward her. She had to make a dash for the barn.

She stood straight but he must have anticipated her next move. He released the light from his palms before she could even take a step. But the beam never hit her. It reflected back to the mage, hitting him with a loud pop and shoving him backward to the ground. His robe sizzled. She stared wide-eyed, wondering what had happened as rain pelted her in the face. Then she noticed her fire pendant glowing.

It must have acted as a shield, turning the power on the mage. He was hit with his own power. Now she had a weapon she could use to fight back.

He was slow to get back to his feet.

"I will kill you for that," he said.

Someone grabbed her from behind. His arms clamped around her upper torso. She kicked, struggling to get free but she knew it was no use. Two more men flashed in front of her. Two more who must be working with this mage.

"Bind her and bring her."

But Allanna continued to struggle. He shoved the hood off his face then and stared at her with eyes that were nothing more than black orbs in the darkness. Gods, he was ugly. When he advanced on her she stilled.

"You will come quietly. Or I will kill you now."

Suddenly he lurched and doubled over. An arrow stuck out of his left shoulder. Allanna looked past him in the driving rain to see Drake fire another arrow and another. The man released her and she ran around the mage to stand in front of Drake, knowing what the enemy meant to do.

He sent a flash of light toward them. She held up her pendant, reflecting the bolt back at them all. It was much bigger than the last one. As though he used more power this time around. The orange-yellow light hit all four of them and they fell to the ground in a heap.

She spun around to Drake, but he wobbled on his feet and fell to his knees.

"You can't stay here," he said.

She watched blood mix with mud and her stomach churned with fear. She grasped him by the shoulders and tried to hoist him up but he wouldn't move.

"Come on, Drake. We have to get out of here."

"Not we. You. Leave me. I cannot ride."

"Bollocks! I'm not leaving you. Get up, Drake. *Get up.*"

"They will wake soon. You have to go."

"Not without you." She blinked, no longer able to see through the haze of raindrops. No, not raindrops. Tears. She hooked her arm in his and pulled with all her might. "You're all I have."

"Go back to Eldrin."

His eyes fluttered closed and he pitched forward, face down in the mud. She screamed out of frustration and fear. Was he dead? Had he died? She didn't know and he was too heavy to roll over.

The rumble of hooves behind her made her turn. She could make out a distant form riding at breakneck speed toward her. But it didn't look like Marath. She squinted in the darkness. As the rider neared, the rain dissipated to a drizzle and then she could see him.

"Eldrin! Thank the gods!"

He halted near her and jumped down. He knelt at Drake's side, feeling for a pulse at his neck.

"Is he…?"

"He's alive. Help me."

Eldrin shouldered most of Drake's weight but Allanna managed to steady his other side. Together they hoisted him on the back of the horse.

"How did you find me?"

"We'll talk about that later. Right now we have to get out of here."

"The other horse is in the stable," she said.

"Fetch it and then we ride."

"Where are we going?"

"Someplace you'll be safe from that monster and where Drake can heal. We're going to see the Skye Elves."

Aesir shook Marath awake, his voice urgent in his ear. Marath peeled his eyes open and looked up at the ceiling with the wooden beams across it. He must have passed out shortly after Lorcann forced him to use the dark magic. Shortly after he and his men flashed away. Aesir peered down at him, concern in his eyes.

"My lord, are you all right?"

Aesir helped him sit up and he ran a hand through his hair. "Fine. I'm fine."

Though he knew he wasn't. Even now he could feel the darkness pumping through his blood. He knew it had nearly overtaken him. Invoking those last bits of blood magic had pushed him closer to becoming Dark. He glanced down at his palms but there was nothing but a faint silvery scar.

Dark magic had healed him, too.

"What happened? You look frightfully pale, my lord."

"I'm all right," Marath said. "Help me up. What time is it?"

"Midmorning. There's been news." Aesir gripped his arm and hoisted him to his feet. "The princess is missing."

The lord-regent halted, not moving. Supreme satisfaction oozed over him and a slow smile spread. "Is she?"

Aesir moved toward the door and closed it. "Is that your doing?"

"My doing?" Marath shook his head. "It is what must be done, Aesir. What I must do to return the glory of the Elven kingdom."

"Forgive me, my lord, but I fail to see how kidnapping the princess will do that."

"Do you remember nothing? As I told you before, the Fomorian mage will take her, kill her and we will lay the blame at the feet of the Fae. I have already planted the seed of suspicion in the king's mind. Now with her dead, he will truly see the horrors the Fae are capable of."

His whore mother had been a Fae. And when he had come into the world, his Elven father had been less than joyful. After his mother's death, his father kicked him aside. Called him half-breed and all manner of other names. It had taken him years to recover. Murdering his vile father was the beginning. And then he fought for and gained all that he had by sheer determination and other persuasive means. He would not live in peace with the dirty Fae.

"You cannot lay blame to all Fae."

"They will all pay," Marath said. "I cannot abide them. They do not deserve to live with us. We *must* be separated."

Aesir cleared his throat. "Shall I prepare a bath for you?"

"Do you not believe me?" Marath sniffed with derision. "Do you think I should allow the bitch to live?" He switched back to the topic of Allanna.

"I have no opinion, my lord. I merely follow your orders."

"You think I should return her safely to her king," he said. "Her father. Her useless father."

"Nay, my lord, I—"

"Well I'm not returning her!"

"As you say, my lord."

"She will die. And I will get my war with the Fae. I will kill anyone who stands in my way. Do you understand?"

Aesir gasped and it was then Marath realized he'd advanced on his servant, pushing him against the wall. He didn't even realize he had clamped a hand around his throat and was squeezing. He released him and stepped away, his hand fisting.

"Apologies."

"It's the sickness. It's beginning to overtake you, isn't it?" Aesir's voice was raspy as he spoke.

"Speak of this to no one," he said.

"Aye, my lord."

"Bring my bath," Marath said. "I will break my fast here."

Aesir gave him a nod and headed for the door. With his hand on the handle, he paused and turned back. "There is one more thing, my lord. Lord Eldrin has left the castle to search for the missing princess."

"He won't find her until it is too late."

Chapter 8

The rain had dissipated to a fine mist. Allanna rode with her brother as they headed away from the crofter's cabin and stable, leaving behind the four men who had tried to kidnap her. She didn't know if they were alive or dead. She didn't care. As long as they didn't follow her, that was all she cared about.

"Why were they trying to take me?"

"I don't know," Eldrin said.

"Who are they, El? They were hideous looking. They scared me. They had magic!"

"I know. I don't know who they are. But I suspect Lord Marath may have something to do with their sudden appearance in our realm."

"Lord Marath?" she repeated. "Aye, of course. He said the Fae were planning to kidnap me. Do you think he's the one behind it?"

"I would assume so. We must hurry. Drake doesn't have much time." Eldrin kept his gaze ahead as they rode hard.

That worried her. She sent a silent prayer to the gods to keep him alive until they made it to the Skye Elves. She had no idea how to get to them as Eldrin had said. They were far away, weren't they? She had never seen a Skye Elf. From what she knew of them, they remained in their demesne high in the clouds and rarely came down. Their blood was thinner than any other race due to the higher altitude of their homes. She trusted Eldrin and knew they would be safe wherever they went.

But something else niggled at her. Before Drake passed out, he'd told her to return to Eldrin. Had he changed his mind about taking her with him back to the human realm? What did that mean? She wouldn't go. She was staying with him and that was final. And if he died— No, she wouldn't think like that. He would live and once he healed they would continue their journey to the Queen's Palace where Queen Elyne would remove her immortality and sift them to Drake's home.

At dawn, they halted near a meadow on one of the high cliffs. In the distance, she could see the churning green water, the frothy waves as they crashed against the sheer rock face. The rain had finally ceased but she, Eldrin and Drake were soaked to the bone. Eldrin dismounted. She followed, sliding out of the saddle and landing in the squishy grass.

"What are we doing?" she asked.

"Waiting."

Eldrin's gaze was pinned on something in the distance. Something far across the sea. The pinkish sky was dotted with heavy gray clouds that still threatened rain. But the sun was rising in the east, giving a golden glimmer to the dark water, which she peered across but saw nothing.

"What are we waiting for?"

"You'll see."

He was maddening. Couldn't he answer one of her questions?

"Eldrin, I think I've been patient. I was good and didn't ask you any questions before. But now—"

He held up a hand to shush her. He merely nodded toward the sky. She looked again and again saw nothing. But then…a small dot appeared out of the clouds. It headed toward them. Closer and closer. She realized after staring for a long while that it was not one small dot but three large ones. Three large, beautiful silver dragons. Their scales glittered in the morning light. They each had a long serpent-like tail with delicate iridescent wings. They seemed to glide upon the air for their wings did not make the usual *whomp whomp* as the other dragons.

"Moon dragons," she gasped. "I thought they no longer existed."

"They still exist. They live to serve the Skye Elves. Very few have seen them."

"But how is this possible? What are they doing here?"

"I sent for them."

"You did? How?"

He sighed. "I will tell you everything soon. For now, follow my lead and try not to ask any more questions."

She frowned but kept her mouth clamped closed. The moon dragons landed on the edge of the cliff near them. Eldrin walked to the biggest one in the middle and placed his hand on its snout. He closed his eyes and she knew he was communicating with it. A moment later he removed his hand, nodded and turned to her.

"Help me get Drake on the back of this one," he said.

She rushed to Drake's side as Eldrin pulled him off the saddle. The dragon crouched near the ground as they shouldered his weight. Drake's skin had a sickly pallor, one that made Allanna fear he could already be dead.

"He can't die." She whispered it more to herself than Eldrin.

"He won't," Eldrin answered.

They exchanged a glance and then Eldrin hoisted him up on the back of the dragon. Then he turned to her.

"You'll be riding that one." He pointed to the smallest of the three. "I'll be riding the other."

"El, where are we going?"

"I thought that was obvious. We're going to the clouds." He nodded toward the sky.

Her heart sped up a little. As a Wood Elf, she preferred to keep her feet planted firmly on the ground. Or at least in her treetop home. Climbing on the back of the beast terrified her. Yet she would not be left behind. Not while that mage could flash anywhere to find her.

She thought she understood why Eldrin was taking her there—farther away from the mage. Away from Marath. Did her father know what had happened to her? Did he send Eldrin to find her and bring her back to the palace? These were all questions she needed answered.

With a deep breath, she climbed on the back of the dragon. A moment later they were airborne. Drenched as she was, when the cold wind hit her it was as though she'd been smacked with an iceberg. She shivered uncontrollably and her teeth chattered. She stole a glance at her brother but he didn't seem bothered at all by the frigid air. As they rose higher and higher the air thinned and turned icier. She gripped the back of the dragon, daring not to look down. But all around her were the wispy high clouds of the realm. As they moved through them, she saw the city of the Skye Elves through the dense haze.

The white palace had breathtaking pointed turrets reaching high into the sky, disappearing into the clouds. It seemed to spread out from there, looming ahead of them as they neared. They flew over the castle in the sky before at last landing on what she hoped was solid ground.

She knew better. She was in the sky. Far above her homeland. Eldrin slid off the back of the dragon and she followed his lead. She would be good and keep silent.

A smooth marble walkway led up to the grand stairs in the front of the castle where three Elves—one woman flanked by two men—waited at the top. As they alighted, the Elves descended and approached. They didn't look so different from her people but they were tall and elegant.

The female in the center had flowing coppery hair with silver eyes. Her gown was of the finest lace with long bell sleeves that went past her fingertips and belted at the waist with a garnet silken cord. A white fur-lined cloak rested on her shoulders and she wore a necklace made of moonstones and matching earbobs dangling to her shoulders. Her skin was smooth alabaster, making quite a contrast with her bright hair.

She was the most beautiful Elven woman Allanna had ever seen.

"Welcome, Lord Eldrin." She curtsied low. Her pale-pink lips curved into a pretty smile. And was that a blush creeping along her cheeks? She seemed quite happy to see him.

"Thank you for allowing us to come to you, Lady Talaiel." He bowed low in response. Something about him softened around all the edges. He took her delicate hand in his and kissed it, lingering far longer than he should. "May I present to you my sister, Princess Allanna?"

Her gaze landed on her then and the smile she gave was one of warmth and friendship. She stepped down the remaining steps and extended her hand. "Allanna. At last we meet. I've heard much about you."

"Have you?" Allanna shook her hand and gave her brother a questioning glance. He said nothing. His face gave away nothing. No hint of any emotion that would reveal his inner thoughts.

They were so high Allanna couldn't help but shiver. The lady noticed.

"You are cold." She gave a wave over her shoulder and one of the men stepped forward with a cloak much like hers. He handed one to Allanna and then one to Eldrin. "I'm afraid our temperatures are not what you Wood Elves are accustomed to."

Allanna pulled the cloak over her body and snuggled into the fine fur inside. It was thick and warm and almost immediately removed the chill that had pressed into her bones. "Thank you."

Eldrin pulled on his cloak to ward off the chilly altitude. But he was still all business.

"My lady, we've not much time for pleasantries. I've come with my friend and knight, Drake. He's severely injured and we need your help. I thank you for answering my call."

"Aye, of course, let us get him to the healer at once. I have him waiting for our arrival."

Allanna glanced at her brother, surprised. He'd told the lady they were coming? How? When?

Lady Talaiel waved to the two Elven men. They jumped into action, removing Drake from the dragon's back and carrying him away.

"I want to go with him," Allanna said, stepping forward.

"Aye, of course. Follow me."

The lady picked up her skirts and walked toward the grand arched entrance of the castle. Inside the castle was much warmer than outside but Allanna still held on to her cloak as they fell in step behind Talaiel, who hurried through the corridors. Allanna gave Eldrin a questioning look, but he kept his eyes on the Elven lady. Never looking at her or even acknowledging her. Who was this woman to him? How did he know her?

The castle floors were made of moonstone. Even as she worried for Drake's safe recovery, Allanna couldn't help but notice the pale iridescent stone as it reflected the candlelight back to them. The walls were a mixture of sunstone, a pale yellow imitating that of sunlight, and moonstone. Each doorway they passed through was arched and trimmed in intricate detail.

As they walked she slid a surreptitious glance at her brother. He kept his eyes pinned ahead and his face passive. His expression would not belie his thoughts but Allanna thought she knew. Her brother was in love with the fair Skye Elf. Who could blame him? She was beautiful.

How did he come to know her? The Wood Elves and the Skye Elves did not cross paths very often. Yet Lady Talaiel seemed to be quite familiar with Eldrin and her.

They arrived at a large chamber where the two Elves placed Drake on a bed. The healer waited for them and rushed to his side.

The two who'd brought him stepped out of the way. The healer peeled back his cloak and then his tunic to reveal the bloodied wound on his side. It was red and still oozed. Drake's tunic was soaked through.

Allanna sucked in a sharp breath. She had no idea how bad it was. He'd lost so much blood. The healer probed the skin around the wound with gentle fingertips. He was a small Elf. His dark hair was pulled back at the nape and tied with a black silk ribbon. He wore a white tunic with the sleeves rolled to his elbows and dark pants held up by suspenders. He had round-glass spectacles perched on the end of his slanted nose and peered through them with brown eyes.

"What was he stabbed with?" he asked.

"I know not," Eldrin said.

"The wound is too hot. As though he's been stabbed with Elven glass," he said, and then looked at the three of them. "Enchanted Elven glass. There seems to be a broken piece inside the wound."

Drake groaned. Allanna's heart tumbled in her chest, plummeting into her stomach. The fear that had been nagging her since they'd left the ground took hold and she started to shake. If he'd been stabbed with enchanted Elven glass, then he would likely die. His blood would be poisoned. She pressed her fingertips against her lips to suppress the sob that wanted to erupt. He couldn't die.

"Can you remove it and heal him?" Eldrin asked.

"I have never tried to heal a human from such a wound," he said. "I will try."

"We shall leave you to your work then, Turin." Talaiel turned to them and gave them both a smile. "Come. Let me get you some refreshments."

"I want to stay," Allanna insisted.

"It's best if you don't stay to watch," the lady said. "Removing the shard can be an unpleasant experience."

"Come, *nethielle*." Eldrin wrapped his arm around her shoulders.

She shoved him away. "No, I'm staying. I don't care how unpleasant it is. I have to be with him."

The healer looked to his lady, a question in his eyes. After a long moment, she nodded. "Let her stay."

"As you wish, my lady."

She ushered everyone else out of the room leaving her, the healer and Drake. Turin turned back to Drake and ripped open his tunic, shoving aside the blood-drenched cloth. Then he turned and opened a large bag, rummaging around inside it before bringing out a knife with a curved blade.

"What are you going to use that for?" Allanna couldn't hide the panic in her voice.

"Be silent, miss. If you're to stay here, I must be able to work uninterrupted." He punctuated the last with a withering stare before turning back to Drake.

Allanna backed from the bed, taking a position far enough away where she could still see. The healer used the tip of the curved blade to touch the wound and then he dug into it. Her stomach tightened and she turned, shoving her fist against her lips to keep from crying out.

The cut must have brought Drake out of his stupor. He shrieked and thrashed on the bed. The healer pulled back the bloodied knife, trying to stay out of the way of his flying fists. He looked at her, his lips in a thin line.

"You must hold him still."

"Me?" she squeaked.

"You are the only one here. I cannot work while he moves. It could cause more damage."

She hesitated, her feet refusing to move. Fear turned into a ball of ice in the pit of her stomach and bile rose to the back of her throat. She wanted to flee, not help. She was not used to dealing with wounds. She wouldn't faint at the sight of blood but she was unsure she could hold Drake steady while the healer worked.

"Come, girl, if you want him to live," he said sharply.

It was all the encouragement she needed. She walked to the bed, staring down at his sweaty, dirty face. But she had no idea what to do. The healer huffed out an exasperated breath.

"Hold his shoulders down on the bed," he said.

She bit her bottom lip as she placed her palms on each of his shoulders, pressing lightly.

"You'll have to hold him better than that. Put some pressure on his shoulders."

Though she wasn't looking at him she could envision the thin-lipped sour look on Turin's face. She perched on the edge of the bed and pressed harder. As hard as she dared.

"When I try to remove the shard it will be quite painful to him. Are you ready?"

Still biting her lip, she nodded. She knew the moment the healer touched the wound again because Drake tried to shove her off. She pushed him into the mattress as tears welled in her eyes. His face blurred as she tried her best to hold him still. But he was fighting her and managed to shove her away. She tumbled off the bed as Drake threw a punch, narrowly missing the healer.

"His hands! Take his hands!"

She jumped up and grabbed his hands, cupping them both in her small ones and pressing them against his chest. She threw all her weight into holding him in place but he was much stronger than she.

"Talk to him," he ordered. "Try to calm him."

A tear dripped from her eye and landed on his cheek. His eyes popped open then. Wild eyes. Eyes like she'd never seen before. She could hear the sharp intake of his breath.

"Drake, it's Allanna. I'm trying to help you."

"Allanna."

"Aye, 'tis me. You have to be still or it will hurt worse."

His teeth chattered but he stopped moving and his eyes seemed to clear. "What's…happening?"

"You were stabbed. There's a shard of glass inside you. The healer is trying to remove it." She said it in the calmest voice she could muster. "You must be still."

His eyes fluttered closed then and he passed out.

"He's unconscious I think," she said.

"It's just as well. I'm sure the pain was too much for him."

She kept her gaze fixed on Drake's face. Every now and then a muscle would tick under his eye. She placed her hand on his cheek. The fever burned hot. A pang of worry sliced through her. All she could do was pray to the gods he would recover.

His face was covered in sweat and every now and then he'd moan in pain. She mopped the side of his face with the edge of her sleeve, wishing she had something better to use.

It seemed an eternity as the healer worked but in that time, she memorized his features. There was an inherent strength in his weathered face. His skin was still pale, making his dark beard a stark contrast. Underneath the hair she could see his square jaw. He had a kind, generous mouth with touches of humor around it.

She traced the line of his lower lip. She watched the flutter of his pulse in his throat and couldn't resist placing her fingertips there to feel it.

Unable to stop herself, she dragged her finger down the length of his throat to his collarbone. She realized she still held his hands in her other one against his chest. Right over his heart where she could feel the slow, steady beat. A dusting of dark hair covered his upper torso. She couldn't stop the schoolgirl blush she felt to her hairline.

"There. I've got the glass out. Now I can cleanse the wound and stitch it," the healer said.

She could hear the relief in his voice. A *tink* signaled as the glass dropped into something. She relaxed, resting her hands on his bare chest, enjoying the feel of him as she waited while the healer stitched the wound. Stealing a glance over her shoulder, she saw him pulling the last stitch, then snipping the end of thread before covering the wound with a bandage. When he finished, he rose, wiping his bloodied hands on a cloth.

"He'll need rest until the fever subsides."

"But he will live?" she asked.

"For now. He'll not be out of danger until the fever breaks."

"Thank you," she whispered.

"I'll let the lady know."

He picked up his bag and left, closing the door softly behind him.

Allanna was alone with Drake. It was the first time since that night by the loch. When he'd held her and kissed her and she'd flung herself at him like a tavern wench. Thinking of it now sent flames to her cheeks. She shouldn't have done that. But she was certain she would never see him again. And now here they were. Together. Alone. In the sky. She would have never foreseen this happening even if she'd had the vision to prove it.

She watched his chest rise and fall with every breath as he slept. There was nothing more she could do for him this night.

Chapter 9

Eldrin paced the length of the hallway, his hands clasped behind his back. He had never seen his friend look so deathlike and had to admit he was worried. The more he paced the more agitated he became. The more agitated he became the more he realized Marath must have had something to do with his injury.

"He is in good hands, Lord Eldrin. Rest assured."

"I know."

He halted abruptly and looked at the Lady of the Skye. The most beautiful lady in this realm or the next. She was the epitome of calm elegance. Nothing seemed to rattle her. She had allowed him entrance into their realm every time he had called upon her.

Despite the distance between them he could not stop his emotions from ruling his heart. He had tried hard to forget her, to pretend she did not exist high in the sky, to banish her from all his thoughts. But she was ever present. And when he thought of her he could not stop wondering what those beautiful lips would taste like. Her eyes were as silvery as the full moon on a cold winter night. Quite often he could get lost in them.

Though they had never spoken of their feelings for each other, he suspected she was as fond of him as he was of her. It was truly a testament of her affection by allowing him to have access to the Skye Elves' realm. She had given him access to her people and her mind. They had never kissed but often exchanged heartfelt glances full of desire. He knew such a match wouldn't be prudent so he never pursued it. Because she deserved better than a man who could only love her part of the time.

"Thank you for allowing us to come. I fear I impose on you too much," he said.

She gave him a soft smile. "Never, Lord Eldrin."

He heard an agonized moan and glanced at the closed door. "I shouldn't have allowed her to stay."

"She wanted to because she cares about him."

"I'm aware of her feelings for him. She doesn't want to listen to reason where he's concerned."

"It is difficult to change how the heart feels," she said.

He met her level gaze. "Sir Drake is a good man, a noble knight and a valiant fighter. And he is my friend. But he is still human and by no means will my father allow them to marry."

"Sometimes, Lord Eldrin, one cannot help who one falls in love with."

His skin tingled and he was powerless to look away from her piercing gaze. Almost as though she spoke to a deeper part of him she understood.

"What is the harm in the princess marrying a human? I see nothing wrong with that," she said.

"There isn't anything wrong with it. I happen to think the match would be a fine one." He took a step closer to her, his fingers itching to brush her fine-boned cheeks. "But my father sees things differently. He has no love for humans. He believes they are dirty warmongers."

"Isn't it wrong to place the same label on all humans? After all, you said yourself Sir Drake was a good man and a noble knight."

Her lips were parted as though ready for kissing. Eldrin could see her pulse fluttering in the long column of her neck and the quick rise and fall of her chest as she struggled to breathe. She was as affected by him as he was by her.

"I agree with you, my lady. However, it is most difficult to break thousands of years of preconception."

"Aye but there is always a way to change the way people think. To make them see the beauty in others despite their differences."

"How?"

"If they love each other, then anything is possible. Change is scary but not impossible."

He had the distinct feeling they were no longer talking about Sir Drake and his sister. That instead the conversation had somehow changed to something more deeply personal. The color was high in her cheeks and he thought he could see her shaking with anticipation. The same anticipation he had. He wanted to reach for her, cup her face in his hands, tilt her head back and kiss her. His hands were halfway to her face when the door cracked open.

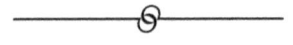

Satisfied Drake was safe for the moment Allanna left his chamber, closing the door behind her. Eldrin and Talaiel waited for her in the hallway standing close to each other. When she stepped into the hallway, they jumped apart and Allanna had the distinct feeling she interrupted something intimate.

Eldrin's brow was pinched with worry. "How is he?"

"Sleeping."

"Good. He needs the rest." He folded his arms across his chest and she knew a chastising wasn't far behind. "Would you like to tell me what you were doing outside the gates?"

She gave a surreptitious glance at the lady standing next to him. "El, now is not the time to discuss this."

"Aye, it is. And you'll tell me everything."

"Lord Eldrin, mayhap you and your sister should have this conversation alone," Talaiel suggested.

"Nay, my lady. You'll stay and hear why I had to call upon your people."

"Then at least allow us to move into a private room. The castle does have wandering ears, my lord. I have one ready for the princess. It's just this way."

He gave a swift nod and followed her. Allanna reluctantly fell in step behind them. She noted they were as far from Drake as they could be. On the other end of the long hallway. She frowned. Did they think the distance would keep them apart? Hardly. This chamber was much the same as Drake's, with the same furnishings. A bed in the center of the room and two chairs on either side of the window. A large fireplace dominated one wall. A wardrobe on the other.

"Allanna, I'm waiting."

"First you tell me how Navin was injured," she demanded.

"I'm not sure. A blow to the head was all Brom knew."

"It was Marath," she said. "You and I both know that."

"We have no proof of that."

"No, but I believe he did it. He attacked me, Eldrin."

"Marath? How? When?"

"After you and the healer took Navin away, he was waiting for me at the top of the stairs. He pushed me against the wall. I don't know what he planned to do but he scared me. I was saved when he touched the fire crystal. It burned him."

"The fire crystal?" Eldrin noticed her pendant for the first time. "Where did you get that necklace?"

"Drake gave it to me." She closed a protective hand around the chain.

"Where would he get something like that? And why would it burn Marath?"

"The fire crystal was forged in the volcanoes of the Hin'dar Rhule," Talaiel said. "It is made of the Light. The Dark cannot touch it."

"What are you suggesting?" Eldrin asked. "That Marath is of the Dark?"

"There is something different about him, El," Allanna said. "I managed to make it to my chamber but he broke through the door. Like he had some kind of super strength. I hid outside the balcony until he left."

"I wonder if he's responsible for stabbing Drake," Eldrin mused. He looked at Lady Talaiel. "How would he be of the Dark? He's one of our own. A Woodland Elf."

"He could turn into a Dark Elf," she said, "by invoking the dark magic of the ancients. It is not unheard of and has been part of our lore for thousands of years. There are still grimoires that exist to teach him how."

"Then he betrayed the king," Eldrin said. "And he's trying to blame the Fae for your kidnapping."

"There were four men men who tried to kidnap me outside the gates. They were no Fae," Allanna said. "They were disgusting, ugly creatures. And they smelled like the sea."

"If they smelled of the sea, they are Fomorians," Talaiel said. "Lord Marath must have released them from their watery prison in the Sorrow Lands."

"By the gods." Eldrin sat down hard in one of the chairs. "Fomorians, of course. I couldn't place the hideous face until now though I should have. They fought with Morrigan against the Fae. He must have released more."

"And the most dangerous," Lady Talaiel added.

"He's mad. I saw it in his eyes." Remembering the way he looked at her in the hallway sent an involuntary shiver through Allanna.

Eldrin ran a hand over his chin. "Why would he release them?"

"Mayhap he thought to take over Urdithane's kingdom with their help," Lady Talaiel suggested.

His gaze swung back to Allanna. "You still didn't answer my question. What were you doing outside the gates?"

"I really don't think that matters now."

"Aye, it does." He glared, his expression uncompromising. "Would it have anything to do with Sir Drake still being near the Woodlands?"

She flushed. Her brother could read her so well sometimes it was maddening. She pressed her lips together and looked away, refusing to answer. She couldn't tell him the truth of it. She didn't want him to know she intended to run away with him. He would try to talk her out of it. He would berate her and tell her that her duties were in the kingdom with them. She was the only princess and on and on and on. And she really didn't want to hear that.

"I knew it," he said.

"You know *nothing*." She snapped her head in his direction. "And you've never told me how you found me in the rain or how you called the Skye Elves."

Allanna thought she saw the color drain from Talaiel's face as she cleared her throat noisily. Eldrin launched to his feet with a growl and prowled the room.

"I believe I have something to tend to," the lady said. "If you'll excuse me."

She whisked out of the room, closing the door with a snap behind her and leaving Allanna alone with her pacing brother. He came to an abrupt halt, his boots scuffing on the floor.

"I heard you and Drake making plans so I followed you."

All the blood drained from her head, leaving dark pricks dancing in her vision. It was her turn to sit down hard in the chair.

"How did you…hear us? I thought we were alone."

"You were not. I was helping Brom take Navin to his chamber but along the way we ran into one of the servants. He took over for me. I intended to return to the hall when I heard the two of you."

The air left her lungs in a heated whoosh of breath, deflating her. Eldrin knew the truth even though she'd tried to hide it.

"What took you so long to get to us, then? If you knew we were leaving together? And why weren't you there when we were first attacked?"

He slumped in the chair and his shoulders sagged. "I was going to let you go. But then I thought this couldn't be something you truly wanted so I came after you. I saw how severely injured he was and called the Skye Elves."

"You called them. Then you've been with them before."

The Skye Elves trusted very few others in the Elven race. It was their way. They preferred their solitude and isolation high in the clouds away from the warring races below. And to call one? It was through mind-speak and something so intimate it was to be shared with only one. Allanna shifted in her chair. She thought she knew who that one person was with whom he shared that special ability.

"Aye."

He didn't hesitate when he answered and the word hung thick and heavy between them. He hadn't wanted to elaborate and she didn't press for information though she suspected it had something to do with the lovely Lady Talaiel. She thought before she'd caught an affectionate glance or two between them but she ignored it. Now she knew she'd seen it.

They were in love with each other. She never imagined her brother to be in love with anyone.

"You can't mean to leave," Eldrin said, breaking into her thoughts.

"I can. And I will."

"If you agree to stay I will see to it you don't have to marry Lord Marath," Eldrin said. "You have my word."

"I appreciate that, Eldrin, but no. I'm not staying."

"Nothing I can say will change your mind?"

"No."

"Very well then. I hope you don't regret your decision." He rose to his full height, pinning her with a glare. "The lady has prepared an evening feast for us. It would be rude if you failed to join us."

That was a demand if she ever heard one. "I can't very well join you looking like this." She waved her hand down the length of her. She still wore her brother's old clothes and was covered in dirt and mud.

He looked her up and down. "I'll ask the lady to bring you a bath and an appropriate dress. Then I expect you to join us in the dining hall without delay."

She narrowed her gaze. "Aye, my brother. I will be there."

He stalked out of the room, leaving her alone and the chamber door ajar. She knew, as he did, that he would never stop trying to change her mind.

Allanna huffed out a breath and flounced in the chair, waiting for the servants to bring her bath. She didn't have to wait long. They arrived with a copper tub and filled it with steaming water and left a lovely gown on the bed. The last thing she wanted to do was attend a feast—hungry or not. Fatigue had hit her hard but she would have to fight through it and make an appearance or suffer the wrath of her older brother.

Once clean and dressed, she headed for the dining hall. How did Eldrin expect her to go to a feast and *pretend* everything was perfectly normal? Her brother knew she intended to leave the realm. Yet the man she loved was injured and had nearly died.

There was nothing left to say between her and Eldrin. She feared her stubborn will had driven a wedge between them and she hadn't a clue how to mend it. Whatever her choice, her heart would break either way. She hated leaving her life here but she was excited to be with Drake in his human world.

If she didn't show up at the feast prepared especially for them, Eldrin would be even angrier with her. And they had helped save Drake. She paused only a moment to peek in on her beloved. He slept peacefully.

Allanna made her way through the corridor to the stairs and found her way to the dining hall. There the Lady of the Skye sat at the center of the long table with Eldrin to her left and to her right a few others Allanna hadn't met before. When Talaiel saw her she smiled and stood, waving her toward them. Eldrin spotted her then and got to his feet as did the rest of the attendees.

"Princess Allanna, I'm so glad you could join us. I trust Sir Drake is faring well?" Talaiel asked.

"He's still sleeping."

"Good. Then he's on the mend. Please sit."

She waved Allanna to a chair on the other side of the table directly across from Eldrin. The lady made the introductions of the other men and women. Names Allanna would never recall for all she really thought of was Drake lying in a bed upstairs. Had he woken? If he had, did he ask for her? Was he confused? Did he know where he was?

A servant filled her goblet with honeywine. Another servant placed some sort of roasted meat on her plate followed by boiled potatoes. The savory scent wafting to her nose made her mouth water. At the sight of the food, her stomach made a raucous noise and she flushed with embarrassment.

"My apologies."

The lady laughed. "No apology necessary. Please, do eat."

It took all her strength not to attack the food with her fork. She kept herself under control, though, and managed to eat like a lady. Like a princess.

"Pray continue, Lord Varras," Talaiel said.

"As I was saying, it is not for us to get involved in," Varras said. "The matters of those clans beneath us do not concern us."

"It should concern you," Eldrin said, his voice hard.

Allanna had never heard his tone so sharp. Not even when he spoke to her moments ago in the chamber. It gave her pause as she looked up at him. He fisted his hand next to his plate.

"Lord-Regent Marath is a real threat. He's used a mage to attack my sister. I believe he's learned how to harbor this dark magic somehow. Should a civil war erupt within my clan—"

"It is still no concern of ours," Varras said in his snooty nasal tone. "Wouldn't you agree, my lady?"

Eldrin clenched his jaw as he swung his gaze to her. Talaiel leaned forward and picked up her goblet. She took a slow sip before returning it to the table and lacing her fingers in front of her plate.

"I believe no clan should war with itself. I also believe Lord Eldrin has brought a very real threat to our attention."

"Are you saying we must act?" Varras' heated tone seemed to warm the entire room.

"I'm saying we should hear him out and consider all our options. Dark magic is nothing to be trifled with," she said. "We saw how the darkness overtook Lord Kieran at the Battle for the Otherworld."

"Is that what we're calling it?" Eldrin asked. "The Battle for the Otherworld? Where were you when we all nearly perished at the Hill of Tara? When Lord Kieran nearly succeeded in using the Stone of Destiny?"

"We were here in the clouds where we belong," Varras said, his tone acid.

"Your kind are not so superior." Eldrin pointed his cold gaze at the man. It was so glacier Allanna even shuddered. "You are equal to the other clans. We are all Elves, after all."

"We mustn't allow this dislike for each other to come between us," Talaiel said. "It will do nothing but destroy us."

"I agree," Eldrin said.

"I would ask, Lord Varras, that you consider helping Lord Eldrin and his king when the time comes."

"The time comes for what? War?" He voice was hard and unforgiving.

"There is a darkness brewing in the west, as we all know," she said, her voice calm and subdued. "Something evil has been released and walks the land once again."

"I believe Lord Marath is responsible," Eldrin said. "He tried to kill Sir Drake and my sister."

Allanna's heart lurched. Eldrin seemed to know this for certain. He must be anticipating war and asking the Skye Elves for their help. Lady Talaiel seemed to want to help while this Lord Varras was steadfast against it. Varras and Eldrin stared each other down, neither wanting to look away first.

"We will table this discussion for a later time," Talaiel said.

"Then it could be too late, my lady." Eldrin wrapped his hand around his goblet, his knuckles leaching of all color as he tightened his grip.

She spread her hands on the table, flattening the palms. "A later time, Lord Eldrin."

Again his jaw clenched. He shoved back from the table, his chair legs scraping along the floor with a loud screech. He left, stomping out of the room. Lady Talaiel leaned back in her chair, taking her goblet with her. She took a healthy swig. No one else said anything.

Allanna didn't understand what she had witnessed. She popped one last potato in her mouth and rose from the table.

"I should check on my brother. Thank you, my lady, for the meal."

She dipped a quick curtsey before leaving the room and searched out Eldrin. It didn't take her long to find him as he hadn't gone far. He stood at the other end of the grand hall, peering through a window into the darkness. Seeing nothing. Or everything. She wasn't sure which.

"Eldrin?"

He turned to look at her, his face devoid of all emotion. He looked back at the window. "Go back to the dinner party."

"What's going on?" She halted next to him. "What were you arguing about?"

He huffed out a breath, fogging the window. "I asked the Skye Elves for assistance with Lord Marath."

"Because he's dangerous."

"More dangerous than I think you or I realize."

"You think he intends to attack Father?"

"I'm not sure but you had that vision about him stabbing Andahar and then Father being poisoned."

"Eldrin, you know as well as I my visions don't always come to pass." Such as the vision with her marrying Drake. Though she fervently wished that would be one of them that did come true.

"But sometimes they do. I believe Marath's allegations against the Fae are unfounded." He turned to face her then, his boot scuffing on the floor. "Tell me, Allanna, do you honestly believe Queen Elyne would try to kidnap you?"

"I do not," she said. "She and Lord Derron have always been a friend to us. You would have never pledged your allegiance to them if you truly believed they were a threat."

He nodded agreement. "'Tis the truth of it. I suspect nothing malicious about the Fae. Why, then, would Marath be so bent on carrying out their destruction?"

"Marath is not a pleasant person," she said. "He strong-armed his way with Father to gain his land and title."

"How do you know this?"

"I've heard the rumors of his bribery of other Elven nobles."

"Rumors that have never proven to be true," Eldrin pointed out.

"Aye but he is a Halfling and that is no rumor."

"How do *you* know that?"

"Eldrin, I've had the run of the realm since Mother died. I know lots of things."

Eldrin smiled. "Indeed. It's known his mother was a Fae and his Elven father disowned him at a young age. It could be what's driving him."

"How was Sir Drake injured?" Allanna changed the subject as she shifted her weight from one foot to the other.

"Only Drake knows for certain but if he was stabbed with Elven glass it leads me to believe there is but one person who would want him dead." He gripped Allanna by the arms and gave her a little shake. "Did Marath at any time see you two together? Could he know about your feelings for each other?"

Heat crept up her throat and over her face. Did he see them? She didn't think so. She and Drake were together in the castle when they brought Navin back injured. But they had been alone then, or so she thought. Eldrin had overheard their plans so it could be possible Marath had, too. He had been waiting for her at the top of the stairs when she went to her chamber. He could have heard everything.

"I...don't think so."

"Yet you're not sure?"

"I... No. I'm not sure."

He dropped his hands. "By the gods, Allanna. If Marath saw the two of you together, as I did, he would surmise what all of us already know."

"Aye, that I love Drake. That is not a crime."

"It is in our kingdom."

Her response was a glare as she folded her arms. "I'm staying here. With him."

"You will have to return eventually." There was a note of warning in Eldrin's tone. "I'm leaving to discuss the situation with Father but I *will* return and when I do you *will* be returning with me."

Anger pricked her veins. If he wanted to go, fine. He could go but she would never leave here without Drake. She knew their earlier discussion wasn't over. Eldrin was determined to keep her in the Woodlands.

"When will you leave?" She tried to keep her voice even and calm. She didn't want to let on how angry she was. The day had sucked the rest of her patience and energy and all she really wanted to do was curl up and go to sleep.

"On the morrow."

He suddenly looked tired as he raked his hand through his hair. For the first time she saw dark circles under his eyes and lines creasing his face.

"Forgive me, *nethielle*. I don't mean to be so hard on you. I just don't want you to make a decision you will someday regret."

She softened then, her rigid body relaxing. "I know that. I truly do. I cannot imagine my life without him. I cannot even think to live another day knowing I would never see him again. Do you know that feeling?" She was reaching. Hoping he would tell her something. Give her some hint of his feelings for the Lady of the Skye.

He leveled his gaze on hers but gave nothing away. "Get some rest. I'll bid my farewell before I leave."

He stalked away. She sagged against the smooth stone wall. He was even too stubborn to admit to her—his favorite sibling—he was in love with Lady Talaiel.

Well so be it. But it would be Allanna's mission to find out the truth. The lady might tell her.

But Eldrin was right about one thing—she was exhausted. She headed back to Drake's chamber for one last peek at him. He still slept but she couldn't resist the urge to climb onto the bed next to him. She curled into a ball and minutes later fell into a deep sleep.

Chapter 10

Drake groaned. The mattress sighed with his weight as he moved. Slowly he came awake, aware of his surroundings. He blinked his eyes open and stared up at the stone ceiling. It was white and smooth and arched overhead down into the smooth white walls. He had no recollection of how he got here or even where here was. The last thing he remembered he was fighting the men and trying to save Allanna.

He heard a sigh and turned his head to see her sleeping next to him. Her dark lashes were a stark contrast to her milky-white skin. Her rose-red lips were parted slightly.

She'd tried to save him but he had told her to go without him. To return to Eldrin. How did they end up here? He had no idea. The last thing he remembered was her telling him he was all she had.

He knew now what a mistake it was to allow her to come with him. He would have to return her to the palace at once. He couldn't allow her to forsake all that she was to be with him. He would never be able to assuage the guilt that swarmed him if she did. If she left her family that she loved. She would never be happy as a mortal in the human realm no matter what she said. There was a hollowness in his chest at the thought of losing her again.

By human standards she was still young, though in her Elven years she was much older than him. She didn't yet understand the consequences of her decision. When she lived without her long life and her crown she would understand. He told her to return to Eldrin and to her kingdom and he meant it.

Glancing over at her, he watched her sleep. The way her long lashes fanned out on her cheeks. He wanted to touch her. He tucked a soft lock of hair behind her dainty, pointed ear. The last thing he remembered was she was dressed in a tunic and breeches. Now she wore a soft gown of ivory. Somewhere she had kicked off her shoes and her bare feet stuck out from under the sheet. Small, dainty, perfect feet.

She stirred and a feminine sigh escaped her parted perfect lips.

Why did he want nothing but to kiss her senseless? Everything about this situation was wrong and he knew it. She shouldn't be here in his bed with him. Alone. It was dangerous to her reputation. If he were a scoundrel he'd pull her underneath him. Good thing he wasn't a scoundrel and he lacked the strength.

He shoved away those lecherous thoughts. What the bloody hell had happened to him? When he tried to sit up, he groaned with the burning sensation in his gut. Then he remembered—that bastard Marath had stabbed him. And then when he tried to save Allanna from the men, he was hit with a strange bolt of light. From the mage. He had never felt anything as powerful as that. It knocked the breath out of him when he fell out of the saddle and landed on the ground. He pressed a hand against his side. Heat penetrated through the bandage. He grunted again.

Allanna woke and bolted upright. Her eyes were bright as she looked at him, blinking away the sleep.

"You're awake."

God, was she a sight for sore eyes. She was beautiful. Her hair stuck out everywhere. He reached for her, placed his hand on the side of her soft cheek.

"I thought to never see you again," he said.

She turned her face into his hand, placed a small kiss on his palm, her eyes bright blue and alert.

She pressed a hand against his forehead. "And the fever seems to have broken."

She bounced off the bed and he groaned again with the pain. When she realized what she'd done, she gave him a wide-eyed, apologetic look.

"My apologies."

"It's all right," he managed.

She walked over to a pitcher and basin sitting on a stand in the corner. She poured water into the basin and then dipped in a cloth and wrung it out. When she returned she dabbed his forehead then cleansed the caked-on mud. She gently scraped away all the dirt and looked as though she enjoyed every moment of it. As if she were happy to take care of him.

"I'm glad you're all right. You gave me a fright," she said.

She went back to the basin, rinsed the cloth and dipped it again. She returned to cleanse the other side of his face, removing the remaining dirt and grime. He had to admit he felt fresher, cleaner and for that he was grateful to her.

He watched her dabbing the cloth with a light touch. So intent was she that she tugged her bottom lip between her teeth. The mere action sent blood rushing to his shaft, hardening it. Now was not the time for that. He may be injured but at least that was proof he wasn't dead. His body was still very much alive and responsive.

"Are you in much pain?"

"Not much." It was a lie but he didn't want her to know that. In truth, his side hurt something fierce. It burned with the fiery agony. What had Marath stabbed him with?

She unfolded the cloth and laid it on his chest, pressing it lightly. Her small hands did nothing to help the hard problem he suddenly had. It was one she would be aware of soon if he didn't get it under control. He wrapped his hand around her wrist to stop her.

"Am I hurting you?" she asked.

In a manner of speaking she was but she couldn't know what she was doing to him. His body's reaction to the way she touched him was beyond his control. Her hand fisted as he held her wrist.

"You don't have to doctor me."

"I want to." She smiled then. Her heart-shaped lips seemed to beckon for a kiss. Then she quickly turned serious. "I was worried about you. I'm glad to see you have some of your color back. You were quite pale."

"What happened?"

"You passed out. My brother found us and brought us here. If it hadn't been for Eldrin, I think you would have surely died."

"Where is *here*?"

"We are in the company of the Skye Elves. This is their castle in the clouds."

"In the clouds?" He blinked, uncertain he heard her correctly.

"We rode the moon dragons to get here," she said. "I'd never thought to see a moon dragon."

"We're in the sky?"

"Aye. High in the sky. Above even my Woodland home."

Incredible. He'd been out far too long. He couldn't quite comprehend being in the sky or riding a moon dragon for that matter. He had seen dragons before so he knew they existed. But he had never seen moon dragons and was sorry he missed that event.

He struggled to sit up. "Help me up."

"The healer said you needed rest."

"I want to see outside. Help me to my feet, Allanna." Before she could object, he was shoving aside the bed linens and swinging his feet to the floor. All he wore were breeches. He had no recollection of anyone undressing him. He did a quick scan of the room but didn't find any of his belongings. No sword, no boots, no tunic. Nothing.

"Where are my clothes?"

"They were covered in muck and blood," she said. "I'm sure we could get you something clean but really I don't think it's such a good idea that you're out of bed."

"I can manage on my own then."

Determined, he held an arm against his bandaged side as he stumbled to his feet and toward the window. Darkness pressed against the glass but he was determined to see outside. He took a few tentative steps toward it and Allanna was there in an instant. She slipped an arm around his waist and helped him walk.

At the window, he unlatched the lock and pushed it open. Cold air blasted him in the face. He could see the first spark of dawn as the deep-indigo sky bled into the pale pink he'd grown so accustomed to in this strange land. Almost as though it were nothing more than a painting where the colors had been smudged, blended together with the deft touch of an artist's brush. The morning light wasn't enough to push out the unfamiliar stars behind wispy clouds or the burning moon that was still in residence and warring with the daybreak.

"Amazing, isn't it?" she asked.

"Aye." It was breathtaking.

"It's beautiful up here."

"It pales in comparison to you, princess."

She blushed and looked away, turning her attention to the open window. A cool breeze fluttered in but he didn't feel it. He was too enamored with her. Too busy watching her face and admiring the curve of her cheekbone. The way the faint pinkish-blue light reflected on the blonde strands of her hair, making them shimmer.

The way the fading starlight glimmered in her blue, blue eyes. Giving her an otherworldly, ethereal glow only she could possess.

Her tiny body shivered and pressed closer to him. He didn't want this moment to end. He wanted to remember the way her arm coiled around his waist, holding him close. How her free hand came up and rested on the curve of his chest. It sent his heart into a fluttering spasm.

Did she realize what she did to him? Did she have any idea how she made him feel? How her touch could make him turn into a weak-minded fool who would do her bidding? No matter what she asked?

"I've never been here before. I knew the Skye Elves existed but they keep to themselves. It's rare they come down from the clouds."

"Why is that?"

She shrugged a shoulder. "They think they're superior." Her tone suggested what she thought about that.

Drake chuckled. "And you believe they are not?"

"Their healer kept you from dying. I will believe whatever they wish me to believe." She gave him a faint smile then shuddered. "Let's close it now. It's freezing."

Indeed the air was chilly. Colder than any English winter he recalled. But he hadn't really noticed it. Not with her warmth radiating over him. She closed and latched the window. He leaned against the frame, pulling her into a tighter embrace as he still peered out at the new day.

Allanna tipped her face up to his, her hand on his chest sliding upward around his neck. Her lips parted and her eyes closed halfway. He couldn't resist her. Those perfect heart-shaped lips. His mouth touched hers, his tongue dipping in for a taste. She met his tongue with the tip of hers. Testing, teasing, tasting.

She twisted her body against him. Molded to him as if she had been made for him and him alone. His arm went around her, gently bending her back to deepen the kiss. Her small, round breasts crushed against his naked torso with a breath of material between them. He had long imagined the moment when he would tug off her gown and taste every inch of her creamy-white skin from neck to ankle.

But he knew it would never be. Not with their current situation and his thoughts drifted back to her desperate plea to take her with him. She was going to run away with him. He broke the kiss but couldn't release her from his arms.

"Allanna, we cannot do this."

"Do what?"

She nipped his chin, her teeth scraping against the growth with a rasping sound. He wanted to die from not being able to bed her. How did she know to do such things? He knew of her innocence. She was not a woman of the world. Could it be pure ardent instinct that took her over?

"You cannot leave your kingdom for me."

She leveled her gaze on his. The starlight had disappeared and now there was nothing more than a hard glint of determination. "I told you before. It is my decision to make."

"Allanna—"

"Why have you changed your mind?" She pushed away from him in a violent shove. Their romantic interlude was over. "First you tell me you want to get me away from Marath and you agree to take me with you. Then you tell me to return to Eldrin. Now you've changed your mind altogether. Why?"

"I do want you away from Marath. He is not the one for you."

"Do you not have feelings for me?"

He huffed out a frustrated breath. "Allanna, I cannot allow you to run away. I cannot allow you to give up all that you are for me."

"Why?" She flung the word at him as though it were an arrow. It pierced through him, through his heart with such violent velocity he thought he might die. Before he could answer, she said, "Because you think you're not good enough for me?"

"I am nothing but a human knight. Once a jousting hero in my world. A man who traveled from one tournament to another looking for fame and fortune to avoid fighting in a war I did not believe in." A war between England and France that had raged far too many years and taken far too many lives. He would not be a party to it. "You should return to your father. I cannot protect you from the darkness in your world."

"No. I won't go." Her fiery gaze seared his. "I'll not go back there. I'm not going to marry that man."

"Allanna—"

"No, Drake. He's a monster."

"You have to return. It's the right thing to do. It is the noble thing to do."

"Nobility be damned! The only one I want is you, Drake. You and no other."

"Allanna, you are a princess. Your brothers can protect you from Marath. Eldrin will help you break the betrothal. You belong here and not in my world. I don't... I can't love you like that."

Dumbfounded, she stared at him. "What do you mean?"

"I mean if you left and we were together, I would forever feel guilty. Despite my feelings for you, it is best you returned with Eldrin to your home. And I to mine. It is the right way of things."

"So you're saying we can't be together then."

"Aye, that's what I'm saying."

He could see the shimmer of tears in her eyes and hated himself for breaking her heart. Her bottom lip quivered. And then she sucked in a sharp breath and regained her composure.

"We will not speak of this now. You are clearly delirious with the pain."

He brushed her cheek with his fingertips. She caught his hand in hers, held it there against her face. Her smooth face. It made all his senses stand up and take notice. Injury or not, there were still parts of him that responded to her in ways he wasn't prepared to follow through. Ways he could never really follow through.

"I'll not go back there," she said. "By now, my father will know I've gone. Once he realizes I'm not coming back, he will renounce me."

"I cannot allow that to happen."

"It's my decision."

"And Eldrin? What of him?"

Pain flickered through her eyes before she concealed it. "He saved your life and mine. For that, I owe him a debt I can never repay."

He admired her inner strength and determination. He loved that about her most. But he couldn't allow her to give up her crown. Not for him. He would try to convince her more later.

She still wore the fire pendant and he remembered how she'd used the necklace to stave off the attack by the mage. He fingered the smooth and unmarred jewel in the center. It was as though nothing had happened to it at all.

"The pendant saved your life," he said.

She glanced down at it, then back at him. "Aye, it did. And yours."

If it could deflect the mage's power, then what else could it do? Was it more powerful than even Elyne knew?

"I don't want to leave you, Drake," she whispered.

"Aye, I know. Nor I you."

She started to protest again but was interrupted when the door to the chamber opened. Eldrin and the healer entered.

"Ah, he's awake." Eldrin grinned at him, clearly glad to see he lived. "Thank the gods you're still among the living."

It reminded Drake of something Finn had said to him before their last tournament together. He'd cheated death numerous times. This time, though, was too close. If it hadn't been for the Elves he would surely be dead. "Aye, I'm still alive." He hobbled back to the bed as Allanna remained at the window.

"'Tis time to change the dressing," the healer said.

"I assume you're the man responsible for saving my life?" Drake asked.

"Aye, that I am. I thought for sure you'd die." He waved him toward the bed.

Drake noticed the woman standing in the doorway, her hands clasped in front of her. Coppery hair flowed over her shoulders. Her silvery eyes peered at him with curiosity. When Eldrin noticed him looking at her, he waved her inside.

"Sir Drake, allow me to present to you Lady Talaiel. She's the one who allowed us to come to her castle so you could recover."

She dipped a quick curtsy. "Sir Drake, it is my pleasure to welcome you here. Lord Eldrin has regaled me with many tales of your adventures."

"Has he?"

"Lie down, human," the healer said. "I need to check the wound."

Drake did as he was bid.

"You're a lucky man," the healer said. "You were stabbed with an enchanted Elven blade. The tip broke off in the wound."

"How did the tip break?"

"Elven blades are made of the finest glass," the healer said. "One can easily break the tip if one chooses or one is not so careful."

"Meaning whoever it was wanted you to experience a slow, painful death," Eldrin said.

"I thank you for your skills then, healer."

"Turin is the name, human."

"Drake is the name, healer," he retorted.

The healer looked at him a long moment before giving a snort of laughter. "As you say, sir."

"Turin is one of the best in the Skye Realm," Talaiel said. "I admit I've long wanted to meet a human. You are not so different than my own kind."

Drake wanted to laugh but the stinging wound hurt too bloody bad. Instead he gritted his teeth. "Is that so?"

"Aye, it is. For many years I'd heard of the cruelty of humans. That you're a warlike people," she continued. "I thought Lord Eldrin mad when he told me how much he respected you and how hard you fought against the Unseelie. He tells me you are most brave."

"I daresay Lord Eldrin exaggerates," Drake said with a thin smile.

The healer placed a clean bandage on his wound and wiped his hands on a cloth. "The wound seems to be healing nicely. I'll be back later to change the bandage again."

"Thank you, Turin."

He nodded toward Eldrin and Talaiel as he left.

"Lord Eldrin, might I have a word with you? In private?" Drake refused to look at Allanna for fear his expression would give away his thoughts. She would know he intended to speak to her brother about her situation.

Eldrin glanced at his sister but she hadn't moved from her spot at the window. She folded her arms over her chest, looking defiant.

"Talaiel, will you show Allanna to her chamber?"

Reluctantly, Allanna followed her out of the room. Eldrin turned to Drake, an expectant look on his face.

"You must return the princess to her father," Drake said.

"No," Eldrin said, matter-of-factly.

Drake blinked surprise, unsure he heard him correctly. "My lord, she should be returned to her rightful place. Despite her objections. You and the king can keep her safe."

"I've been thinking about this a lot and I've decided I'm not taking her back. Not yet. My father doesn't know she ran away, though I suspect he would have been alerted to her disappearance by now. I'm the only one who knows why she left and I intend to tell him differently. I cannot return Allanna to marry a man of such evil."

"But what of the betrothal—"

"The betrothal will be dissolved. Marath sent men to attack and kidnap her."

Anger rose in Drake so violently he clenched his fist. The man would pay. He would make sure of it. Marath would never touch her again. Drake agreed with Eldrin—he couldn't send Allanna back to that. He'd thought Marath's attack on him was to get him out of the way. But clearly Marath had a more diabolical plan in place if he tried to kidnap and kill Allanna.

Another reason to kill Marath.

"I will kill him for that," Drake vowed.

"Not unless I kill him first. The truth is, Sir Drake, someone tried to kill my baby sister. She was attacked as were you. I think you and I know who that someone was."

"Marath stabbed me," Drake admitted. "He threatened me. Told me to stay away from her and that the princess belonged to him. I thought he wanted me gone so he could marry Allanna. She told me they were betrothed."

"There is more to it than that."

"I believe you have the right of it. He told me he had spies in the land."

"That may be true," Eldrin agreed. "That's why I had to bring you here. The Skye Elves admit those they wish by moon dragon. Moon dragons are controlled by the Skye Elves. They'll not be able to get to us here."

"Not even if they flash here?"

"Not even. The Skye Elves' magic is powerful. They closely guard their realm with numerous unbreakable wards in place. They cannot flash here."

"That's comforting to know we'll be safe then. However, Marath wasn't the one who attacked Allanna when she tried to run."

"He may not have been the one but he sent the men after her. A mage. A Fomorian mage," Eldrin said.

"How do you know this?"

"I recognized his race."

Drake wasn't all that familiar with the Fomorians but he sensed they were not a pleasant people.

"The Fomorians were banished to the sea long ago. We call it the Sorrow Lands. They were hidden away from the land and the people because of their vile and evil deeds. You'll recall Morrigan used some to attack Queen Maeve. Most were killed in the battle at the Sacred Forest but a few escaped. Marath must have released them all," Eldrin said. "There is only one way they could have been freed from that prison."

"How is that?"

"Dark magic," Eldrin replied.

"And you believe Marath had something to do with that?"

"Aye, I do. I intend to find out the truth. I need your help. You're the only one I trust with my sister. She will do what you ask."

"And what would you have me ask her to do?"

"I want you to keep her here where it's safe. I don't believe that will be difficult since she refuses to leave your side. Lady Talaiel and her people will protect you."

"If you intend to go after Marath, I cannot allow you to do that alone. The man is dangerous and I believe he has learned how to flash."

Eldrin stared in disbelief at him for a long moment. "You saw this?"

"I did. When he attacked me in the stables. He flashed to me and then flashed away after he stabbed me."

"That presents a bit of a problem."

"Why is that?"

"Because Elves cannot flash," Eldrin said. "They don't have the power. We are not like the Fae who can sift from one place to another. A skill such as this would have to be learned by dark magic."

"Why kidnap the princess, though? What does he gain?"

"Because my father would give him anything to save his daughter. I suspect Marath wants more than marriage to my sister. He also mentioned how dangerous the Fae were and that the Treaty of Separation should be reinstated."

"Then by kidnapping Allanna he could demand the treaty be put back in place for her safe return. I daresay he intended to make it look as though the Fae were responsible," Drake said.

"I believe you may be right," Eldrin agreed. "I must return to my father and warn him."

"I cannot let you return alone."

"You're injured, Sir Drake. Stay here. Rest. Recover. And protect my sister. I will be back as soon as I can with news. Hopefully to return you both to the palace."

"And should you not return?"

Eldrin flashed a smile. "I don't think that's a possibility, my lord."

"I hope you're right." Drake smiled, admiring the man's courage and confidence. "Thank you, my lord, for saving my life. I owe you a debt."

Eldrin gave him a wide grin. "Mayhap someday I can collect it."

The Lady of the Skye waited for Eldrin in the hallway after sending Allanna on her way. She'd wanted a moment alone with him. She gave him a small smile as he closed the door behind him. Gods, she was lovely. He had always thought so. She grew more beautiful every time he saw her. And now he would have to leave her again. He hadn't even spent any time alone with her.

"I trust the human is doing well?"

"He's better," Eldrin said.

"Good."

"I'm leaving them in your care," he said. "If you approve. I know you'll be able to protect them from the mages hunting my sister and Sir Drake."

Her smile quickly faded. "You're leaving again? So soon?"

"I have to return to the Woodlands. I have to deal with Lord-Regent Marath. My sister cannot marry that man. He tried to kill her."

"This is her betrothed?"

"Not for long if I have anything to do about it. As soon as I have the situation in hand, I will be back for Drake and Allanna."

"To return with them to the Woodlands."

"Aye."

"I understand, of course. They are welcome to remain here as long as they need."

"You have my thanks, my lady."

"It is not your thanks I require."

He knew what she meant and he wanted to give that to her. Oh, how he did. He had loved her from the moment he rescued her from the hunter. From the moment he saw her, he wanted her. She spoke to his heart in a way no other Elven woman had or ever could. He took her hand, planted a soft kiss on her palm.

"I cannot give you want you want."

"You can." She flattened her hand on his cheek.

"I can't. You cannot leave your kingdom and I am bound to my own." He released her hand and stepped away. "I will return, my lady."

He started down the corridor, his boots echoing on the walls.

"Lord Eldrin," she called.

He paused and turned to look at her. She took slow steps toward him, her hands clasped in front of her. Light from the candles in the wall sconces shimmered in her coppery hair, sparking a bright flame in the strands. Strands he longed to touch and run his fingers over.

"Let me make myself clear, Lord Eldrin. I love you. I have always loved you and I think you love me too. We can find a way. There is always a way."

His heart lurched. She had never said the words until now. She had never acknowledged her feelings. The feelings they had both tried to bury. But now it was clear she had no interest in trying to hide them anymore.

Eldrin clenched his fists. To hell with rules and decorum. He'd waited long enough. He took two large steps toward her. She must have known what he intended to do before he did it, for she relaxed her hands and shoulders. Desire sparked in her silvery gaze as he took her in his arms.

His mouth met hers with such a fierce savage hunger she whimpered. Her lips yielded with such willingness his knees nearly buckled. He angled her body and pushed her backward a few steps until she bumped into the wall. He pressed against her, feeling her long, lithe body against his for the first time. Feeling the weight of her bones as she wrapped her arms around his neck. Feeling her pliant, soft lips part against his. His fingers twined in her hair that reminded him of Elven water silk. He imagined it would be that soft.

It was a kiss of longing, of desire, of lust. As though their souls fused and forever entwined with each other. Never to part. Never again to be separated. And he knew in that one instance, that one exchange of breath, that he could never live the rest of his days without being able to kiss her. To love her. His thirst for her would never slake. Not after one kiss. Not ever.

When he parted from her, color stained her high cheekbones. Her lips were plump and pink from his brutal onslaught. She fought to catch her breath.

"I will return for you." He whispered the words against her mouth.

"I will wait for you."

It took all his strength to release her and walk away.

Chapter 11

Allanna waited for Lady Talaiel at the bottom of the stairs, hoping to get a word with her. But it wasn't the lady who came down first. It was her brother. He paused briefly as he looked at her and halted.

"I'm returning, Allanna. I leave you in Lady Talaiel's care."

"May the gods be with you, brother."

He gave her a nod and departed. She watched him walk away and knew that part of her was dying with every receding step. He would return and expect her to come home to the Woodlands and then she may lose Drake forever. What would become of her then? Would she be forced to marry Marath, that evil, vile man? Gods, she hoped not.

Seconds later, the Lady of the Skye descended the stairs, her fingertips pressed against her dark-red lips and a dreamy look on her face. Somehow Allanna knew she and her brother must have kissed and possibly even exchanged words of love. She smiled to herself, glad to know her brother had finally found someone. Lady Talaiel was beautiful and perfect. No wonder Eldrin was in love with her.

When the lady saw her, Allanna gave a nod of greeting. "My brother goes back to the Woodlands."

"I know," the lady said. "But you will be safe here, I assure you."

Allanna looked to the door Eldrin had disappeared through. "May I ask you a personal question, my lady?"

She chuckled. "Of course."

"How did you come to know my brother?"

"We have known each other for quite some time, your highness," she said. She gave her a sidelong glance with a smile.

"I thought the Skye Elves remained here in the clouds," Allanna said. "It is said they never leave their heavens."

"That is mostly true," Talaiel said with a nod of agreement. "Would you like to hear the story?"

"Aye, I would."

"You look tired. I will escort you back to your chamber while I tell you the tale. I had gone riding on one of my moon dragons." Allanna fell in step with her as they headed back up the stairs once again. "It was very dark that night. There was no moon. I was beckoned by the cool, crisp air. I love to fly, you see. And knew the risks I took by going with no moonlight.

"I flew close to the ground to feel the wind in my hair and face and see all the trees sped by. It was exhilarating and always took my breath away. I knew how dangerous it was but I was arrogant enough to think I would be safe. I never anticipated the dragon hunter to come after us."

Allanna gasped. "But dragon hunting has been outlawed for quite some time."

"Aye, you have the right of it. But there are still a few who hunt them. Especially the silvery moon dragons. Their scales are worth the most in trade. The hunter struck down my dragon. He couldn't maintain his flight and we fell from the sky. I was lucky I didn't get crushed when he landed. However, I broke my leg so I couldn't flee.

"As soon as we were on the ground, the hunter charged. I knew by the evil glint in his eye he intended to kill me and then my dragon. As the hunter tried to attack, he suddenly fell to the ground, several arrows in his back," she said.

"My brother saved your life," Allanna guessed.

Talaiel smiled and flushed a little. "He did. He killed the hunter and saved me and my dragon."

"Then what happened?"

"Your brother knew some first aid and was able to set my leg to get me to the healer. He helped me back on the dragon and we flew back here. Naturally, my kinfolk were curious to see a Wood Elf here in the sky. We allowed him to stay while I convalesced. He was wonderfully attentive—"

She halted there and flushed again.

Joy spread through Allanna's chest as she looked at the lovely Talaiel and she suddenly *knew* for sure the lady had feelings for her brother. She smiled slowly and stepped closer to her, dropping her voice.

"You're in love with him."

Allanna could tell by the way she talked about him. She never imagined her brother in love with anyone. She was not displeased, though. Talaiel had helped Drake. Plus the Elven lady was nothing short of elegant. She had a strength and beauty Allanna admired and one she imagined her own mother had possessed. How could Eldrin resist her? He'd be a fool.

"I...I hope that doesn't come as too much of a shock," she said.

"Does he know?" Allanna asked. Because what if her dolt of a brother didn't? He could be thickheaded sometimes.

The beginning of a smile tipped the corners of her mouth. "I believe he may have an idea."

Allanna blew out a breath. At least he wasn't unaware of her adoring glances. "Sometimes he can be blind to things that are right in front of him."

The lady stifled a chuckle. "I do not think that's the case. Ah, here we are. Your chamber."

"I thank you." She curtsied.

"Rest, your highness. And then join us for a meal in the dining hall."

"I should like that," she said.

Talaiel gave her a final smile before heading back the way she'd come. Allanna backed into her chamber. The room was palatial. It dwarfed that of her own. There was no balcony like she had at home but one wall of windows that stretched from floor to ceiling. She could see nothing but puffy clouds and a glimpse of pink sky.

She yawned. Fatigue hit her hard as she backed toward the bed and sat. She thought she would lie down for a moment. But the next thing she knew her eyes drifted closed and she was fast asleep.

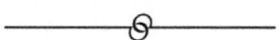

When Allanna finally awakened, the room had darkened. She must have slept away the day. Someone had come into her chamber and lit all the candles and started a fire in the oversized fireplace. It was a good thing too, since the room was chilly. Standing, she walked to the windows and peered into the night. Twilight had deepened and the stars winked back at her on their background of deep indigo. Moonlight slashed through the panes, spilling over her in a blue-white veil. She could feel the cold air pressing against the other side of the glass and shivered.

As she looked out at the deepening twilight she thought of Drake. That morning they had stood together at the window in his chamber. And she had leaned against him with her arm wrapped around him, snuggled up to him for warmth from the chilly morning air. She had pressed her hand on his chest over the wild beat of his heart. And she had valiantly tried hard not to glance at anything below his waist.

Tried but was unsuccessful. Even though she got a glimpse she could not get the image of his corded abs out of her head. Nor the way his waist tapered down into the top of his breeches. Nor the way a thin line of soft hair trailed downward into the waist of said breeches. A thin line she wished to trace with the tip of her finger and the tip of her tongue to the hardened length she so desperately wanted to touch. And taste.

It was an absolutely scandalous thought.

How could she forget the way he looked at her? The way he told her she was beautiful? How could she forget the way he kissed her with such reckless abandon? His lips were soft as velvet. His kiss full of white-hot heat that sent her senses reeling. What would his kisses feel like on her throat?

She couldn't stop from scraping her teeth down his bearded chin. She had no idea what made her do that—all she could think about was doing it. And when the coarse hair whispered against her lips she had become weak in the knees.

Thinking of that now made the blood rush to her cheeks. She pressed her palms against them. It devastated her when he told her he couldn't love her *like that*. When he tried to ease her away from him. But nothing in this world or the next could make those feelings she had for him go away. *Nothing*. Not Marath. Not her brother. Not her father.

What if her brother returned on the morrow and demanded she go back with him? If he did, what if these were her last moments—alone—with Sir Drake? She may never get another opportunity to be with him. Despite his determination to set her free, she was not so ready to release herself of his affections yet.

She needed more time with him. One more night. One more kiss. One more caress. And then she would go peacefully. She would hold the memory close to her heart for the rest of her long days.

She had promised Lady Talaiel she would join her for a meal in the dining hall. And indeed her stomach rumbled at the thought of food. But she couldn't go there. Not yet.

She stepped to her chamber door and opened it, peering into the hallway. She spied a few guards walking past, mayhap heading for their guard duty. When they didn't stop to stand guard, she made her move.

She walked toward Drake's chamber with a purposeful stride. But when she got to the door she halted, losing her nerve. Her stomach twisted into a tight knot as a wave of dizziness accosted her.

Was she really going through with this? She must be mad. But she also knew she could not go another day without being with him. Near him. Her lips tingled in anticipation of his kisses. Her body reacted at the mere thought of his hands touching her again. There was a swooping in her lower abdomen as she stood there, her hand raised, ready to rap on the door.

A moment's hesitation came over her, thinking of everything she had done in the past and everything she would do in the future. Drake had refused her once. He had pushed her away. Would he refuse her again? Would he remain the noble knight? Or would he fall to her seduction?

She smiled and knocked on the door.

To her surprise, the healer answered. He gave her a nod of greeting.

"Ah, princess, do come in. He's been asking for you."

Her heart jumped. Drake had asked for her? She suppressed the smile that wanted to erupt. The healer closed his bag and turned to Drake.

"The wound looks good. It's healing well."

"When can I get out of this bloody bed?"

"Soon enough. You don't want to be too quick about it." He tipped his head in a nod.

"Thank you, Turin."

And then they were alone. The healer closed the door behind him leaving Allanna standing in the middle of the room. They stared at each other a long moment. She was afraid to approach him. She was losing her resolve. Her cheeks heated as she looked away, suddenly interested in her shoes.

"I'm happy you came," he said.

Gods, she was happy to see him. More than any words could say. Her stomach clenched again. Tendrils of heat spiraled downward. Her lower body warmed with his words.

Which did nothing but make her flush again.

She dared a peek at him through her lashes. "I'm happy to see you."

Gods, she sounded like a dolt. Her voice was a weak whisper. He must think her nothing but a silly girl with a crush. After everything they'd been through. After everything they'd done. Moments ago she had decided she would be with him. Now she wasn't so sure.

"I didn't think you'd come back after what I said to you earlier."

She met his gaze. His unwavering gaze full of desire and sorrow. He hadn't wanted to push her away. He was doing what he thought was best for both of them.

"I couldn't stay away. Not from you. Not ever."

She didn't miss the sensuous light that passed between them.

"Come closer." His voice was husky, demanding. Like nothing she had ever heard from him before.

Her heart hammered a painful, rapid beat as she looked at him. He held a hand out. Her feet refused to move as she took in the sight of him. He was still shirtless and the bed clothes were tucked around his waist. She could clearly see the outline of his legs underneath the cover. His dark hair was mussed about his face, which was still covered in a beard. His eyes were bright and shining, glinting with an emotion she had never seen before. Something dangerous and seductive.

She swallowed hard and took a tentative step. She placed her hand in his and his fingertips closed around hers. The warmth of his touch assaulted her senses, making her reel. It took all her self-control not to swoon.

"How are you feeling?" she asked, finally finding her normal voice.

"Better." He smiled and she could have sworn his eyes twinkled.

"I'm glad."

"Closer," he demanded.

"Closer?"

"Aye, closer. Like you were this morning. Let me look upon you. Let me memorize your beautiful face. Let me see all that you are."

His hand trailed up her arm and he gave her a little tug toward him, pulling her down to the bed next to him. Now her heart raced, pulsing in her chest with reckless abandon. He reached for her, both hands cupping her face. She lost her balance and fell forward. Her hands landed on his chest as she stopped, their faces inches apart. A breath shuddered out of her.

"You speak as though you will never see me again," she whispered.

"I may not. We may not have another moment together. I wish to remember how you are."

She had come here intending to seduce him but somewhere along the way, he had managed to seduce her. He had managed to bring her to the edge of her senses. She could see the spark of desire in his piercing blue eyes. Eyes that searched her face for it did indeed seem as though he were memorizing her. She sat next to him, uncertain now what she should do. She was unskilled in the art of seduction but she knew what she wanted with Drake. She knew how she wanted to feel with him. She knew she never wanted to be with another.

She bit her lip.

His eyes landed on her mouth. He groaned, pulled her to him and kissed her.

Their mouths fused in a heated kiss of passion. Each one tasting the other. She relaxed her arms and fell into him. His hands tangled in her hair, fisting her locks as his tongue pushed into her mouth. She tasted back, their tongues doing a sort of sinful duel for control.

He won. She wanted him to win. She wanted him to always win.

His mouth moved to her throat. Her skin burst into flame as he made his way around to her earlobe and nibbled. This was what she dreamed of, what she wanted. Now that it was finally happening, her mind exploded with more possibilities. Little pinpricks of light pierced her vision as her eyes fluttered closed. Heat flooded her body and pulsed dampness between her legs, making her feel things she never expected.

And, oh gods, she loved the velvety feel of his mouth.

"Sir Drake…"

"Aye?" His breath wafted over her skin, sending heated chills over her.

"I…came to…to…" Oh gods, she couldn't think. Her mind wouldn't form the words. She knew what she wanted to say but how to say it was another matter. And her tongue swelled into a thick, useless muscle.

"To?" His eyes glinted almost as though he knew what she wanted to say.

Oh, bollocks. "To kiss you back."

She swept her tongue over his lower lip then sucked it gently between her teeth. He groaned again. His body felt good under her hands, the way his chest curved and the sprinkling of coarse hair. The tips of her fingers trailed down his corded abs to the edge of the waistband of his breeches and halted. She couldn't go forward even though she wanted to. Fear clasped her, made her stop. She knew what she wanted to do yet she couldn't force her hand to move.

Breaking the kiss, she dropped her head to his chest, inhaling the deep, masculine scent of him. A woodsy scent. Something that was inherent to him. Mayhap because he was human. She didn't know.

He stroked her hair as he held her and then dropped a kiss on the top of her head. It was then she remembered his wound and bolted upright.

"Did I hurt you?" Her gaze landed on the bandage on his side. She was relieved to see there was no blood.

He chuckled. "No, princess. You didn't. You couldn't."

"I meant your…your wound. Is it better?"

"Almost healed like Turin said."

"That's good." Her gaze flickered over him and she blushed when she saw the hardened length between his legs. The length she had stopped herself from running her fingertips over.

"I came to check on you," she said. "I'm glad you're better."

"Is that the only reason you came?"

Could he read that on her face? Was she so transparent? She bit her lip again.

"Ah, you really shouldn't do that."

"Do what?"

"*That.*" His gaze fixed on her lips.

"Why?" She blinked.

"Because I like it too much."

A smile tugged at the corner of her mouth. Her confidence soared. "You like it?"

"Aye, I do."

"And what would happen if I did it again?"

"You really shouldn't do it again."

"Shouldn't I?" She did it again.

He reached for her and dragged her to him. "Are you trying to torture me?" He said it against her mouth, his breath mingling with hers.

"No. Am I?"

"You are."

"Should I apologize?"

"Nay."

"Do you intend to do something about it?"

He growled.

"Is that an aye?" She grinned, enjoying teasing him.

"Princess—"

"Do you want to deny me again?"

"I will not take what does not belong to me."

"I do belong to you, Drake," she whispered. "I've already given you my heart. Isn't that enough?"

She could see the flash of pain in his eyes before he regained his composure. "I wish it were, princess."

"What more do you require of me?" she asked.

"I require marriage vows. You are too precious to me. I would not ruin your innocence."

"Oh, Drake. It wouldn't be ruining my innocence. I give myself to you freely." She pressed her hands against his chest, slid them upward to his shoulders. "I'm prepared to love you. Here. Now."

"Allanna—"

"Please don't deny me again."

A moment of indecision flashed through his eyes and then he pulled her tight against him before he pushed her to the mattress. His body pressed against hers. Her breath caught in her throat as she looked up at him, into those deeply penetrating eyes. Was he going to forget all that he was? Would he make love to her here? Oh gods, she wanted him.

"I do not deny my feelings for you," he said.

"Then—"

"You are still chaste. And I'm still a knight."

"But—"

"I'm still a knight but by Saint Mary you drive me mad."

"I—"

"You challenge my honor with every flutter of your lashes."

"Drake…"

"And with every flutter, I find you harder to resist."

His mouth covered any retort she had. She was conscious of every touch. Every movement. He leaned on his good side, kissing her. His hands slipped over the curve of her body, over her small breasts and flat abdomen. Flames followed by a warming shiver swept over her.

She was here. With him. And he was kissing her. And touching her. She had no idea what he intended to do next so she remained perfectly still and waited. She held a breath as his tongue moved against hers.

His kisses made her feel as though she were drunk on honeywine. Like something she could no longer live without. She needed them—him— like she needed air to breathe. When his mouth turned to a whisper against hers, she swept her tongue over his lower lip. He growled in response. He fisted her skirt and the shift beneath and crunched it within this hand. He inched it up slowly, his fingers doing a little walking dance along her thigh.

Her head exploded with new sensations. When his fingers brushed her bare skin, her breath hitched in her throat and she thought she would go mad. And all the while his mouth had never left hers. Her heart pattered quickly, threatening to burst from her chest as his fingers moved to her inner thigh and up and up and up.

And then he stopped kissing her. His searing-hot gaze met hers.

"I've gone too far," he said.

"No."

"Aye, I have and we must stop."

"No. No, don't stop."

She pressed her hand against his, pushing his palm down on her thigh. Her eyes fluttered closed as she memorized the way his hot hand pressed into her.

"Touch me."

She whispered the words against his mouth, her eyes still closed. She didn't want to see the denial in his face. Her throat had constricted and it was difficult for her to get the words out. Still she managed to push them past the lump in her throat. Past the fear of what would happen next.

Drake hadn't moved. Her fingers tingled. Why hadn't he moved?

"I shouldn't."

His deep voice floated over her. She had to look at him, to see the need and desire in his gaze.

"You should," she urged.

The piercing blue depths of his eyes sizzled with a spark of savage inner fire. It sent her reeling. She throbbed at the apex of her thighs. A curious pounding she had never experienced. Damp heat radiated from her core. She bent her knee and opened to him in invitation. His hand slipped from under hers and his fingers trailed over the curls hiding her sex, teasing her. Testing her. As though he were unsure he should touch her there when all she really wanted was him to touch her *there*.

A breath trembled on her lips.

"May I?"

Oh gods, he was going to do it. Her only response was to keep her eyes on his and nod.

His fingers slid into her curls, dipping deep into her folds and touching a secret place she never even knew existed. Heat exploded all over her at the heady sensation. And the pulsing between her thighs increased tenfold. He slid back and forth, enhancing the now ever-present ache. Her hips rocked against his hand with some deep-seated instinct. All she knew, truly, was this was exactly what she wanted him to do. And she never wanted him to stop.

"Does this please you?"

She whimpered as a mewl escaped her. She couldn't speak.

"Good," he said.

His fingers worked over her, never going any farther. She whimpered and rocked her hips against his fingers, wanting more. So much more but something she didn't know to ask for. She didn't know what she wanted only that she needed something else. Something deeper.

"Not yet," he whispered against her cheek before his kisses trailed down her neck and nibbled her earlobe like a murmur of love and adoration with every graze. There was a dreamy intimacy now. Something she had not thought possible with this man for their worlds had been so far apart only moments ago. In one secret moment he had shaken her to the core, shattered any thought of ever leaving him. She would never let him go. Not now. Not ever.

All because he had tasted her. All because he had touched her. All because he had dared to love her.

"So soft. So sweet."

He breathed the words against her neck, heating her overly chilled skin. Her fingers slipped through the silken strands of his dark hair, tangling them in her fist. Her hips moved in concert with his rotating fingers, building her to heights unimagined. The build was slow at first but had rapidly increased. Dizziness accosted her as her eyes closed again, concentrating and memorizing the way he stroked her.

Her world tilted on her axis. She would never be the same.

Her muscles contracted suddenly, her legs closing together on his fingers. Her body convulsed as she cried out. The vibrations sizzled through her from where his hand rested between her folds to the tips of her fingers.

Drake's mouth found hers again. When their lips met she was buffeted by the winds of his savage desire. A savage desire she returned with her own eager response.

When she finally relaxed he stopped kissing her and slipped his hand away. He rolled to his back next to her, his chest rising and falling with his labored breathing. She curled against him, snuggling against his side. He slipped an arm around her and held her close. Her fingers trailed through the fine hairs on his chest.

"I never want to leave this room," she said.

"But you must."

"Why?"

"There are those who will be looking for you. And to find you with me in my bed…" His voice trailed away.

She didn't give a whit if anyone found her in his bed. She was with him. That was all that truly mattered.

"I care not for that," she said.

"But I care." His hand trailed through her locks.

But Allanna knew every moment with Drake was a step she took further from her family and her old life. It was a step closer to him. He was her new life. Didn't he understand? Couldn't he see? She would gladly give up everything for him.

"It was a moment of weakness and I gave into it. I cannot allow myself to be swept away by your charms again, princess."

"I would marry you today if you asked."

"Ah…princess." The deep timbre of his voice rumbled in his chest under her ear as he continued to stroke her hair.

As much as she knew he was right she still did not want to leave this room. For if she did the spell would truly be broken. She feared they would never be this close again.

"I would marry you. If I could."

Her heart did a wild tumble before falling into her stomach and making her nearly come undone. The heated flare of desire and need and want burned through her. How could he say such things to her?

But then how could they *not* marry? Marath was not the man she wanted and she would do anything to keep from marrying him. Even…defy her father. What more could she lose? And she'd had the vision she'd seen their wedding.

"I regret nothing. Do you?" She rose to look at him.

He cupped her face. "Nay, my princess."

She could see the love burning in his eyes. But she could see some other emotion there too. Mayhap it was regret and he didn't want to tell her the truth of it. She would regret nothing. She would never want another man to touch her the way he touched her. To kiss her the way he kissed her.

"I'm glad," she said at last.

"But, Allanna, I fear we cannot be like this again. I fear next time I will not be able to stop."

"I don't want you to stop."

"Again I say you don't belong to me."

By the gods, she hated when he said that. She also hated the burn of tears at the backs of her eyes. "What if I did? What if we exchanged marriage vows?"

"Then things would be different."

So he would have her no other way. She should walk out of his chamber and never return. She should keep herself locked away until Eldrin returned to take her home. That's what she should do.

She had another plan. She wanted more. She needed more from him. Now was only the beginning. How could he continue to deny her after that? What was she going to do? What if Drake continued to deny her and refused to take her with him?

A sense of calm washed over her as she came to a decision.

"I should let you rest." She slipped away from him and slid off the end of the bed.

"Will you return later?"

She paused at the chamber door, breathless and lightheaded. As she turned to look at him one last time she couldn't ignore the tingle of excitement that went up her spine.

"Aye, I will."

Allanna left him, closing the door behind her. She leaned against Drake's closed door and pressed her hand on her roiling stomach. Her knees went weak and she hadn't fully recovered from what had happened. He had...touched her and given her pleasure she had never known before. And now that he had stoked the flames within, bringing them to a roaring blaze, she knew she would never again be the same.

Even remembering sent her cheeks flaming.

She would speak with the Lady of the Skye. Mayhap she would have a solution for her. She first sought her in the dining hall but the evening meal had long since ended. She'd missed it. And even though she should be ravenous, she wasn't. So she wandered through the castle halls, searching for the lady. Asking any random servant who happened to pass by. One at last directed her to the library.

Allanna halted in the doorway, awed by the enormous room.

The Skye Elves' library rivaled that of the one in the Woodlands at her father's palace. Allanna had never seen so many books before. The shelves soared upward to a twenty-foot domed ceiling where painted frescoes depicted silvery dragons in flight with moonlight upon their wings and an Elven warrior upon their backs. There were battle scenes and a depiction of a king who had once ruled the heavens. These were images of the Skye Elves' history.

In one corner, a wrought-iron spiral staircase took the visitor to a loft far atop the books where a window in the shape of a clover peeked out and soft cushions invited the reader to stay a long while. Skye Elves, clearly, had no problem with heights.

The furnishings of the room were elegant and feminine, which included a rug woven in fine fibers in bright colors with an intricate floral pattern, oversized stuffed chairs and matching settee in one corner in front of a fireplace with smoldering embers and the lady herself seated in a high-backed chair, her legs tucked under her and a tome with yellowed pages and a crumbling binding in her hands.

Allanna hesitated, not wishing to disturb her but she must have sensed someone in the room for she looked up. Golden firelight danced over her delicate features as she granted a smile, closed the book and rose.

"Ah, Princess Allanna. Come in." She waved her inside the library. "Are you hungry? You missed the evening meal but you were so tired I was hesitant to wake you."

"No, thank you. I find I'm not very hungry at all."

"If you change your mind, please do let me know. I'm sure the cook would be happy to get you something. How are you finding your accommodations?"

"Oh, my room is lovely," she said. "I was wondering if you could...if I could talk to you about a...a delicate situation." Allanna glanced down at her fingers twisting in a knot at her waist.

Talaiel cleared her throat. "A delicate situation?"

"Aye, regarding Sir Drake." She braved a glance at her and saw one pale brow rose to her hairline.

"My dear, are you with child?" she asked point-blank.

"Gods, no! I am...I mean to say we haven't...I don't know him *that* way." Flustered, Allanna blew out a heated breath. "It's complicated."

"Love often can be. Honeywine?" Talaiel asked.

"No, thank you."

She poured a glass of honeywine for herself and waved Allanna to the chair opposite her. "Come sit and tell me what this 'delicate situation' is."

Allanna shivered and hugged her elbows. It was from the cold in the room as well as the conversation she was trying to have with the lady. Mayhap she was wrong to come to her, to try asking her advice. But in truth she had no one else to turn to since Eldrin had left her in the lady's care. And he didn't really understand anyway. She knew what he'd say—that he wouldn't want to see her give up her crown for the knight.

Yet what would he do should their situation be reversed? Would he give up all that he had for the love of a woman? For Talaiel? Obviously he hadn't since she was still in the sky and he was still a ranger. Allanna would work on those details later. At the moment she had her own dilemma to solve.

Talaiel went to the fireplace, which had grown cold. As Allanna took her seat, the lady poked the embers until they managed to come alive once again. She added more wood and watched the flames crackle and burn.

"I hadn't realized it'd grown so cold in here. I'm so accustomed to the climate I forget how chilly it gets." She took a sip of her wine as she sat on the edge of the chair next to her. "Now, why don't you tell me what this is all about?"

"I shouldn't, really," Allanna said. "My father would not approve of me discussing our family matters with someone else."

"Someone like me, you mean?"

"Someone not of our line," she clarified. "I came to you because…my mother has been dead for many years and I have no one else."

The lady worried her lower lip through her teeth. "I see." Though it seemed as though she didn't.

"I'm to be married to that monster of a man, Lord-Regent Marath."

"Aye, your brother mentioned him before he left. I agreed to keep you and Sir Drake under my protection until the matter can be dealt with."

"Then you understand why I cannot marry him."

"I do. That and you are clearly in love with Sir Drake."

Allanna flushed. "Is it that obvious?"

"Any Elf with eyes can see that." Talaiel gave her a kind, understanding smile. "And you refused to leave his side while he was injured and recovering. Were I in your position, I doubt I could leave his side."

"Then you know how I feel. I love him. I do," Allanna said. "It's why I've come to you for advice."

"My advice?" She didn't hide the incredulous look as her eyes went wide.

"I don't know who else to turn to. When Eldrin returns, he will expect me to go back to the Woodlands with him. I fear when that happens I will never see Sir Drake again. My father betrothed me to the lord-regent to make me forget about him and because he is an Elf. He doesn't want Drake and I to marry because he is a human."

"That does present a problem," the lady said. "Is this the delicate situation you mentioned?"

Allanna nodded.

Talaiel sagged in the chair in relief. "Thank the gods. I thought you were going to ask me how a man and woman created a child. I wasn't prepared to give you *that* speech."

As they looked at each other, they shared a laugh. It eased the tension between them and Allanna knew she'd made the right decision to come to her for help.

"Sir Drake was to return to his human realm but I begged him to take me with him." She lifted her head and looked the lady in the eye. "I am prepared to give up all that I am for him."

"But?"

"But my father will never speak to me again nor allow me back into the palace if I decide to leave with him."

"And you don't wish to lose your family," she said.

"Eldrin is my closest brother. He understands me and he treats me as more than a sister. He treats me as his friend. It would be difficult if I lost him."

"So what do you wish of me? What advice can I provide you?"

"I suppose I want to know if I'm making the right decision."

"Only you know that, princess."

"I know. But if you were in my place, what would you do?"

Talaiel didn't respond for a long moment as she took another sip of her honeywine. Her hand tightened around the tankard as she gripped it. She inhaled slowly through her nose before exhaling as slowly, as though considering her next words carefully. "I would follow my heart. What does your heart say, Allanna?"

"My heart says to go with Sir Drake. I would marry him faster than a dragon can breathe fire if he asked."

"Then you must decide if losing your family is worth the price of loving a human. If you believe it is the right one then never look back, Allanna."

"I'm scared."

"Aye. That's why you must find the courage within you. Does he know you love him?"

"He does."

"And he loves you as well?"

"Aye, he does." Though he had never spoken the words, she knew it to be true.

"So your decision should be easy."

"But it's not easy," Allanna insisted. She twisted a corner of her sleeve around her finger. "I still don't know what to do."

"What do you want to do?"

She considered, knowing the answer within her yet too afraid to speak it.

Talaiel took another sip of her honeywine. "There is the old custom of handfasting."

"Handfasting?" Hope bubbled inside her. "What do you mean?"

"Aye, handfasting. Not quite marriage vows but you would indeed be married after a year and a day."

"I've heard of this custom, my lady." Her heart palpitated at a rapid pace. "I know of it."

"And if you and Sir Drake were to exchange vows during a handfasting…" She paused, considering. "Well, it would make the betrothal invalid." The Lady of the Skye tapped her chin with the tip of her finger. "Aye, it may be the perfect solution." Then she gave the princess a pointed look. "If, that is, you are truly willing to give up all that you have to be with him."

"I am." Allanna said it with all the sure calm she possessed.

"Then leave all the arrangements to me."

Chapter 12

King Urdithane had not stopped pacing his private chamber since the moment he discovered his daughter was missing. He had refused any sort of food or drink. He had refused to see anyone but his son. And when he had learned Lord Eldrin was also missing and Lord Navin injured, his worry had increased tenfold. What was happening to his kingdom? His children were missing or injured, save Andahar. And he had sent his elder son on an errand to discover the truth.

Andahar, like him, had decided it would be best if he remained alone in his private chamber. Lord Marath was still in the palace and despite giving him Allanna's hand in marriage, he wasn't all too sure he trusted the man anymore.

What a fool he'd been. How could he have agreed to such a betrothal? It was clear Allanna had no love—or even like—for the man. And Marath was...he didn't know what Marath was but he didn't like what he'd discovered about him. It pained Urdithane to think him a traitor after all he'd done for Marath. After all he'd given him, trusted him with.

A swift knock on the door before it opened and Andahar stepped into the room, closing it behind him.

"Have you found anything, Andahar?"

"No, Father. Allanna has disappeared without a trace as well as Eldrin. I've had men out looking for both of them. I also sent a raven to the Fae queen asking her if they had arrived there. I thought, mayhap, Allanna followed the human knight there." He paused, color draining from his face. As though he had news he didn't want to tell.

"Well? Did she reply?"

"Aye, she did. And she hasn't seen Eldrin or Allanna...or Sir Drake. He never arrived at the Queen's Palace."

"Gods." Urdithane sat down hard on the edge of his bed. "What's happened, Andahar?"

"I know not. Marath has been asking for you."

"Marath." He snorted. "I want you to go to the High Druid immediately and have that betrothal broken at once."

"Father, are you sure?"

"You heard me. It was a mistake to agree to that marriage in the first place. I don't want her married to that man."

"He'll not be happy about that."

"I don't give a hang what he thinks," the king said. "See that it's done."

"Aye, I will make sure it's taken care of immediately."

"Good."

"You should eat something, Father. You look pale."

"I can't eat until I know my children are safe."

A knock on the door interrupted them. "Come," the king called.

When it opened, one of his guards stepped inside. "My king, Lord Eldrin has returned to the castle. He was spotted riding through the gate."

"Was the princess with him?" He couldn't deny the hope swelling inside him.

"No, your majesty."

Fear replaced that hope. "Bring him to me at once."

"Aye, your majesty." When the door closed again, Urdithane turned to the prince. "Go to him. Make sure he gets here safely to me."

"As you wish, Father."

When he was gone, Urdithane went back to pacing. He had gone a few steps, turned, a few more steps and turned again. When he did, he stopped short at the surprise appearance of Marath. He stood in the center of the room, holding a brass ewer. Urdithane took a step back. He hid his scowl as he crossed his arms.

"How did you get in here?"

"Through the door." He motioned toward it.

The king's brow wrinkled. "The guards would not have let you in. Aside from that, I'm not receiving visitors." He went to the door and opened it. His guards were nowhere in sight. He spun back toward Marath. "Where are they?"

"They took a break."

"You're lying. They have orders to remain."

Marath appeared in a flash of light in front of him. He kicked the door closed.

"Come now, my king. Allow me to help. I understand you've refused your food and drink." Marath held up the ewer. "Honeywine? I understand you've had difficulty sleeping as well."

Urdithane narrowed his eyes. There was something different about him. He couldn't quite decide what it was. A shadow, a darkness, haunting Marath's features. A fine sheen of sweat covered his face. "Who told you this?"

"It is the talk of the castle with the princess and the ranger missing, your majesty."

The king watched as the lord-regent walked to his table and poured two tankards of the honeywine. His hand shook ever so slightly. Was he ill? Marath handed one to Urdithane.

"Do you know where she is?"

"My king, I'm afraid I have some…difficult news about your daughter."

"Oh? And what is that?"

"I saw her with that human knight. Sir Drake, is it?" Marath ran the tip of his finger around the rim of his tankard.

"What do you mean you saw her with him?"

"There was no mistaking the look of adoration they exchanged shortly before they kissed."

Urdithane's hand tightened around his cup. "What are you telling me, Lord Marath?"

There was an eerie glint in Marath's eyes. "I'm telling you she and the human have run away together."

"Impossible."

"Oh, it's quite possible. I saw them leaving together."

He couldn't believe it. His daughter had forsaken all that she was and all that she had to be with a *human*. Eldrin must have discovered the truth and returned to break the news to him. The thought disgusted him. Now he would have to renounce her. Forever banish her from the Elven kingdoms. She was no longer one of their people. One of the Light.

"My condolences, sire," Marath said.

"My daughter…" He sat on the edge of the bed, still holding the cup. "I cannot believe she has done such a thing. Queen Elyne said she hadn't seen Sir Drake or Allanna."

"Mayhap they didn't ride off to the Queen's Palace," Marath suggested. He wiped sweat from his forehead with the back of one hand. "It could be they are still in the Otherworld. Or they found another way to return to the human realm. There are still portals that can be used if one knows how."

"And Elyne could have told her how to use them," Urdithane said.

"Aye, she could."

"Then the queen lied to me." Urdithane lowered his head as his chest tightened with the disappointment.

"A trait common to the Fae," Marath said. He seemed to be lost in thought for a moment then snapped back to the present. "Mayhap you should taste the honeywine, sire? It will help you sleep and put your worried mind to rest."

He stared down into the pale liquid as the ache of fatigue pressed into his bones. Aye, he was tired. He wanted to sleep. He took a deep quaff of the drink.

"The betrothal—"

"Broken, of course, sire. I expected that." Marath waved away the thought as though waving away an annoying gnat. Again Urdithane saw his hand tremble.

Urdithane yawed as the room suddenly tilted. The cup slipped from his hand, the remaining liquid pouring out on the stones. It clattered to the floor with a resounding *bong*. He could hear Marath talking but he couldn't understand what he was saying. It was as though he were in a long tunnel with nothing but an echo. His eyelids turned heavy and he could no longer keep them open.

His stomach clenched into a tight knot as he passed out.

As soon as the king was out, Marath flashed away from the bedchamber and to his own. He fell to his knees, sweat trickling down the side of his face and back. He sucked in a sharp breath, trying to stave off the illness. Stave off the effects of the black magic. His stomach cramped, threatening to heave.

After several deep breaths, he managed to push back the flood of magic trying to regain control of his mind and body. The power was strong—so strong—but he was stronger. The darkness had totally consumed him although he had resisted at first. Now he embraced it. He had never been so free or alive before. All he need do was control the way it affected his mind.

His chamber door opened and Aesir entered, balancing a tray of fruit and cheese on his arm.

"My lord?"

Marath wiped his brow with the back of his hand and got to his feet. He waved him inside, a tremor shaking his hand. "I'm quite all right," he lied. "Come in."

Aesir closed the door behind him and placed the tray on a nearby table. "The Fomorian has been lurking outside the gates all morning, my lord. He wishes to speak with you. He is quite agitated."

"Aye, I know. What of the prince?"

"He has gone to greet Lord Eldrin."

Hearing that, a chill froze his veins. His mind buzzed with warning, the dark magic once again fighting to control him. "Eldrin has returned?"

"Aye, my lord."

"Any sign of the princess or the human knight?"

"No, my lord."

He ran a hand over his chin, then squeezed his hand into a fist to hide the tremor. "The ranger returning poses a problem."

He had intended to rid the kingdom of the meddling Andahar next. Now with the ranger back, he wasn't so sure he could do that. The king would be discovered shortly and he needed the spare moments to intercept the prince before he found him. That would likely not happen now.

"May I ask what your plan is?" Aesir kept his tone even and light.

Marath opened his eyes wide. What did Aesir say? "Plan?"

"I thought this was merely about reinstating the Treaty of Separation. But now you've attacked the princess and tried to murder the king."

Aye, he had altered his plan and he hadn't shared it with Aesir. Something inside him had changed. Though he knew it was due to the dark magic—and he knew he would soon become a Dark Elf—he couldn't stop it. He was compelled to do these things. As though a small sinister voice urged him, telling him what to do.

Somewhere along the way he had realized he would not be happy as long as King Urdithane or his useless son sat on the throne. He would crush the hated Fae and rule the entire Woodlands. Aye, that's what he wanted. What he *needed* to do. What the darkness compelled him to do. The betrothal to the princess had merely been a way into the royal family. Her disappearance had been fortuitous.

"Do you intend to take control of the Woodlands, my lord?" Aesir asked when he didn't answer.

Marath met Aesir's level gaze. The man could always read through him so easily. Another quiver ran through him. He squeezed his fists tight. It was all so clear now. "That *is* what I intend."

"Why?"

"Why not? When I can have so much more. That Treaty was useless anyway."

He walked to the tray of fruit Aesir had brought. He picked a small purple grape and held it between his thumb and forefinger.

"It is clear to me neither Urdithane nor Andahar have the Woodlands' best interests in mind. I do. I intend to rid this place of those royal fools. And once I control the palace, I intend to crush the Fae."

"But what of Lord Eldrin and Lord Navin?"

"They will be killed as well." Lorcann would help him.

To punctuate his point, he squished the grape between his fingers and let the shell of it land on the floor. "I have done nothing but good for this realm and how am I repaid? With a small parcel of land in the far-reaching corner of the Woodlands."

"But the princess—"

"The princess will be found and dealt with accordingly," Marath said. The darkness had plans for her. "She defied me. She and that *disgusting* human knight."

"By your command, my lord." Aesir merely nodded but Marath didn't miss the look of worry creasing his face.

"Tell Lorcann I will see him at once," Marath said.

"Aye, my lord. It will be done." He gave a quick bow of his head before leaving the chamber.

He could do nothing to soothe the Fomorian mage. Nor could he put his plan for Andahar into action due to the untimely arrival of Eldrin. He cracked his knuckles, closed his eyes again and listened to the black magic whispering inside him. They both had to be disposed of at once.

———————————⊙———————————

Eldrin was glad he had left the horses in the nearby meadow when they took off for the Skye Elves. As soon as the moon dragon landed, he mounted his horse and rode with a fury toward the Woodlands. He hadn't stopped until he reached the gate.

Another Elf had taken over Navin's duties while his brother healed and admitted him right away. He relinquished his mount to one of the stable hands and took the stairs two at a time to the palace. His thighs burned and his chest heaved by the time he reached the top. Yet he never slowed his pace. He walked swiftly through the halls when he came upon his elder brother standing outside his father's chamber.

Prince Andahar's brow wrinkled with lines of worry and he ran a jerky hand through his hair. His normally pinkish skin had lost all its color. He was speaking in low tones to the healer, Brom. When Andahar saw him, relief flashed across his face.

"Eldrin, thanks be to the gods you're here. Where have you been? Where is Allanna?"

"Allanna is safe," Eldrin said. He would save the details for later. He knew by the look on his brother's face something was terribly wrong. "What's happened?"

"It's father…he's…" Andahar faltered. He pressed his lips together in a thin line.

"He's ill, my lord," Brom said.

"Ill? How serious is it?"

Andahar sagged against the door of the king's chamber. Eldrin had never seen him so distraught.

"He's unresponsive. As though he's in a deep sleep," the healer said. "I believe he was poisoned, your highness."

Fear prickled the back of Eldrin's throat. All he could think about was Allanna's vision. She had told him not long ago about the ones she had with their father and Andahar. She was certain it had something to do with Marath.

"Will he live?" He glanced between Andahar and Brom.

"I know not, my lord," Brom said.

"Then you know what must be done, Andahar. With the king indisposed, you must take over the realm."

"Nay," Andahar said, shaking his head. "I'll not do that. Father will recover and be fine. He'll still be able to rule."

"And what if he doesn't recover? You are crown prince, Andahar. It is your *duty*. You must take over the realm before anything else happens," Eldrin said.

"Lord Eldrin is correct, your highness," Brom interjected. "The kingdom cannot go without a ruler and you are the next in line."

After a moment, Andahar at last nodded. "All right."

"Can I see him?" Eldrin asked the healer.

"I don't think he'll be able to hear you but, aye, you can."

"I want you to begin searching for a cure for him at once, Brom," Eldrin said.

"There may not be much I can do for him. His symptoms are vague at the moment."

"See what you can do." Eldrin patted him on the shoulder.

The healer nodded as he trudged off. Eldrin opened the door to his father's chamber and stepped through. Andahar followed, closing the door. The king lay upon his bed under the bedclothes, his face ashen. He had never seen him look so pale.

"How did this happen, Andahar?"

"I don't know. I was coming to meet you at the gate. Before I could get out the palace, the healer had been summoned. One of the chambermaids found him. There was spilled honeywine on the floor with a discarded tankard next to the bed."

"Where is the tankard now?"

"I had the healer take it and examine it. He found a grainy residue in the bottom. That's why we suspect it was poison. I don't understand how this could have happened. He had been in here, guarded, for days. No one saw anyone come in or out of the chamber."

"Father had been in here for days?"

"Aye, since the day you and Allanna disappeared. I thought it best if we take precaution and add guards. No one knew where you had gone. It was almost as though you had disappeared without a trace. Where have you been?"

"Allanna was attacked by four Fomorian mages," Eldrin said, cutting to the thick of it.

"Is she all right?" Concern flickered over the prince's face.

"She is safe for now. I took her to the Skye Elves."

"The Skye Elves? Is that even possible?"

"I know the Lady of the Skye," Eldrin admitted.

And that was all he intended to admit. He had no intention of telling his brother he was in love with the lady. The memory of their kiss still burned hot under his skin. He itched to return to her but he quickly shoved away thoughts of Talaiel. He couldn't afford to be distracted by her now.

"Andahar, Allanna had a vision not long ago that involved you and Father. She told me she saw the king poisoned and you stabbed with a sword. By Marath."

More color drained from his face, as if that were possible. "When was this vision?"

"The day of her betrothal."

Andahar clenched his jaw. "She told me of the one where I was killed but not of Father's poisoning. Why did you fail to tell us?"

"Neither of you readily believe her visions. She told me because she knew I'd listen and because she knew I would believe her."

A silent moment passed between them. A flicker of annoyance passed through his eyes before he quickly squashed it. But Eldrin knew as Andahar did that he and their father never believed in her visions. That was why she and Eldrin had formed such a solid bond. He had always believed her and always treated her as though her visions were normal. And they were for her.

"She saw it was Marath in both cases?"

"She suspected about Father. She said she saw him stab you in her second vision. In light of the current situation, you should be guarded from dawn to dusk, your majesty."

He frowned. "You speak as though we are not brothers."

"I speak as a ranger," Eldrin said. "It's for your own safety."

"I will not cower behind guards," he growled. "Lord-regent or not, I will have him brought to me."

"Do you have proof he poisoned the king?" Eldrin asked. "You said yourself the guards saw no one enter or leave the chamber save for you. And none of our servants would do such a thing. They're all too loyal."

"Aye, that's true. I have no proof."

"There is something else you should know." Eldrin had to decide how best to tell his brother. "Sir Drake remains in the realm. Marath tried to kill him."

Andahar stared at him a long moment. "Where is he now?"

"Safe."

"Is he with Allanna?" he demanded, hands still fisted.

"He is. Without the Skye Elves' healing, he would be dead."

He looked thoughtful. "I have no love for the human knight, Eldrin. This you know. But tell me something. Do you trust him?"

"With my life."

"And he will protect our princess?"

"With his life."

"Very well, then. You and I will handle the situation here with Marath."

"May I recommend we have the betrothal broken immediately?" Eldrin asked.

"Father has already requested it. So, aye, I'll visit with the High Druid." Andahar glanced at their father lying still on the bed, his hands folded over his chest one on top of the other. "Hopefully Brom will be able to find a cure for the poison."

"I pray to the gods he does."

Once Aesir summoned Lorcann, the mage wasted no time flashing to his chamber in the Elven palace. Marath was uncomfortable with that but he had no other choice but to admit him.

As soon as the mage appeared in the center of the room, Marath gave him his best smile. But Lorcann wasn't interested in pleasantries. His hand clamped around Marath's throat as he shoved him backward against the nearest wall. The point of a dirk jabbed the underside of his chin.

"You lied to me."

"I did nothing of the sort," Marath gasped against the man's hand around his throat.

"You failed to deliver the princess to me. She got away. Taken by the human."

"I can get her back. The human couldn't have gotten far. I can find them both. He will be punished."

"Why should I believe you? You have yet to deliver any of the promises you've made to me."

"Give me one last chance."

Lorcann's eyes narrowed, making his hideous face even more so. He removed the dirk and stepped back. He still clutched the blade in his hand as he looked over the man. "One more chance?"

"The ranger, Lord Eldrin, has returned. Mayhap he will know where the princess is. Allow me to speak with him."

"Speaking to him will not produce the princess." Lorcann twirled the dirk between his fingers. "Bring him to me. I will wait for you at the edge of the loch."

"Why?"

"If you wish to have one more chance to make things right with me, then you will do as I say. Bring me the ranger. I will use my powers to get into his mind and find out the location of the princess."

"As you wish."

"If you fail me again, our alliance will be broken. I have released my brethren from their watery depths. They will be joining me and my other friends soon."

Fear poured through Marath's veins like acid, poisoning his blood. Fear that quickly turned to rage. Or mayhap that was simply the dark magic blending with his blood. Shadows clouded his vision, staining the edges. Lorcann had released the remaining Fomorians without his permission? How dare he?

"You dare defy me?"

"I do not need your permission to release my people. They are *mine* and *mine alone*. And I will not let you or anyone else stand in my way."

Something deep, dark, dangerous inside him cracked. He brought his hand up to Lorcann's chest. A pop and a flash of light had the mage flying backward across the room. He crashed into the side of the bed. The dirk clattered to the stone floor. Lorcann retaliated with a pop and flash of his own. Marath doubled over with the impact and clutched his middle.

Lorcann was already on his feet as though the impact hadn't hurt him at all. He snarled, showing off his stained teeth. "You thought me not so powerful, didn't you? Or did you not realize the blood rite we shared gave me a resurgence in power? For that, I thank you. And I thank you for waking me from my prison in the Sorrow Lands. It has allowed me and my people to come back to the land. To once again show our power and our might."

Marath collapsed to his knees, his body vibrating with the residual effects of the attack. "What do you intend to do?"

"You assured us we would have a war. A war is what we want."

"You intend to declare war on the Elves?"

"Should you fail, I do. And, my lord Marath, we will win."

Before Marath could form a reply, the Fomorian flashed away.

The deal with Lorcann had spun quickly out of control. He had never intended for a war with the Elves to happen. He had once wanted the Treaty, now he wanted to rule. But to rule he would have to do away with the royal family and he needed Lorcann's help with that.

Now that he had lost his command over the mage that would be impossible. Finding the princess was more imperative than ever. Marath opened the door to the corridor where Aesir waited.

"Find Lord Eldrin. Tell him to meet me by the loch. I have an urgent message for him."

"As you wish."

Using his new power, Marath thought of the loch and flashed there in an instant. When he arrived, he glanced around but saw no one. Not even Lorcann. Was he here? Did he hide among the shadows?

He waited there until Lord Eldrin came. He had one hand on the hilt of his sword as he approached with caution.

"Lord Marath, I received your message. What's so urgent?"

"I worried about the princess's safety. Is she all right?"

Eldrin hesitated before he answered. "She's quite safe."

"Do you know where she is?"

"You tried to harm her. Why should I tell you?"

Marath started to reply. A flash of light appeared between them and then everything happened so fast he couldn't process it all. Lorcann had flashed to Eldrin, placed a hand around the ranger's throat and backed him into a tree so hard his head bounced against the wood. He grunted as Lorcann got in his face, nose to nose.

"You'll tell me," Lorcann said.

"Never."

The ranger wasn't going to be taken so easily. He pulled a dagger from his waist and stuck the mage in the side. Lorcann wailed and released the ranger, stumbling backward. Eldrin held the dagger, the blade coated with blood. But Eldrin didn't wait for him to recover.

The ranger charged him again but a moment later Lorcann flashed behind Eldrin. He had his arm wrapped around his throat and squeezed. Eldrin's face turned red as he gasped for breath.

"Don't kill him, Lorcann. We need him," Marath said.

Lorcann released some of the pressure, allowing the ranger to breathe. "Tell us where the princess is and we'll allow you to live."

"I'll…never…tell…you," he said through gasps.

"Then I will be forced to take the information from your mind."

Lorcann flashed around him, clamping his hand around his throat again. Eldrin fumbled with his sword, trying to get his hand on the hilt but the mage had shoved him backward against the tree again.

Marath knew what the mage intended to do—he would get into his mind and extract the information he wanted. The information they sought. And once they found the location of the princess they could find her and bring her back.

And then…she would be his once again.

Eldrin's eyes were wide and round as the mage pressed his long, claw-like fingers into his throat. Eldrin gasped, trying to take a breath. Then his eyes closed and he went limp. Lorcann released him, letting him fall to the ground in a crumpled heap. He turned to Marath.

"I have the princess's location," he said. "She is with the Skye Elves and her human knight."

"The Skye Elves?" Marath asked.

"I know how to summon the moon dragons."

"I'm coming with you."

"No. You will remain here and remove the prince from power. I will return with the knight and the princess. Then you may do with them what you wish."

"You won't be able to get into the gates of the Skye Elves. They're too heavily guarded. And Skye Elves only allow those they wish. Certainly not the likes of you."

"But they will if I look like someone they trust," Lorcann said.

Lorcann used whatever dark magic he had to change his appearance. He no longer looked like the hideous creature Marath had released from the underwater prison. Now he looked like Lord Eldrin. The mage had manifested somehow. It was a power Marath had no idea the man had.

In another instant, he flashed away. Eldrin's neck showed the puncture wounds from the mage's claws. Blood seeped from the injury. Marath knelt by Eldrin and touched his neck and found his pulse barely a flutter. He would die soon enough. One less Elf to get in his way. Lorcann was right. Prince Andahar must be dealt with immediately.

Marath flashed away.

Chapter 13

The moment Allanna had left his arms, the emptiness and loneliness pressed against Drake's heart.

And the guilt. Oh, it was there, too.

How could he have allowed his desire to overcome him? He was stronger than that. More in control. He should have resisted but she was so *bloody* hard to resist. With her big blue eyes fringed in dark lashes. Her perfectly heart-shaped lips. The way she fanned those thick lashes at him as she lay in the bed next to him and all but begged him to take her.

He had asked her to come closer in a feverish moment of need. She had acquiesced so prettily when she flushed, turning her pale skin a lovely shade of pink. All the way to the tips of her pointed little ears and the hairline of her golden locks.

She had kissed him back with such fervor he thought he would go mad. The way she swiped her tongue over his bottom lip still sent zings of pleasure through him. His shaft stood at rigid attention for her, begging for her sweet touch. Even as he held her next to him in his bed not so long ago, his body had protested it was not getting more action.

More action was all he could think about. All he could dream about. He could still smell her on his skin and taste her in his mouth. He would never be satisfied until he had her underneath him, his shaft pushing inside her petite body while she wiggled beneath him. She'd done it against his hand—though if she knew what she was doing it wasn't apparent. Some instinct had taken over. Her nipples had beaded the bodice of her gown, tempting his mouth. Her body was wet and slick and oh so ready for him. When his fingers slid easily inside her folds, the heat that lashed through him rivaled that of anything he had ever experienced.

She had begged him not to stop. What was a man to do? He knew it was merely a matter of time now before he would bed her.

Drake had enough of loafing around in the bed. He'd regained most of his strength and intended to finish what he had started with the princess. He shoved aside the bed clothes when Turin returned to his chamber with his healing bag.

"What do you think you're doing?" he demanded. "I haven't allowed you out of bed yet."

"I've had enough of this." Drake waved his hand over the bed. "I'm ready to get up."

"Not without my permission, you're not."

"I don't need your permission," he retorted. "I'm getting up and finding something suitable to wear."

As Drake stood, Turin shoved him back to the bed with more strength than the man looked to have. It surprised the English knight.

"Nay. You'll not."

"Turin, I grow tired of lying abed. Release me so I may be of some use here. I swore an oath to Lord Eldrin I would protect his sister. I cannot do that while here."

The healer heaved a sigh. "As you wish. But I'll have a look at the wound one last time."

"If you insist."

"I do."

Drake swung his legs back onto the bed. He still had no tunic, which made getting to his wound easy for the healer. He pulled away the bandage and pressed his fingertips lightly against his skin.

"The wound is all but healed. There will be a slight scar." He admired his handiwork as he replaced the bandage. "A few more days and this can come off and the stitching can come out."

"Thank you, Turin. Had it not been for you, I would be dead."

"Had it not been for Lord Eldrin bringing you to me, you *would* be dead," he said. "Never forget that."

"It is a debt I will gladly pay one day," Drake said. "Now I'm getting out of this bed."

"Your tunic was ruined and blood-soaked. I'll see about getting you some fresh clothing," Turin said.

"And a bath," Drake said. For all he could think about was kissing and making love to Allanna. "And mayhap a razor."

"As you say. I'll speak to Lady Talaiel."

The healer packed up his bag and left the chamber.

It wasn't long after he left servants brought a copper tub to him and filled it with steaming water. Two servant boys also brought him new clothes. A long tunic, clean trousers and his boots that had been cleaned and shined. His sword was returned also.

A manservant had been sent to assist him with bathing and dressing. One look at his scraggly face in the looking glass had him cringing. How had Allanna kissed him looking like that? His beard had grown unruly. It would have to go.

An hour after the healer left him, he was clean-shaven and dressed and smelling of lemons. How long had he been here? Days? It seemed forever. And he'd never stepped foot outside the chamber.

"Lady Talaiel has asked you join her and her guests for a feast in the dining hall if you're up to it, my lord," the servant said. "Or I can bring food to you if you prefer."

"No, I'd like to join her."

"Very good, my lord. I will send word to her at once. She also she welcomes you here along with Princess Allanna."

"Thank you. Where is the dining hall?"

"Down the stairs to the left, my lord." He gave him a stiff bow before exiting the room.

Drake took one more look at his reflection in the looking glass. He smoothed his hands down his tunic and strapped his sword to his side. He was ready to leave his sick bed behind.

He had regained most of his strength but still tired easily. However, when he had the princess in his bed he hadn't noticed any fatigue. Funny that. But then the princess seemed to give him a strength he couldn't explain.

By Saint Mary, he loved her. She was everything to him. And he hadn't the courage to tell her. Knowing they couldn't be together seemed cruel to tell her how much he truly loved and wanted her. How much he wanted to spend his life with her.

He found his way easily to the dining hall. Music wafted from a small group of Elves who played tunes on their instruments, which weren't so different from those in his own human realm. A lute, a dulcimer, drums. Sounds with which he was familiar.

Several people already crowded the room, mingling and holding tankards of ale or honeywine. He spotted Lady Talaiel across the way. She smiled, excused herself from her conversation and headed toward him. She walked as though she floated on air, her steps were so light. She possessed an air of confidence and charm he'd seen in Queen Maeve and Princess Elyne. As she approached him, she extended her hand.

"Sir Drake, 'tis wonderful to see you up and about at last. You had us all quite worried."

"It's good to be up and about." He took her hand, bowed low and kissed it. "Thank you for everything you've done for me, my lady."

"No thanks are necessary, Sir Drake. I'm pleased you could join us. When Turin told me of your recovery and how you wished to get out bed, I planned a feast in the hopes you could be here with us."

"Thank you, my lady. Your hospitality is much appreciated."

Despite his conversation with the Lady of the Skye, he couldn't help but scan the crowd for Princess Allanna. He hadn't seen her yet.

"I'm sure the princess will be joining us shortly," she said.

He flashed her a sheepish smile. "I daresay your eyes are keen, my lady."

"Anyone could see how she fretted over your injury. She refused to leave your side the first night you were here."

He hadn't known and it touched him.

"She's a lovely girl," she said.

"She is," he agreed. One he wished he could marry. But her obstinate father stood in his way like a blockade.

"She cares for you a great deal," Talaiel continued.

"As I do for her."

"Aye, I know." She gave him a surreptitious smile as a glint of mischief twinkled in her eyes. "She came to me. She is prepared to give up all that she has for you."

"Aye, I know. But I don't want her to do that. I wish there was another way."

"Do you?" She sounded as though she had a secret.

He met her gaze. "What are you about, my lady?"

"I believe I have a solution to both of your problems," she said.

"Our problems?"

"It is apparent to me you wish to remain with her. Is that correct?"

"Aye."

"She asked for my advice. She wanted to know whether she should indeed give up all that she is and all that she had to remain with you."

His stomach suddenly had a fluttery, empty feeling. "And what did you tell her, my lady?" The words came out scratchy and a little breathy.

"I told her she should follow her heart."

Words left him as he stared at her. He blinked, unable to respond. His palms broke into a heated sweat. His mouth turned desert dry. Could it be the lady was about to hand him everything he wanted? She had tried to run away with him before they were attacked outside the gates of the Woodlands moments before Marath stabbed him. Was Lady Talaiel about to make being with the princess a reality for him?

"There is one way to make sure she doesn't marry the lord-regent."

"And what is that?"

"Marry you instead."

Now his heart dropped into the pit of his empty stomach, his chest burning with the ache of such a promise. He pressed his fingers against his temple. He couldn't think straight.

"I have made the arrangements with my High Druid. He will perform a handfasting. It is no longer in practice with the Elven people, however the Fae still perform them to bind themselves to the one they love."

He recalled seeing such a ceremony between Lord Derron and Queen Elyne. They had handfasted in their official bonding ceremony and he had been one of the honored guests. He remembered it quite clearly. He also remembered thinking of Allanna. He had given her a sly glance and she had given him that bashful smile she always had ready for him.

At the time, he had thought someday they would be able to exchange such vows. But with the developments with her father and how he was against the match, he had put all thoughts of it out of his head.

He had soothed his ragged nerves with a new idea—simply making love to her would be enough. He told himself this over and over. Now, Lady Talaiel dangled the fruit of something more in front of him—taking Allanna as his wife.

"If you exchange these vows and consummate the marriage and remain together for a year and a day, the king must recognize the marriage is valid," she said.

"Are you certain? Even though he is against the match?"

"It is an old Elven law. One, I believe, that has been forgotten by most," she said. "I admit it is an old custom and not performed as much these days. However, once handfasted, it cannot be refuted. The king will have no choice but to accept you as his daughter's husband."

"And the betrothal with Lord-Regent Marath?"

She paused, looking thoughtful. "I do not believe that will be an issue much longer, my lord. The king will have no choice but to end it."

She thought as he did Eldrin would take care of that when he returned to the Woodlands.

"Why would you do this for us?"

She looked away but he caught the flicker of pain in her eyes. "Because I know what it is to love someone and be separated from them. I don't want the same thing to happen to either of you. I rather like Allanna. Lord Eldrin would give his life for yours." She turned her gaze back to him, her eyes piercing. "He speaks highly of you. He trusts you. Therefore I trust you."

"My lady...I'm not quite sure what to say."

"You say thank you. Now will you come with me? Your bride awaits."

How could he refuse?

Lady Talaiel led him from the dining hall. Along the way, she briefed him on the ceremony. What he would do and the words they would exchange. The lady assured him she would help if he needed it.

They arrived at the small chapel that served her people. Candelabras blazed brightly, giving the room a warm, ethereal glow. And standing at the front of the chapel next to the High Druid was Allanna.

The sight of her nearly stole his breath. His stomach clenched. She was dressed in an ivory gown, the scooped neckline dipped low enough to entice him. It was belted at the waist with gold braid. A wreath of flowers—where did the Skye Elves get flowers?—perched upon her head to hold the opaque veil in place. All that golden hair seemed to glow beneath the material as it cascaded down her back.

The color was high in her cheeks as she gave him a shy smile, looking at him through her lashes. That look he had come to know so well. That look she had given him so many times that had rent his heart in two and made him weak in the knees. That look that made him want to do anything for her. Was her heart racing as fast as his? Did she feel the blood pumping in anticipation through her veins as well? As the distance closed between them, he tingled all over.

Their eyes never left each other as he stepped next to her. He'd lost all coherent thought.

"I will bear witness to the handfasting," Lady Talaiel said.

"Very well. Please join hands."

Allanna placed her hands in his. His fingers closed around her softness. The High Druid wrapped a silken cloth around their hands, making an infinity, and tied a loose knot.

"Is it your wish today, my lady and my lord, you be joined and your hands be fasted in the ways of auld?"

"It is," they answered together.

"Princess Allanna and Sir Drake, know now that your lives have crossed, your paths are forever linked and you have formed an eternal and sacred bond. Your hands are bound in the infinity, forever linking your souls to each other. Do you declare your intent to be forever bound to one another?"

"We do."

"Sir Drake, if it is truly your desire to become one with this woman present her with the symbol of your pledge and token of your love." Drake removed his sword and placed the flat side of the blade across their hands. Candlelight winked off the steel, reflecting back at them.

"Princess Allanna, Sir Drake has pledged his sword to you. The pledge of his sword is the pledge of his soul. A symbol of his power, his passion, his fire, his strength, his courage. His ability to protect, defend and care for you. The strength of his blade and endurance of his sword represents what is in his heart. Do you, as his beloved, accept his pledge of heart and steel?"

Color crept up her neck and into her cheeks. She ran her tongue over her lips, dampening them. "Aye, I accept his pledge of heart and steel. Now and always."

Drake took his sword away and replaced it back into its sheath. Then the High Druid looked at her.

"Princess Allanna, if it is truly your desire to become one with this man present him with the symbol of your pledge and token of your love."

She turned to Lady Talaiel, who had picked up a nearby chalice. It was a pewter goblet encrusted with jewels around the rim. She took it from the Lady of the Skye and held it over their clasped hands.

"Sir Drake, Princess Allanna has pledged the chalice, a symbol of all that is within her, her rapture, her devotion. Yours is the voice of reason and steadfast support. You are the spark of her passions and yours are the arms in which she will come to rest. The red wine within foretells the richness of your future together. Will you, as her beloved, take the chalice in which she offers and drink from the bounty within?"

"Aye, I will accept the chalice. Now and always." Drake took the chalice and sipped. Afterward, he handed it to the High Druid who passed it off to Lady Talaiel.

"Turn to each other and speak the vows."

When Allanna looked up him, he knew he would never be able to live without her again. She smiled.

"I, Allanna, bind myself to you, Sir Drake. I pledge to you my heart, my love, my soul. To love and care for each other as the fires burn within and never to go out. I forever bind myself to you with all my heart's affections and all my love."

The warm heat of joy washed over him. He knew he could never remember all the words so the High Druid helped him and he repeated the same thing to her. Forever pledging their hearts to each other.

"Blessed be this union between Sir Drake and Princess Allanna. May it forever endure." The High Druid, who had been stoic and serious throughout smiled then. "You may kiss your bride, Sir Drake."

He happily sealed their promise to each other with a kiss.

"You are handfasted, then," the High Druid said.

He slowly unwound their hands but Drake was reluctant to release hers. Talaiel clapped wildly once the ceremony was done. She wiped a tear from the corner of her eye.

"You have my heartfelt congratulations."

The Lady of the Skye hugged each of them, placed a kiss on each cheek before stepping back to admire her handiwork.

"You have my heartfelt thanks, my lady," Sir Drake said. "Without you, I daresay this would not be possible."

"I was happy to do it. You are welcome to join our feasting now, or—"

"With all due respect, my lady, I'd rather not." Sir Drake gripped Allanna's hand tighter. Then brought her hand up and kissed her knuckles. The princess flushed.

"I understand, of course." She granted them both a knowing smile. "Follow me then. I'll see that you're not disturbed."

It seemed an eternity before they would be alone. Allanna had waited for this moment her entire life. She had waited for this day since the first moment she realized Sir Drake was the man for her. Happiness consumed her.

No one spoke as the Lady of the Skye led them through the corridors. Allanna's heart pounded hard with anticipation, with need, with excitement. She had never thought this day would come and yet she knew—knew from her vision—it would. Even though the real-life version had differed from her vision, it had still happened. She had married Sir Drake. She was his and he was hers. Forevermore.

Her senses reeled. She was aware of everything around her. The way he held her hand. The way his steps beside her seemed to be unhurried yet every step was in concert with her beating heart.

At the chamber door Talaiel merely gave them a smile, a swift curtsy and then started back down the corridor, leaving them alone. She never looked back as she walked away. They stood together a long, quiet moment before he swept her up into his arms and kicked open the door.

She didn't question him. She didn't want to question him. She merely loved the way he carried her across the threshold of the chamber and then kicked the door closed with his boot. It clanged shut, rattling the hinges.

It was quite possibly the most romantic thing that had ever happened to her. Aside from the handfasting.

His chamber had been prepared for them. Fresh linens on the bed and a fire crackling in the hearth. A tray of fruit, bread and cheese. A tankard of honeywine. And candles. So many candles all lighting up the chamber in a warm, golden glow. The bed had been turned back. A silent invitation of what was to come.

"The Lady of the Skye is indeed quite the hostess," he commented.

He set her to her feet, turned to slide the bar into place to keep others out and then pressed her against the door. His hungry mouth found hers and when she kissed him she tasted his urgency and need. A gentle passion that fused between them in a way she could never forget.

Oh gods, she had wanted him for so long. Her knees were weak. The weight of him pressing against her was all that kept her upright.

"You are my wife." He murmured the words against her lips and then trailed kisses along her jaw.

Her arms slid around his neck, pulling him closer, closer, closer still. She hated the material separating them.

"You are my husband. Mine."

"Aye, mine. Forevermore."

Forevermore.

It could not be forevermore. Not really. He was mortal and he would, one day, leave her. He would age, weaken and die. But for now she would relish this time together. She would not think of such a thing. And mayhap on the morrow she could address his mortality with the Lady of the Skye. She would know what was to be done. For Allanna could not bear to be parted from him. Not ever.

His lips trailed down her neck, nibbled her earlobe. This is what she'd wanted. What she'd waited for. What she had imagined doing with him for so long her body had ached with the need and desire. Now the moment was here and she wanted to savor it. She didn't want to think about anything else but Drake.

"You shaved." Her fingers trailed across his smooth jawline and to the cleft in his chin. She liked his smooth skin against her palm. Even though she liked the way he looked with the beard, he was dashing without it.

"For you. Do you not approve?"

"Oh I approve. Wholeheartedly."

He whisked her up into his arms, holding her against his chest. "Good. But if you want me to grow it back, I will. I will do whatever my lady commands."

She couldn't stop the blush the bloomed under her skin. "I command you to take me to bed."

Drake grinned and walked toward the bed. He set her on her feet, but kept her in his embrace. "All in good time, my princess."

She pushed her hands under his tunic, felt the hard muscles there and the edge of the bandage that still resided on his side. "Are you sure you're all right?"

"Nothing will stop me from being with you tonight. Now. I want to take pleasure in you. All of you."

He plucked the wreath of flowers off her head and the veil slid away, revealing soft waves of golden hair. His hands tangled in her locks as he bent to kiss her. A swooping low in her belly tightened then throbbed with the yearning for his touch once again. The ache inside her grew exponentially until it was nearly painful. Until all she could do was whimper her need against his mouth.

She watched, with her heart in her throat and her breath ragged, as he slid the gown off her shoulders and down her arms. The material pooled at her feet. He had bared all of her. When the cool air in the chamber breezed over her skin, it raised gooseflesh from head to toe and she fought the urge to shiver. Her nipples stood at rigid attention, puckered into stiff, almost painful peaks, waiting for his touch. He looked her over, his appreciative gaze taking in the sight of her fully nude body for the first time. His breath shuddered out.

"So pretty. Like I always imagined."

She blushed and crossed her arms, trying to cover her bare breasts. He reached for her, gently pushed her arms back to her sides.

"Don't do that. I want to look at you. At your perfection. At your loveliness."

"No one has ever looked at me that way."

"I daresay no one else ever will. You are mine."

Aye, his.

Her heart pattered wildly. An uncontrollable beat she could not stop. Did he hear it too? When he reached for her again, the tips of his fingers landed on the heavy pendant she still wore around her neck, grazed the chain and over the jewel in the center.

"You still wear it."

"Of course I do. I will always wear it simply because you gave it to me," she said.

He gave her a smile of satisfaction as he brushed over her small mounds. His deft, perfect hands lingered over the dusty tips. And then he bent his head to take one into his mouth. Flames flickered behind her closed eyelids. Her heart fluttered with the intimate touch and her knees threatened to buckle. To steady herself, she pressed her hands on his forearms, her nails digging into the sleeves of his tunic.

Drake tugged his tunic over his head and kicked off his boots. She pulled at the tie at his waist, watching it come undone. Like her. She'd come undone. But he halted her progress by covering her hands with his.

"That can wait."

Drake slipped his hands over her small waist, pulling her to him. When she didn't look at up at him, he tilted her chin back. Their lips met the same time their skin touched for the first time. Blood rushed from her head, making her lightheaded, and she thought she might swoon. But his mouth on hers, his arms around her, kept her on her feet. His skin was warm with a fresh, clean scent she'd not noticed before.

As they kissed, he backed her toward the bed.

The bed. The bed that had been so carefully prepared for them. Her heart sped up to an even quicker pace and a little mewl echoed in her throat. He sat on the edge and pulled her into his lap. She could feel his hardened length beneath her. His mouth found her neck again as he kissed down her to her shoulder. His fingers trailed over her skin, leaving a heated trail in their wake.

"You intoxicate me." His breath whispered over her skin as he spoke. "It seems I cannot get enough of you."

His hand landed on her breast, palming it as his fingers closed over the soft mound. Taking his time.

"It seems as though I have waited a lifetime for you. For this," she said.

Allanna flattened her hand on his chest. She traced his muscles down to his abs where she paused again at his waist. She twined a finger around one of the laces on his pants and tugged.

"There is time enough for that."

He nudged her hand away as he turned and placed her on the mattress. "Right now I want to see you. Touch you." He kissed the hollow of her throat. "Worship you."

His deep timbre with the English lilt rumbled over her, warming her. She loved his voice as much as she loved his hands, his kisses, his caresses. His hands roved over her breasts but he didn't linger there. He moved downward, sweeping over her skin to the flat plane of her belly and the curves of her sharp hipbones and rounded thighs.

And all this she watched through half-lidded eyes while her heart pounded a drumming tempo that seemed to keep time with the throbbing of need between her legs. How she wanted him to touch her there again. To press a finger inside her. To kiss her...*there*.

As though he heard her thoughts, he moved her to the bed, placing her gently on the mattress. He leaned next to her on one elbow, his hand sweeping down the length of her, brushing over every inch of bare flesh. He nudged apart her thighs, opening up her most secret place. But he did not move for a long, breathless moment, as though he couldn't stop looking at her. And when she lifted her gaze to his face she could see the adoration and the love in his gaze as he looked at her—really looked at her. The way she had opened herself to him. She trembled.

"Drake?"

"Your skin is the color of moonlight. So pale. So perfect."

His fingers danced along her inner thighs. Her hips rocked to and fro, as though the motion could urge him to move faster, to touch her or kiss her in that secret place. That place she had so longed for him with some deeply buried carnal desire he had awakened.

When Drake slipped a finger through her ashen curls and down her dampened folds, a ragged breath escaped her. A ragged breath of reckless abandon and dire need. White-hot lust fired through her skin, pushing through to her bones, setting her aflame. Engulfing her. He parted her folds with a tender touch. His fingers roved over her, teasing her and touching her like he had before. She opened to him, wanting so much more. He shifted, moving to nestle between her thighs and then bent toward her. She could see the wicked glint in his devastating blue eyes as he lowered his head.

She stilled. So still she could not breathe. So still she could not think. Her skin prickled, gooseflesh popping out over every inch.

The tip of his tongue tasted her, slipped into her dampness. She gasped air back into her lungs in a sharp, cold breath. A cold breath that burned through her, stoking her fire, sending her to higher heights.

She fisted the sheets, closed her eyes and bit down hard on her lip to keep from crying out. She was unable to form any coherent thought. All she could think about was his mouth on her, kissing her, tasting her. She dared to glance down her length. Her milky-white length with his dark head at the juncture of thighs, taking his pleasure and sipping her desire through supple lips.

The sight made her unravel. Every last piece of her control split, frayed and she could no longer hold it into place. The threads slipped away as she breathed out a heated breath while he kissed her, his tongue sliding in and out of her in a way she had only imagined. In a way she never wanted to end. This pure longing of desire and need and ecstasy.

And love.

She arched her lower back and opened her legs wider for him. He moaned his delight as his tongue continued the onslaught.

He kissed her with urgent tenderness, taking his time as though they had all the time in the Otherworld. As though time stood still for them. As though she were not coming apart at the seams and her old life was ending and her new life was beginning. He took his time sipping her, tasting her, as though he could not get enough of her. As though he never would.

She was acutely aware of his freshly shaven face as it brushed against her sensitized skin. Acutely aware of the tip of his tongue swirling, dancing, caressing between her folds. Acutely aware of the way his finger moved into her, stroking her and touching a deeper part of her she never knew existed.

She was consumed in flame and fire. Her skin was surely ablaze by now. She whimpered as her hands found the soft, dark strands of his hair and she didn't know if she wanted to urge him on or pull him away. She didn't know if her body could take much more, if she could allow herself to feel any more pleasure than she already felt. For if she did, she surely would be consumed by the fire licking its way across her bare flesh.

"Release yourself to me, my princess. Come for me. Let me taste you."

Oh gods. Should she? Could she? She had experienced that release only one other time with him. Her body seemed to know what it wanted even if her mind didn't. Even if she didn't understand all that was happening to her or all that he was doing to her.

Pinpricks of light exploded against her closed eyes. Like a starburst. A flash of amber light in the night sky. Heat burst through her, engulfing her in the threatening flames at last. Nothing had ever been so divine or beautiful in her life. And when she thought she was at the end of the wave, he stopped.

And suddenly his hand was gone as he kissed his way up her body. He paused at each breast where he paid homage. Where he took one hard little peak into his mouth. His tongue did a little dance over it before he took the bud in his teeth. And sucked. Her body reacted with a pulsing, throbbing heat dampening her core. She writhed against him, her nakedness brushing his hips still clad in the trousers.

Her hands fumbled between them until she found those ties again. This time she would not be pushed away. She pulled open his breeches and slipped her fingers underneath the material. His body was hot to the touch. As though he too were engulfed in the flames. When the tips of her fingers brushed the tip of his hard length, he groaned approval, rumbling through his thick chest and into her body.

Drake's hand moved, slipping between her dampened folds and running over her heated core. Her hips vibrated with the touch as he pushed his palm against her mons. She rode his hand, her body responding as it had when he'd touched her before. She couldn't get enough. She needed more. She needed him.

Her hand closed over his shaft, moving it back and forth in concert with his ministrations between her legs.

"Drake." Her voice was so breathy she hardly recognized it.

"You're almost ready for me," he said.

When he removed his hand, she whimpered. He'd left her feeling empty. As though she were missing some crucial touch to sate the yearning within her. She heard the quick shuffle of clothing and knew he'd shucked his breeches. Her eyes cracked open as he slid on top of her, his body covering hers from head to toe. The glorious weight of him pressed her gently against the mattress, covering her. Consuming her.

His hands found hers and pushed her arms over her head, their fingers lacing. He settled between her legs, the head of his shaft tentatively probing her opening.

"I wanted you ready for me." He kissed her. She could smell the sharp tang of sex on his lips. "Are you?"

"I'm ready. I've waited long enough for you, Drake. My husband." How she loved calling him that.

"As have I, princess. My wife."

His mouth landed on hers again, their tongues dueling as he pushed deep inside her. Their bodies fused for the first time and heated pain lanced through her. She bit down on his bottom lip but he didn't stop moving. Nor did she. She rode the wave of pleasure-pain as he pulled out quickly then dove back in again. Moving in and out of her. Over and over. Stroking her with his body, filling her up, touching her deep inner core. The pain was forgotten and replaced by bliss and that sweet, sweet undulating heat washing over her.

Her hips rocked against his and they quickly found their rhythm. Her legs snaked around his hips as she arched against him, her body growing taut like a bow. She could not ignore the way his hipbones bore into her thighs with every thrust. Nor could she ignore the demands of his mouth as he kissed her with a fierce possessiveness. His tongue pushed inside her mouth as his thrusts pushed inside her body, moving her toward the edge of passion. A cry of pleasure vibrated her throat and he responded in kind.

His hands had moved from hers and into her hair, tangling in the soft locks and fisting the strands. Her hands pressed against his bare back, her fingers curling and her nails scraping against his skin. Digging through the tender flesh until he bowed upward, pushing away from her. His big body hovered over her, the shadows from the candlelight spilling over her pale skin. Those piercing eyes of his met her gaze and she could see all the love, the passion, the tenderness in that one look.

She unraveled completely then and that starburst was upon her. The last vestige of her control was gone. She gasped as she allowed it to take her over. He pushed inside her one last time, his body shuddering against hers. He held there, looking at her for a long moment before kissing the tip of her nose.

Somehow she found the strength to unwind her legs from his as he moved next to her, the mattress sighing with his weight. He gathered her close, brushing his fingers through her hair, then over her face as though his fingertips wanted to commit to memory every angle, every curve, every plane of her face, her shoulders. The hollow of her throat. Then down to her breasts where he circled the still-peaked tips.

Her eyes remained closed all the while he touched her. And all the while she knew she had never loved more deeply than she did then.

Chapter 14

"I love you."

Her eyes blinked open and she turned her head to look at him. His hand rested on her ribs, his thumb tracing the slight curve of the underside of her breast. It sent warm, wonderful tingles through her. And the look he gave her…oh, it was one of utter abandon and naked longing. One that would be forever burned into her memory.

"It occurs to me, princess, I have never told you."

The threat of tears pulsed the backs of her eyes. He was right— he had never said it to her. He had expressed his affection for her on numerous occasions but never had he uttered those three little words she had so longed to hear. Never, even, when they were handfasted. She parted her lips to reply but he pressed two fingers over them to quiet her. She dropped a soft kiss on the pad of his forefinger.

"There is more I wish to say." He traced the outline of her lips as his gaze lingered there. "You have perfectly heart-shaped lips. Did you know that?"

"Is that what you wished to say?" She almost giggled with her joyful delight yet the tears still threatened.

"No." His gaze met hers and turned serious. "I never thought to be with you this way. It is truly a gift I will always cherish."

"What gift?" she whispered. She blinked, refusing to allow those impending tears to fall.

"The gift of you. Your innocence. Your sweetness." He kissed her cheekbone and breathed the last words against her skin, "Just you."

Her heart hadn't had a chance to recover from their lovemaking and now it sped up even more, if that were even possible. It pounded so wildly she thought it would burst from her chest. She reached for him, slipped her hand through his dark hair, her nails gently raking across his scalp. He sucked in a sharp breath.

"I have always belonged to you, Sir Drake." She placed her palm against his smooth cheek.

"And now you really do." He grasped her hand and dropped a kiss on the tip of each finger.

"I have never loved anyone but you."

Saying the words and seeing him look at her with such heartrending tenderness stirred something deep inside her. Swooping through her, making her want him again.

"Rest, princess. I'll watch you sleep."

"Nay. I don't want to close my eyes. For what if this is all a dream?"

He smiled, the light of the candles twinkling in those blue depths. "It's not. I assure you."

"I don't want this night to end. I want it to go on forever."

"I know," was all he said.

She had never experienced such happiness. It cascaded through her body, warming her and then—

Allanna took in a sharp breath as she shot to a sitting position. The warmth was replaced by sharp pain and she knew a vision was upon her. She pinched the skin at her temples between her fingers as she struggled to breathe. Drake sat up next to her, an arm around her shoulders.

"Are you all right? What is it?"

He knew she had visions. He knew she saw the future and sometimes the present. But he had never been with her when she had one. And before she could answer, it burst through her mind, playing out before her mind's eye.

This one was of Eldrin, her beloved brother. Something horrible had happened to him. He slumped against a tree, unconscious. He had purple bruises on his neck. As quickly as the vision appeared, it was gone.

She panted, struggling to take air into her lungs.

"A vision," she said at last.

"Does it always come on like that?"

"Aye." She curved into him, a sickly fear gripping her stomach. He wrapped his arms around her. "It was of Eldrin."

"What did you see?" He stroked her back, calming her.

"He was… I think something is wrong. He was slumped against a tree. At home."

Home. She hadn't given so much as a thought to the Woodlands. She had never even thought of Eldrin until this moment, when now he could be in danger or dying. Her heart burned with fear and an urgent panic that made her want to return as soon as possible. The only thing keeping her rooted was Drake's arms around her.

"Shh. I'm sure Eldrin is fine."

"We have to get back," she said. "We have to go back to the Woodlands, Drake."

She jerked against him, ready to bolt from the bed but he held fast.

"There is nothing to be done now. We'll go in the morning."

"But—"

"Eldrin will be all right, Allanna. I promise."

"What if he's not?"

"Let's not think about that now." His hands pushed through her hair as he cradled her against him.

"I'm worried. What if Marath has done something to him?"

"Then I will deal with Marath myself. We can do nothing right now. Let's rest and head for the Woodlands in the morn."

Reluctantly, she nodded. "All right."

He lay back down, taking her with him, holding her against his chest. Even though she felt safe and warm in his arms, she couldn't help but think about her brother and worry about him. What if he was dead? He had returned to the Woodlands to deal with Marath. What if he'd killed him?

It was her last awful thought before exhaustion overtook her.

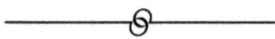

"My lady, one of the moon dragons has been called."

Lady Talaiel looked up from her book at her servant standing in the doorway of the library. If a moon dragon had been called and drawn down then Eldrin would be returning. She hadn't expected him so soon.

"That must be Lord Eldrin. I will meet him on the grand stairs."

"As it pleases you, my lady. Shall I notify Princess Allanna?"

"Not yet. Let's give her a little more time with her knight. Bring some refreshments to the grand hall so that I may receive Lord Eldrin there."

He nodded and left to do her bidding.

She smiled. Eldrin had returned for her as he promised. She hoped he came with news of the broken betrothal between Lord-Regent Marath and the princess. It would make telling him Sir Drake and the princess had handfasted much easier. She, alone, would take responsibility for that.

Talaiel rose from her chair and put the book aside. She gathered her gown in her hand and headed for the grand stairs that led to the entrance of her castle in the sky. She paused a moment to take her fur-lined cloak with her. At this hour of the morning, the temperatures were quite cold.

As she stood at the top of the stairs, she could see the grand gates opening to allow the dragon inside. Eldrin returned alone, which she hoped meant good news. The situation in the Woodlands must be in hand. He alighted from the back of the dragon as soon as he landed.

Her heart skipped a beat at seeing him again. Especially after their last encounter when he'd kissed her so fervently and vowed to return to her.

"Lord Eldrin, we welcome your return," she greeted with a warm smile. "Though I confess I didn't think it would be so soon. However, I'm not displeased at all."

He ascended the steps one at a time. Mayhap he intended to drag out their reunion with his slow pace. When he reached the top, he didn't rush to her as he had in the hallway. Nor did he take her in his arms and greet her with a kiss. No. He stood at the top of the stairs, his hands fisted at his sides as he looked at her with unfamiliar eyes.

"I have come for the princess and the human knight," he said, his voice flat.

She drew up tall and stiff, her shoulders pushed back. Her smile of expectancy disappeared quickly. Her guard went up. This man may look and sound like Lord Eldrin but something was off. How was it he looked so much like him yet he wasn't him?

"The human knight, my lord?" She raised a thin eyebrow. "I've not heard you call Sir Drake that before."

"Is that not what he is?"

She stared at him a long moment, trying to decide how to respond. Of course that was what Sir Drake was—but that was not what Eldrin called him. He had fought alongside the man in battle. They respected each other and it was clear to her this imposter did not know that.

The best thing to do would be to bring him inside and try to find out who he truly was. Her guards would be able to detain him but in the meantime, she needed to warn Drake and Allanna.

She cleared her voice. "Aye, of course. Please come this way. I will show you to the grand hall where you can wait for them while I have them summoned."

The Lady of the Skye motioned for him to follow her to the grand hall where she paused. "Could I offer you some refreshments?"

She waved to the nearby cart full of cakes, scones and sweets. She poured a tankard of honeywine and offered it to him. He snatched it from her hands and quaffed the entire thing, the sticky-sweet brew dribbled down his chin. He dropped the tankard, letting it hit the floor with a clang.

Then he attacked the sweets with a sort of barbaric hunger. He crammed the delicate treats in his mouth. Icing stained his fingers and smeared across his face. Crumbs tumbled to the ground on her handwoven Elven rug she'd brought from the Hin'dar Rhule.

She noticed the blood staining his side, the gaping hole in his tunic. He had been stabbed and recently. He seemed not to notice or care. And the more he crammed food into his mouth, the faster he seemed to heal. As though the food helped him to somehow regenerate.

Talaiel stared at him in horrified silence. No, this was not her Lord Eldrin. Who was he?

"If you'll excuse me, I'll see what's keeping Sir Drake and Princess Allanna."

With her heart in her throat, she turned and hurried toward the staircase, taking the steps two at a time.

Allanna knew it was morning. She hated to open her eyes lest she break the spell she was under with Drake. For when she opened her eyes, the night would surely be over and the new day would be upon them.

So she kept her eyes closed and listened to his rhythmic breathing while he gently stroked her arm. Soothing her.

"Good morrow, wife."

That deep voice of his rumbled beneath her ear. She couldn't help it—she smiled.

"Good morrow, husband." Yet she still kept her eyes closed.

"I trust you slept well."

She hadn't. She'd been haunted by visions of Eldrin. Dead or dying. She didn't know which. And despite the fact she wanted to stay in bed with Drake, she also fought the urge to leap from it to dress and leave this place to get back to him.

"You didn't, did you?"

"I—"

A loud rap sounded on the door then Lady Talaiel's voice floated through the wood. "Sir Drake?" Her voice sounded thin and urgent and both of them knew something wasn't right.

They sprang apart as though they were caught doing something they shouldn't. As Allanna pulled the sheet to her chest to hide her nakedness, Drake jumped out of the bed and jerked on his breeches. When he opened the door she charged in and slammed it shut, her back to it. She had a wild, panicked look in her eyes. Her chest rose and fell with every ragged breath. She kept her gaze firmly on Drake's face.

"My apologies for the untimely intrusion."

"What's wrong?"

"Lord Eldrin has returned."

"Eldrin is here?" Relief flood through Allanna, glad he'd returned unharmed.

"Aye, but I believe the man in the hall is not your brother."

"What do you mean?" Allanna asked. Her relief quickly turned into fear.

"He may look and sound like Lord Eldrin, but it is not." She clasped her hands together in front of her, her fingers clenched tight. Allanna could see the worry lines in her face and an alarm bell sounded through her mind. Worry she also felt. Worry that her vision had come true.

"You know this for certain?" Drake asked.

She gave him a pointed look. "I know Lord Eldrin's mannerisms and this man does not possess them. He did not greet me as I expected him based on our last encounter. And..." She cleared her throat. "He called you 'the human knight'. Also this man has been stabbed. I offered him food and the more he ate, the faster he healed. He is *not* Eldrin."

Allanna's heart did a wild pump. Eldrin would never call Drake that. Her brother had more respect for him. She slid to the edge of the bed, her feet touching the cold stone floor as she kept the sheet clutched to her chest.

"Who is he?" She couldn't hide the fear in her voice.

"I don't know."

"A Fomorian is my guess," Drake said. "Eldrin thought they were the ones who attacked Allanna. But he also said they couldn't flash here."

"He did not flash. He rode in on a moon dragon."

"How is that possible?" Worry gnawed at Allanna now and her fear escalated.

When Talaiel met her gaze, she could see the uneasiness in her silvery eyes. "He must know how to draw down the moon dragons."

"If he looks like Eldrin then..." Allanna couldn't finish. Her throat constricted. All she could think about was her vision. "Something's happened to him. Drake, we have to return at once."

"Aye, I agree."

"As do I," Talaiel said. "But I'm not going to let you go with...whatever that is down there."

"But Eldrin could be injured. My vision—"

Drake pulled Allanna to him in a fierce hug. "Don't say that. He'll be all right."

"What about your vision? You had a vision of Eldrin?"

"I saw him slumped against a tree."

Talaiel drew up tall and turned all business. "Then you must find him. I can secret you out of here. But we must hurry. I will stall the Fomorian for as long as I can."

"And then what?" Drake asked. "I can't leave you alone with him."

"I will be fine," she said. "While I stall him, I'll send Turin here to show you the way out. There are many hidden passageways in my castle."

"I can't ask you to risk that much for us," he said.

"I'm willing to risk it for you. I promised Eldrin I would keep you both safe. Let me keep that promise." She glanced between the two of them and then her gaze landed on Drake. "In return I ask for one as well."

"Anything."

"Please save Lord Eldrin, wherever he is."

"You have my word."

When she closed the door behind her, Allanna reached for her gown. The one she'd wore to marry Sir Drake. It was all she had. But she couldn't get the vision out of her head and she couldn't stop the tears that blurred her vision. Her hands shook. If anything happened to Eldrin, she would never forgive herself. Her refusal to marry Marath sent him back to the Woodlands to deal with him. And now...now he could be dead.

They dressed quickly. As Drake strapped his sword to his waist he turned to her, gripped her shoulders.

"He'll be all right."

"I hope so."

A knock sounded on the door and a moment later Turin opened it. He waved them into the hallway.

"Come quickly."

"Where is Lady Talaiel?" Drake asked.

"In the grand hall with the imposter." Turin walked briskly down the hallway.

"Where are we going?" Allanna took long strides to keep up with the two men. Already her muscles burned.

"I'm leading you to the chamber at the end of the corridor. Inside that chamber is a passageway behind the fireplace. Take that and follow the winding staircase down. It will lead you out through the library. From there you can exit the castle to the grand staircase where a moon dragon awaits. Good luck."

Turin turned to go but Drake stopped him. "Thank you, Turin. For all you've done."

"You're welcome. Now I must quietly alert the guards to the imposter's presence. Our walls have not been breached in thousands of years. We do not wish to see them breached by more of the enemy."

"Good luck."

With a nod, Turin left them in the corridor. They watched him disappear and then Drake grasped her hand.

"It's you and me, princess."

"We cannot leave Lady Talaiel behind."

"I agree," he said. "But she insisted."

"If he truly is a Fomorian, he will kill her. We can't leave her here with him."

She could see the hesitation in his face. He looked back up the hallway where Turin had disappeared.

"Drake…she loves him."

"I suspected."

"Please."

"We cannot defeat the Fomorian."

"No," she agreed with a slow nod. "But I have the fire pendant." She held it up.

His eyes lit with hope. "Aye, you do, don't you?"

They took off for the grand hall, hurrying back up the corridor. At the top of the stairs, Drake pushed her behind him. Then pressed a finger against his lips to remind her to keep silent. She nodded.

He started down the stairs and despite his heavy boots, his steps remained quiet. He had the advantage of stealth. At the foot of the stairs, his hand gripped the hilt of his sword as he glanced through to the grand hall. Allanna stood on the bottom stair and peered over his shoulder.

A female whimper echoed from the grand hall. It was all Drake needed to draw his sword and rush into the room. Allanna followed on his heels as close as she could but his long legs far outpaced her.

They found Lady Talaiel on the floor, struggling to get to her feet. Drake rushed to her and gently took her by the arm, helping her to a sitting position. She had a lump on her forehead but otherwise seemed unharmed.

"Are you all right?" he asked.

Allanna knelt next to her.

"I believe so. I hit my head." She placed her fingers on her forehead.

"What happened?" Allanna asked.

"The mage came into my mind. He tried to find you both. I fought him when I realized what he was doing. He hit me with something. You should not be here. He's after the princess," she warned. "Please go before it's too late."

"Let me fetch the healer," Drake said.

"No. Turin will be along soon with the guards. Go while you can."

"Are you certain?"

She nodded. Drake stood and held his hand down to Allanna. "It's against my better judgment, my lady."

"And mine," the princess added.

But Talaiel waved them on. "Go."

Reluctantly, she grasped his hand and they rushed out of the grand hall into the bitter morning. She shivered, wishing she'd thought to grab her fur-lined cloak. The air was cold, burning through her skin and right into her bones. They could see the moon dragon at the base of the grand staircase. Her heart leapt, knowing they would soon be airborne and back to the Woodlands.

As they stepped off the last stair the Fomorian flashed in front of them, standing between them and the moon dragon. He looked at them with unfamiliar eyes. He was the ugliest creature Allanna had ever seen. Jagged, yellowed teeth. Small black eyes too close together. Thinning hair showing his shiny bald head through the strands. A crooked nose. She remembered him from before. He had attacked her outside the Woodland gates.

"Surrender."

A heartbeat of silence passed then the stranger added, "If you do not, the Skye Elves will be destroyed."

Drake drew his sword but the Fomorian hit his hand with a flash of light, burning the skin.

"Do not fight me or you will die. You and the princess will come quietly."

"To be delivered to Lord Marath? Never," Allanna said.

The imposter's eyes narrowed as he looked at her. Fear pumped through her but knowing Drake stood beside her gave her strength. She edged closer to her husband.

The attack came with no warning. There was no way either of them could anticipate it and react. The mage flashed first to her and then sent a blast of magic at Drake that was so powerful it knocked him off his feet, backward and up several of the steps. Allanna screamed as she turned, trying to run toward Drake.

The next thing she knew the mage's strong arms clamped around her upper body. She struggled against him, but he put a dirk to her throat and pressed it against her skin. She felt the prick and knew he'd drawn blood.

"Do not struggle. You do not wish to arrive to Marath as his damaged prize, do you?"

Drake wasn't moving. She had no idea if he was alive or dead. The mage dragged her to the moon dragon and shoved her toward it. She had no choice but to get onto the back of the beast.

When Drake awoke, he had a raging headache and groaned. He tried to sit up, but strong hands pushed him back down.

"Steady. You need to stay still." Turin. The healer. Drake blinked his eyes open and saw him standing over him. "You're lucky to be alive."

He shoved Turin away and sat up. His head exploded into a thousand pin pricks of light. The pain was almost intolerable as he grunted and put his head between his legs. The back of his head throbbed with intense pain. He remembered getting hit with the power from the mage. Looking down, he saw his tunic singed but his skin seemed uninjured.

"I told you to be still."

"Where is Allanna? Where is my wife?" His voice was muffled against his knees. He tried to sound angry, but he couldn't muster the strength.

"The Fomorian took her," Lady Talaiel said. "I'm so sorry, Drake."

"And you're lucky he didn't kill you," Turin added. "You're lucky all he did was knock you in the head."

Blinding red rage clouded Drake's vision. But he was too weak to move. It took all the strength he had to lift his head. "I will kill him."

"Why didn't you leave when you had the chance?" Turin's angry words wafted over him.

"Tried." Groaning, he pressed his fingers against his head. "What happened to me?"

"You were struck with the Fomorian's magic. You fell back and hit your head," she said. "It's a wonder you're alive."

"He didn't mean to kill him. If he had, the knight would be dead." Turin again. He didn't bother to hide his disappointment and his anger. "My lady, the wards have been breached by the Fomorian. There will be no stopping them now."

"We'll deal with that when the time comes, Turin." Her voice was calm, soothing. And it seemed nothing could shatter her composed exterior. "Right now our more immediate need is to find Princess Allanna."

"What do you mean 'our'?" the healer snapped.

"By that I mean I intend to go with Sir Drake. Along with as many guards as I can spare."

"My lady—"

"Do not try to change my mind, Turin. We are helping the Wood Elves whether or not you or any of my council likes it."

He huffed out a sharp breath as he stomped away.

Drake pushed to his feet but his stomach revolted. He doubled over, waiting for the dizziness to subside. Talaiel's hand pressed against his back in reassurance.

"We will find her, Drake."

"I hope."

"I know."

When he regained control, he righted himself. "Tell me the truth. You're going because of Lord Eldrin, aren't you?"

She looked away to the sky. And when she spoke, she couldn't meet his gaze.

"I am a woman who happens to have feelings for the ranger, sir. I must see with my own eyes he's safe rather than stay here and wait. And worry."

He smiled. "I understand." He felt the same way about Allanna. He couldn't stand the thought of being separated from her.

"I knew you would."

Chapter 15

The ride back to the Woodlands was short yet the longest one of Allanna's life. They landed outside the gates of her home. The dragon flew away as soon as they alighted and Lorcann grabbed her by the arm and dragged her through the gates.

Her home had been transformed. It was a place she did not recognize. There were Fomorians as guards and very few of her kinsfolk. Where had they all gone? How had this many of them infiltrated the security of her home?

Lorcann took her through the wooded area to the stairs inside the tree that led upward to the palace. Where her father and brother and—hopefully—Eldrin would be. If there were this many Fomorians, though, she feared for her family. Would they be alive?

The mage delivered her to Marath's chamber. He didn't even knock when he entered. He gave her a violent shove. She fell right into the lord-regent's waiting arms.

"Ah, the lovely princess has returned at last. I'm happy to see you, Allanna."

She spit in his face, making him release her. She stumbled away, cowering close to the wall as far from both of them as she could get.

"Lorcann, where is the human knight?"

"I left him with the Skye Elves."

Black rage crossed Marath's face. It scared her. "You were told to bring them both."

"I brought the princess. She is the most important."

"I want that human!"

"I doubt he'll be coming back," Lorcann replied.

"Why?"

"I took care of him."

Marath stared at the mage. Allanna though she might retch. She pressed a hand against her roiling stomach. Drake couldn't be dead. She refused to believe that.

"He better be alive." As he spoke, Marath advanced on Lorcann.

"Why do you care?"

"Because I intend to kill him myself! Bring him back to me at once."

They stared each other down. Allanna held her breath, watching the two of them and waiting. She had never seen Marath in such a state. He was not the man she remembered or knew as she grew up. He was different. More violent. More angry. More dark.

Lorcann flashed away without another word. Marath unclenched his fists and exhaled. He raked a hand through his hair and turned to her. She flinched.

"Please don't kill him." She hated that she begged but she couldn't stand the thought of Drake, her one true love, gone.

"Why should he live? He is nothing but human slime." He advanced on her, standing a few inches away. She could smell the stench of something emanating off him but didn't know what it was. All she could think was it smelled like evil, death and rot. "I know your little secret, princess."

She met his gaze dead on, even though the terror sliced through her like a broadsword. "What secret?"

"Do not play me for the fool. I saw you together. The way he looked at you and you looked at him. I saw you in the great hall when you thought no one was looking. When you thought you were alone." He leaned toward her as he spoke, his face a breath away from hers. "I saw him put his mouth on yours."

Her heart turned numb. So he knew that much but nothing more. Thank the gods. Her mouth had gone bone dry. Her lips suddenly parched. She swiped her tongue over them and noted with some disgust he eyed her lips a long moment before meeting her gaze once more.

"I had thought it would be more prudent to dispose of you and blame the Fae. My ultimate goal was to put the Treaty of Separation back in place and having you conveniently murdered would convince the king the Fae were dangerous."

"Why do you hate them so? The Fae have done nothing to you."

"Stupid girl," he snarled. "My mother was a Fae whore. She gave herself to my father in a weak moment and when he no longer wanted her, he cast her out. Filthy Fae that she was."

So it was true. He was a Halfling.

"My Elven father eventually tired of me. He threw me away as he did my mother." He regarded her with an oily smile. "Now I shall repay the Elves and Fae by taking control of your kingdom. I will marry you now that the king and your brothers are indisposed." He paused as he eyed her from head to toe, making her skin crawl.

Her father and brother were indisposed? What had the man done to them? She couldn't worry about that now. All she could do was hope Eldrin and Drake were all right.

She regarded him with cool contemplation. Or at least she tried to project that sense of coolness to him but she wasn't sure if she pulled it off. She had married Drake and Drake was her true husband. "I will never marry you. My heart belongs to another."

That enraged him. The dark shadows in his eyes flared to life. "You will marry me or the human knight dies."

Her stomach twisted into a knot and she knew he was deadly serious. He tilted his head and for a sickly moment she thought he was going to kiss her.

"We will take our vows at once so you will be mine. I fear I cannot wait another moment to have you. To seal our pledge to one another." He twined a lock of her hair around his forefinger, careful to avoid the fire pendant around her neck. She recalled how it burned him the last time he touched it, though she noted he eyed it with caution. "To taste your innocent sweetness. And sip upon those sweet lips."

Bile rose to her throat as she forced back the gag. She would not give this man the satisfaction of knowing how revolted she was. She didn't know how to react, what to say. She stood rigid, not moving. Wishing she had the strength and courage to slap his hand away. But she couldn't. She feared his retribution.

She wanted to tell him, in the smuggest voice she could muster, she had already lost her innocence. That it belonged to Drake and no other. That he would *never* steal that from her because she had given it freely out of love. Because she *loved* and deeply and she never would again. Even if he were dead.

Instead she heard herself say, "I will not."

He pushed away from her then, his eyes black orbs. "Then he dies. And I take you by force." His gaze, so lascivious and immoral, pierced her. She shuddered. "Lorcann will return with the knight and when he does you will witness his death. You will watch as I cut him to pieces and feed him to the wolves."

She stared at him, horrified by the thought. Marath had once been nothing but a simpering fool who wanted his own way—and often got it by strong-arming, manipulating and sucking up to the right people, including her father. But he was not this violent, cruel, wicked man. She choked off a sob.

"What's happened to you?"

Marath opened and closed his fingers into a tight fist, clearly agitated. "Lorcann will soon return." He said it again as though he tried to convince himself. As though he *hoped* Drake were still alive so he could kill him in front of her.

She pressed against the wall, thankful he had retreated. But the stench of his evil still clogged her nose.

"But Lorcann cannot flash to the Skye Elves' realm," she said, sounding almost triumphant. "There are too many wards in place."

"He can call the moon dragon as he did before. He *will* bring me the knight and you *will* marry me."

When he faced her again, she could see that darkness rooted in his gaze. Pulsing with some sort of wicked light under his skin. It sent a cold chill to her bones much like the cold air of the Skye realm. She pressed her icy fingers to her lips to keep from sobbing, from crying out. In her most level voice, she said, "I will never marry you."

She wanted to tell him she was already handfasted to Drake, to needle him further. But she feared it would push him to an uncontrollable edge and he seemed too close already.

Marath charged her, gripped her so hard his fingers bit into the fleshy part of her upper arms. He gave her a violent shake, rattling her back teeth.

"You will be mine. Do you understand me? Even if I have to take you by force! You *will be mine.*"

Allanna couldn't move. She couldn't think. And she was stuck there while he gripped her, leaning against the wall. She had no escape. No way to get away from him. All those tips Eldrin, her ranger brother, had given her had fled her mind. She was simply paralyzed by fear.

His face relaxed then and he loosened his grip and dropped his arms. He glanced at the fire pendant. It was almost as though the dark cloud had receded as he stepped away from her. But she still cowered against the wall. Watching him with a careful eye. A brass ewer stood on a nearby table. If she could somehow get her hand on it, mayhap she could use it as a weapon.

"Forgive me, princess."

Sweat beaded his forehead. He swiped at it with the back of his hand. Allanna inched toward the table, her fingers itching to land on the ewer.

"I didn't mean to frighten you."

But she didn't accept his apology. She dove for the table, snatched the ewer and swung with as much force as she could. It connected with the side of his head with a loud *clang*. Marath cursed and grabbed his head, stumbling to the side. It took him moments to regain his composure and then he turned to her, his face a dark mask of terror and rage.

Before he could attack her, though, something curious happened. The fire pendant soared to life, the orange-yellow crystal in the center pulsed and flared. Light shot out of it and struck him. He dropped like a stone and smacked his head on the edge of the table. Had she killed him? She didn't want to stick around to find out. Her heart raced as she released the ewer and fled the man's chamber. She wanted as far away from him as possible.

She wanted to find Andahar and Eldrin and her father. Where were they? She hadn't seen them as Lorcann dragged her to Marath. And the people she did see averted their gaze, afraid to look at her. Somehow her Woodland home had been transformed into a Fomorian haven. It was almost as though there was some kind of dark spell hanging over the place, forcing the inhabitants, a generally peaceful folk, into hiding or cowering in fear.

Allanna ran through the corridors to the royal quarters and burst through the door to her father's chamber. What she saw made her stop short. She didn't know if she could take any more frights.

Her father was unconscious. She rushed to the bed, tears blurring her eyes. He looked as though he had aged years since she'd last seen him. His cheeks were sunken and his skin was colored a sickly pallor. With a gentle touch, she took his ice-cold hand in hers.

The vision she'd had of her father's poisoning rushed back to her. It had come true. She could feel the faint flutter of his pulse beneath the frail skin so she knew he still lived. But barely. She regretted the anger she'd had with him for betrothing her to Marath.

When the chamber door opened, she flinched. Relief sputtered through her when she saw Andahar enter. They stared at each other in shocked surprise. But it was too much for her and the thin control she'd maintained deteriorated. She collapsed into a heap on the floor, her face in her hands and tears streaming down her face.

"Thank the gods you're safe." The relief was evident in his voice as he closed the door and sagged against it.

Andahar and Allanna had often had a strained relationship but she could tell he was glad she was here and unharmed. There was no rushing together for hugs—that's not how they interacted. Had it been Eldrin, though, she would have.

"What's happened to him?" Her voice was muffled against her hands. She swiped at the tears, whisking them away.

"Poisoned."

A chill went through her. Her vision *had* come to fruition.

"By Marath we think," he added.

Marath. She knew it had to be him. "What's being done for him? Will he live?"

"Brom is working on an antidote. He hasn't found one yet." He took a tentative step toward her and kneeled to her level. "Allanna, Eldrin said you were attacked by Fomorian mages."

A million thoughts skittered through her mind in that one moment. Was Eldrin safe? Did Andahar still expect her to marry Marath? Why were all the Fomorians in the Woodlands? All she could think to say was, "Where is Eldrin? Is he alive?"

"He was found by the loch. He's injured but he's all right. How did you know he was injured?"

"I had a vision. He's alive then?" She squeaked the words.

"Aye. Allanna, how did you get here? Where is Sir Drake? Eldrin was going back for you when he was attacked."

Allanna cried harder. "I thought he was dead."

Andahar reached for her and in a very uncharacteristic move, hugged her. "He's all right. What happened to you? Is it true you were attacked by the Fomorians?"

"Aye, it's true. Eldrin saved me. Drake..." His name clogged in her throat. Drake...was he all right?

"He was stabbed. Aye, Eldrin told me that, too. He said he took you to the Skye Elves." His voice quivered with awe.

Not many had seen the realm of the Skye Elves. In fact, not many had seen Skye Elves themselves. They were something of a mystery, hiding in their clouds. Keeping to themselves with their superior egos. Save for the Lady of the Skye. She was endearing and sweet and kind. And she'd made it possible for Allanna to marry Drake.

"What's it like there?" he asked and his voice held a tone of reverence.

"Beautiful. Enchanting. Perfect."

She would never forget it. Never. Not for all the days of her long life. It would forever hold a sacred place in her heart. That and the Lady of the Skye.

"That…Fomorian mage. He came to the Skye Elves' realm on a moon dragon disguised as Eldrin."

"Where is Sir Drake?" he asked again.

"The mage…Lorcann, I think, attacked Drake. I don't know if he's alive."

"And Lorcann took you from the Skye Elves?"

She nodded.

"That's how you got here." He sat back on his heels.

She met his level gaze. "Marath has to be stopped, Andahar."

"I know but something has happened to him. Allanna, I believe he has turned Dark."

"Turned Dark?"

"He is now a Dark Elf."

She stared at him, her stomach clenched into a tight knot. As though someone had a fist around it and squeezed. "What's happening, Andahar? When we arrived, there were Fomorians everywhere."

"Aye, I know. Marath's doing. Our people are afraid of them. And most of them know the king is indisposed."

Anger flashed inside her. "Why don't you get rid of them? They don't belong here."

"Marath has some sort of hold on our people. Our nobles. Our council. There's some…dark force that surrounds the Woodlands. I don't know what it is and I can't explain it."

"You can force them out."

"I can't without bloodshed. Marath knows that. He's threatened to destroy the Woodlands if I don't comply with him."

"Then you must attack. There must be bloodshed to save our kingdom. You cannot allow him to continue his hold on you or us."

"I cannot ask our people to fight dark magic," he said.

"Why not?"

"Because it's a losing battle. Don't you see? He knows our weakness. And he's exploited it. And now with Father poisoned—"

"You are the rightful leader, Andahar. You have to take care of our kingdom now." She placed a hand on his arm. "And I will support you."

He smiled and blew out a heated breath. "Thank you, Allanna, but the problem remains. How do I fight against Marath and his Fomorians?"

"I don't know but you won't have to do it alone. The Lady of the Skye can help us. And her people," she said.

He looked at her as though she'd grown a second head. "The Skye Elves? They won't come down for anyone. They're far too superior."

"Aye, that's what I thought once. But 'tis not the truth of it. Lady Talaiel is most kind and generous." And in love with Eldrin. She would do anything for the ranger. "She wants to help us. I heard her say so when I was there."

Andahar ran a hand over his smooth chin. "If they'd help us then we might have a chance."

"Aye, we might."

"Come, then. Let's go to Eldrin. He knows the lady. He can help us get a message to her."

He helped her from the floor. She gave one last glance to her father on the bed and sent a prayer to the gods to help him.

They stepped into the hallway and saw Marath stumbling down the corridor with blood dripping down the side of his face and a sword in his hand. He snarled when he saw her. His eyes had turned into black orbs again and she could see the darkness in his face. That same darkness she had experienced up close. The stench of his evil wafted to them and she knew Andahar was right—he had turned Dark. Never to return. He would have to be banished to the Unseelie realm or killed.

She shrank behind Andahar as he stepped in front of her. He pushed her back with his arm to keep her behind him.

Allanna was reminded again of her vision of Marath stabbing Andahar.

"Don't let him come near you," she said. "He's going to try to kill you."

Andahar drew his own sword as Marath halted in front of him but said nothing in response. He gripped the hilt, holding it so tight the veins in his hand popped under the skin.

"You cannot hide behind your brother, you little bitch."

"Leave her be, Marath."

"She did this to me." He waved a hand down the side of his face. "She'll pay."

Marath raised the sword and charged. Andahar reacted quickly and their swords clanged against each other.

"Allanna, go!" He nodded back toward their father's chamber.

She hesitated. Not wanting to leave him there alone with the Dark Elf. But how could she help him? She was unarmed. She had no bow or quiver of arrows. Even if she did, she doubted she could help her brother.

He was right. She could escape back to her father's chamber. But where would she go then? She couldn't climb down from the balcony. It was too high. And yet she really had no other choice. She couldn't help Andahar fight. She had to trust that he would be all right, that he could defend himself against the madman.

She ran back inside and slammed the door, sliding the bar across it. Though that hadn't stopped him before in her chamber. She wasn't sure if it would stop him now.

Her father hadn't flinched or moved on the bed. He lay there and all she could think was how much he looked like a corpse.

Allanna shoved that thought away as quickly as it came. She shouldn't think that way. Her father was *not* dead. He was merely sick.

Shouts outside could be heard through the balcony doors. She flung them open. Men ran everywhere. Her kinsfolk as well as the Fomorians. And whatever terrified them came from above. Her heart kicked into a speedy throb as she glanced skyward. It took a moment to see them but slowly the outline of the moon dragons came into view. A whole army of moon dragons.

She almost cried when she saw them. Lady Talaiel had sent help. And if she sent help, mayhap Drake was with them. A scream of pain outside the chamber door made her heart sink. It was Andahar. She knew it.

She opened the door a crack. Andahar was on the floor, a pool of blood spreading on his tunic. She clamped a fist against her mouth to keep the scream lodged in her throat. Marath must have fled for he wasn't there. She stepped tentatively into the hallway, tears blurring her vision.

"Andahar..."

Before she could sink to her knees at his side, Marath flashed in front of her. He clamped his arms around her and pulled her to him. And when he smiled, he smiled with all the evil he possessed.

"Now you are mine, princess. Your father will soon be dead. Your crown prince and ranger brother, too. And then I will have my prize. You. And your kingdom."

He intended to wipe out her entire family? He was insane. She wiggled against him but it was useless. He wrapped a strong arm around her and dragged her down the corridor. She would not go without a struggle, though. She fought him all the way by dragging her feet. When he tired of pulling her along, he hoisted her over his shoulder and carried her down the winding stairs, down into the great hall.

"The High Druid awaits to perform our wedding ceremony, my princess."

Oh gods. She couldn't go through with that.

"It's high time you make good on that betrothal," he said.

"I'll never marry you!"

"You have no choice."

They had arrived at the great hall where he set her on her feet in front of him. His hands landed on her shoulders. Hot, burning hands that scorched through the material of her gown. The same gown in which she had married her beloved. Her stomach cramped, swirling with nausea. Her feet refused to move. She would *not* take another step toward her doom.

But Marath was behind her with those hot, burning, fiery hands and shoved her forward. She stumbled, nearly landed face first on the floor, but he caught her. This time he had flashed in front of her. He gave her that wicked smile as he pulled her into his arms and steadied her feet.

"Careful, my sweet. I don't want you damaged before I can have you."

She swallowed the bile rising in her throat.

Aesir stood to the left of the High Druid. He held a shortsword to the man's back. So the High Druid was being forced, too. His face had turned ashen. He held the ceremonial silken handfasting cord.

"It's to be a handfasting, dearie. An old custom, aye, but I'm old-fashioned."

But she was already handfasted to Drake. She was already married as far as she was concerned. She didn't want to tell him that. She didn't want to reveal it until she had to. If she had to. "You'll never get away with this."

"Oh, but I already have." He looked to the High Druid. "Get on with it now. Along with the handfasting I want the traditional marriage vows as well." His evil stare turned back to her. "I intend to make sure you cannot escape from me. For once we are wed, I mean to consummate our union quickly. I have waited a long time for you, princess."

So he intended to make her his wife under all the Elven laws, both old and new. Her heart pounded a wicked tattoo as her mind raced to come up with a stall tactic. Anything to keep from binding her hand with his. She knew Drake—or at least the Skye Elves—were on their way. And where was Eldrin? She had yet to see him. If she could stall long enough, mayhap it would give them enough time to get here and get her out of this mess.

Marath turned her toward the High Druid and pushed her, forcing her to walk toward him. He held her hand in his, the heat of his skin burning into hers. She jerked, trying to get free but he held fast.

"Bind us," Marath said to the High Druid. "And quickly. I wish to take her as soon as possible."

"No." She jerked her arm again but he wouldn't let go. "Please don't do this, Marath. You don't want this."

"Oh, aye, I do. I want this." His black eyes met hers. "I want you, my sweet. All of you." And then he raked his disgusting gaze down her body in that same way he had in his chamber.

A lump formed in her throat. A lump of fear and anguish. Tears threatened to fall again. "No, you don't. You can't have me."

"And miss the taste of your sweet innocence?"

She bowed up straight, knowing the truth of it. Did he want her simply because he thought she was still a virgin? "That is something you will *never* take from me, Marath." She smiled.

"Oh, aye, it is." He sounded so sure, so confident, so bloody arrogant.

She needed to knock him down a peg or two. "You'll never have it because someone has already had the pleasure."

Oh, she would forever remember the way he looked at her. The way his face darkened into an evil, horrible mask of terror and anger. The way his hand tightened on hers. The way he jerked her to him, making her press against his scorching body as his free arm wrapped around her.

"You little whore." His rancid breath fanned her face, making her gag. "You fucked the human."

She winced at his harsh language. That was not what it was to her at all. It was something magical and wonderful and romantic and she would never let this monster take that away from her. No matter what happened.

"You let me go." She pushed against him, trying to get loose. She prayed the moon dragons would hurry.

Marath took her hand again in his and pushed her in front of him. He held her in place and extended their joined hands.

"Marry us. Now."

Indecision flashed through her. If she told him she was already married to Drake, would he kill her on the spot? She thought he might. If she kept it to herself she had a better chance of getting away from him. Of surviving. Of the Skye Elves riding to her rescue. The marriage wouldn't be valid anyway. And when Marath learned that truth? She hoped to the gods her brother—or someone—would have gotten to her by then.

Allanna watched, horrified, as the High Druid twisted the silken cord around their hands, winding it into the shape of the infinity symbol. The very symbol the Skye Elf High Druid had done when he handfasted her and Drake. She pulled and jerked and tried to get free, even though she knew it was no use. As the High Druid tied the cord, tears burned her cheeks.

As Eldrin awoke he sensed the moon dragons were coming. He pushed out of his bed with a groan and stumbled to the balcony where he stood, shivering and half-naked in the cold morning breeze. Waiting and watching the sky for the telltale signs that they were here. If they were coming, then something must be wrong.

He pulled on his tunic, tucking it into his breeches and then reached for his boots. He hadn't quite recovered from the mage's attack. A quick glance in the mirror showed him he still bore the wounds from the man's hand on his throat. He still felt so weak but he had to find out what was happening. He had to find Andahar. Had Lorcann returned? Did he capture Allanna and Drake?

He didn't know if he would ever forget the way Lorcann had invaded his mind, scraping through his memories and his thoughts, shifting through them to find the one thing he wanted—Allanna. When Eldrin realized what was happening he had tried to shove the whereabouts of his sister and her lover to the far reaches of his mind. To hide them and their location into the depth of shadows. But it hadn't worked and Lorcann found them anyway.

It couldn't be helped. It was done now.

He prayed that Lady Talaiel's wards would be unbreakable. Even if Lorcann tried, her guards would kill him on sight. No one made it to the gates of the Skye Elves undetected.

But now…the moon dragons were coming. And he knew deep down there was something terribly, terribly wrong. He strapped on his sword, snatched his bow and arrows and left his sick room. When he came upon the body of his brother, he rushed to him. Andahar had a gaping wound in his left side, bleeding profusely. As though whatever happened had only been moments ago. A cold chill went down Eldrin's spine as he recalled Allanna's vision—first the king and now him.

His brother's eyes fluttered open. Relief flooded his face when he saw him and he reached for him. He gripped his tunic, pulling him down to his level.

"Eldrin…Allanna…here…"

"Allanna's here? Where? How? Who has her?"

"Marath." It was all he said before he passed out.

Cold fear settled through his bones. If Allanna was there and Marath had her, then it could only mean Lorcann was successful in capturing her and Drake from the Skye Elves. That meant Talaiel's wards had been breached. That meant she could be dead or injured, too.

Eldrin couldn't leave Andahar there. He had to find his sister. Adrenaline pumped through his tired veins, giving him the strength he needed to find her. And then he would find his lady.

He picked up his brother and wrapped an arm around his waist, dragging him down the corridor. He had to find Brom before it was too late. Before Andahar couldn't recover from his wound. Should the king die, gods forbid, then Andahar would rule. And should Andahar die—no, he would not think such thoughts. As he limped, burdened by Andahar's weight, Brom rounded the corner. He rushed forward when he saw them.

"Gods, what happened?"

"I don't know but I suspect Marath had something to do with it."

"That bloody man. He's been nothing but trouble since he arrived. Take him in there." Brom pointed to the nearest empty bedchamber. "Put him on the bed. Let me see how bad it is."

Eldrin did as he commanded and then stepped away while Brom took over. "I need my medical bag at once and some help. Send a chambermaid or anyone you can find."

"I need to find my sister."

"She's here?"

"That's what Andahar said before he passed out."

"Go then. Find her before that madman does."

"You can save him, can't you?"

"By the gods, I'm going to try."

Eldrin couldn't stop the panic welling inside him as he left the healer behind, knowing his brother was in good hands. But even still, he worried. Marath had managed to take out both his brothers and his father. If he got his hands on his sister, he feared the worst.

As he ran toward the stairs, he grabbed one of the king's servants and ordered her to help the healer. She nodded despite the wide-eyed look of fear she gave him. Eldrin hurried down the stairs to the great hall. When he saw Marath and Allanna in front of the High Druid, their hands corded together he knew what was about to happen. Allanna sobbed uncontrollably while Marath tried to make her respond, to accept him as her husband.

Enraged, Eldrin wielded his sword.

"Take your damn hands off my sister, you bloody knave."

Chapter 16

The Lady of the Skye told Drake he had ridden on the back of one of the moon dragons to her castle. However, he didn't recall that since he had been wounded and unconscious at the time. The flight was exhilarating and beyond anything he had ever experienced. Their iridescent wings were nearly silent on the wind as they glided with elegance, soaring on the breeze.

She'd brought with her a hundred guards but Drake had a feeling deep in his gut that would not be enough. She assured him with a confident smile a hundred men would be plenty to fight the Fomorians. He prayed it would be, though, and that something horrible hadn't happened to Allanna. As they neared the Woodlands the temperature went from frigid to balmy.

Lady Talaiel rode next to him, the wind billowing in her red-gold hair. She kept her gaze forward, intent on scanning the ground as though she could see Lord Eldrin from the back of the dragon.

They landed not far from the gate of the Woodlands. He knew she intended to walk the rest of the way. From the sky he could see the gate was open and he knew right away that something was amiss. So did she.

As soon as all the men were on the ground, the moon dragons flew away, disappearing as if they had never come. Talaiel met his gaze.

"We must be cautious." She started for the gate.

Drake stepped in front of her, halting her progress. "You should not be allowed to enter first. It's too dangerous."

She considered for a long moment but then nodded. "Aye, I agree." She waved several of her men in front of her. "But I will not stand out here and wait, wondering what's happening."

"Nor would I ask you to," he said. "But should anything happen, then I want you out of harm's way. Allow your men to bring you back here."

"No." Her voice was hard as ice. "I'll not stand idly by. I'm coming whether you like it or not."

There was no use arguing with her and he knew that. Still, he had to try to keep her away from danger. "If anything happens to you, Lord Eldrin will have my head."

"I can take care of myself," she assured. "And your head will stay firmly attached."

"As you wish, my lady." He wielded his sword.

They headed for the gates with Drake in the lead followed by several of her men. At the entrance, they paused and peered into the wooded area. The guard was nowhere to be found. This gave Drake pause as well, for he knew King Urdithane would not leave the gates unattended.

"Where is the gatekeeper?" Talaiel asked.

"I don't know but I don't like this at all," Drake said.

Before anyone could move, several Fomorians burst from the trees and attacked. Drake shoved the lady behind him as he took on one. Talaiel's guards immediately went into attack mode, fighting against them with a power he had never seen nor experienced. Not from the Fae or the Woodland Elves. When he managed to dispose of his own foe, he turned to see each of the guards—no, warriors was a better word—had killed the remaining Fomorians.

He stared at them, shocked, as the woods descended into silence.

"That was too easy." Talaiel peered around the trees, as if trying to see more foe hiding in the shadows. "There were a few of them. I sense there to be more."

"You sense them?" Drake asked.

"Can you not feel the darkness hanging over the Woodlands? It is because of the Fomorians."

He could sense something was different about the place but he didn't know what. He looked at the treetops and he had to admit he could see some darkness, some shadow hanging in the air overhead.

"It is everywhere around us," she said.

"How do we get rid of it?"

"We must kill the mage who is responsible for the dark spell. That should release it."

"Then let's get to the palace," Drake said.

He could see no other signs of the Woodland Elves. Where had they all gone? He hurried toward the tree that would take them up to the top where the nobles lived. The guards and the lady were right behind him as he took the steps two at a time.

As soon as they reached the top, they were attacked again. Several Fomorians were ready and waiting for them. Almost as though they knew they had arrived. Drake did his best to keep up with the Skye Elves, but they were a force he could not match. When he looked closer at them, he could see their swords glowed with a strange ethereal light. He was so mesmerized by the sight he nearly took a sword to the gut.

Drake saw the movement out of the corner of his eye. The Fomorian narrowly missed him but he blocked the blow in time. He shoved his sword into the man's gut and then tossed him, head over heels, over the side of the rope bridge.

A scream behind him and he turned to see one of the Fomorians with his hands on Talaiel. He launched toward her but was intercepted by another enemy. He quickly disposed of the Fomorian. Shoving the dead man out of the way, he started again for Talaiel.

Her attacker lurched suddenly and she gave him a shove backward. He fell against the rope handrail, his weight making the material sag. She held a bloodied dagger in her hand and flashed Drake a triumphant smile.

"I told you I could take care of myself." She sounded exhilarated, as though this were the most fun she'd had in her entire life.

"Aye, I see that. Let's find Eldrin before you get yourself killed and I have to explain that to him."

"I won't get myself killed, Sir Drake. You have my word on that." She flashed him a broad smile.

But Drake wasn't so certain. He kept her behind him as they headed for the king's palace.

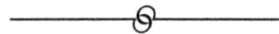

Thank the gods for Eldrin. Allanna craned her neck to see her brother standing on the other end of the great hall, sword in hand and blind rage on his normally passive face. She spotted the faded bruises on his neck and knew her vision had not been false—she had seen those very same bruises on his neck. She did not miss the quiver of arrows on his back of the bow slung over one shoulder either. He had come armed, dangerous and ready to do battle. She'd hoped to be saved by one of the Skye Elves, but Eldrin was there now. He would help her.

Marath jerked her around in front of him, making her face her brother.

"I'm keeping her. She's mine."

"You're not marrying her. I won't allow it."

"It's already done." He turned to the High Druid. "Say the final words."

The High Druid hesitated. "But my lord the vows—"

"Say the final words!" he shouted.

The High Druid flinched. His gaze landed on her, a look of regret and pain in his eyes. She knew what he was going to say— that they hadn't exchanged the vows. But it didn't matter anyway since their union wouldn't be official.

"Blessed be this union between Lord-Regent Marath and Princess Allanna. May it forever endure."

"No!" she shouted. "I do not agree. I didn't say the words! It's not binding."

Marath pulled her against his chest, holding her tight against him. But Allanna never took her eyes off her brother, who in turn never took his gaze off Marath. The Dark Elf's hand landed on her breast, cupping it, holding it as though he possessed it. His hot, blistering hand that burned through the material of her grown. It was an awkward position with their other hands still bound together and there was nothing she could do to free herself.

"I intend to take her here. Now."

"By the gods, you will *not*."

Eldrin charged, sword held aloft. Marath flinched but quickly regained his control. He put his hand up, palm out, sent a bolt of magic right toward her brother. He turned his sword with the flat edge out and when the magic hit the blade it dissipated.

With some relief, she realized Marath's magic was not as strong as Lorcann's.

Marath emitted a howl of frustration. Eldrin charged but his Fomorian men seemed to come out of every nook and crevice in the palace to intercept him. Marath, still bound to her, dragged her backward away from the ensuing melee.

"Come, my princess. It's time I take what belongs to me."

She dug her heels in. "I will never submit to you."

"You will or you'll die." He looked at her as he said it and his eyes were dark and menacing and she knew he meant business. She knew he would kill her should she refuse.

She glanced toward Eldrin to see him fighting against the Fomorians. There were so many and he had no help. How would he survive? Marath dragged her away from there, outside onto the rope bridge that connected the palace to the other treetop edifices.

Chaos abounded outside. She had never seen so many Fomorians. They were all fighting but not against her kinfolk. When she looked closer she realized they were the Skye Elves. They'd made it.

She quickly scanned the men, hoping to get a glimpse of— Yes! There was Drake.

Marath dragged her farther from them, though. She had no idea where he intended to take her nor did she wish to find out.

"Drake!"

Marath spun to see the dark head of her human knight—her true husband—bob through the men, hacking any Fomorian who stood in his path. And there, behind him, was the Lady of the Skye. He growled low in his throat and started dragging her away again.

"Let me go, you barbarian. Drake!"

He spotted her then and their eyes met for a brief moment. And then Marath pulled her around a corner, hiding them from view. He shoved her against the south wall of the palace and clamped his hand over her mouth. Fear clawed through her.

"You will not scream or I'll slit your throat. Is that clear?"

She nodded. He removed his hand a second later and went to work at the knots on their bound hands. Good, he was releasing her. Then she might have a chance to get away.

But then he halted and his gaze, that frightening gaze, met hers. His eyes narrowed and the color had darkened so much she could no longer see the pupil. His skin had turned a white, sickly pallor. Sweat beaded his top lip and the angry crease in his forehead. She could see the evil there, smell it coming off his skin.

"The last time I let you go, you hit me in the head. I shall not make that same mistake twice."

His free hand clamped down on the neckline of her gown and yanked. The material, being of the finest Elven silk, held fast. He snarled as he tried again. She put her free hand up in defense, trying to shove him backward off her. Or at least away from her.

"Let me go!"

He yanked again and this time the material ripped, revealing her shift. Hot tears spilled down her cheeks. She tried to slap away his hands but he was bigger, stronger. He went for her shift this time, gathering a handful of cloth.

Finally Allanna was able to act. She lifted her knee and embedded it in his groin as hard as she could. He grunted and doubled over, her shift forgotten. But when he doubled over, he took her with him since their hands were still bound together. She collided against him, against his heated exterior. Their heads smacked together with a sickening crack. Pinpricks of light exploded in her vision and her head immediately throbbed with the pain and her stomach cramped.

He tried to stand straight and succeeded, if only a little. He slapped her so hard she tasted blood on her lips. Her head had whipped to the side so she felt rather than saw Marath pushing against her. Pushing her into the wall and clawing at what was left of her gown. His rancid breath wafted over her face as he panted against her.

The next thing she knew, Marath howled and reared back. He stumbled. She stumbled. She had to put her hand on his chest to keep distance between them. That's when she saw the arrow sticking out of his back.

Eldrin stood at the other end of the rope bridge, having somehow gotten away from the attackers in the great hall. When he released the second arrow, she froze and gasped, watching in amazed horror as the arrow headed right for them. Knowing her brother was an excellent marksman, she knew not to move and she prayed Marath wouldn't stumble or jerk to cause the arrow to hit her instead. Luckily he was still trying to recover from the arrow in the back and hadn't seen Eldrin release the second projectile. It breezed by her face so close the fletching scraped her cheek before it pierced Marath's shoulder with a wet *thunk*.

It was that exact moment the fire pendant around her neck decided to come to life again. The crystal pulsed, flashed and exploded between them, hitting Marath square in the chest. She cringed as he started to fall backward over the rope handhold.

Allanna knew what was happening but was powerless to stop it. She screamed as he tumbled over the side, his hand still bound to hers. He took her with him but she managed by some small miracle to hook her arm over the rope handhold as she tumbled over. The force of his weight as he fell, though, caused a rope burn to her forearm all the way to her wrist. She grasped the handhold and dug her nails in. But her nails didn't have much strength and bent backward, shooting sharp pain through her fingertips to her wrist.

Below her Marath kicked. He clawed at her, as though trying to climb up her to get back to the bridge. A second later Drake's head came into view.

"I've got you."

His hand clamped around her wrist as he tugged, trying to pull her up. But Marath's weight pulled her down. She whimpered—relieved to see Drake unharmed but terrified Marath would fall and take her with him.

"Eldrin, hurry!" Drake shouted.

"She's mine. She belongs to me, you bastard."

Marath still clawed at her with his free hand, snatching pieces of her shredded gown and pulling at her. If not for Drake's sure grip, she'd be falling to her death with the Dark Elf.

Eldrin came into view then, a dagger in his hand. He hooked his boot around a piece of rope and leaned far over the side of the railing to saw through the silk cord binding their hands together. Allanna released her fingers from Marath's but he still insisted on holding tight. He still insisted on keeping her all for himself. He still insisted on trying to climb up her when he realized what Eldrin intended to do.

With every thread Eldrin cut through, Marath doubled his efforts to hold on to her. And when the last of the silken cord was cut and fluttered away, the Dark Elf clamped on to her wrist. With Drake holding her other one, she could feel the tug of war on her body, pulling her in two directions. And for a moment she thought she might be torn in half with Marath getting a piece of her, too.

But Eldrin wasn't going to allow that to happen. He disappeared for a brief second and then reappeared with bow and arrow in hand. He shot several off at Marath. She could hear the *thunk thunk* of arrows smacking into his body and his subsequent grunt. Arrows stuck out of his chest and shoulders. Blood pooled around the tips. But even still he would not let her go.

"Allanna, look at me," Drake said. And she knew Eldrin was about to do something horrific.

Allanna met his gaze. His beautiful blue eyes that made her heart melt. Another close-range arrow fired from Eldrin's bow and it seemed as though everything moved into slow motion. She could hear the distinct reverberation of the bow string with the release of the arrow as it sprung back into place. The swish of the arrow as it slid through the air, spanning the short distance. The damp *thwack* as the arrow found its mark followed quickly by a blood-curdling scream from Marath. His nails scraped down her skin while his other hand clamped on a fistful of her gown, ripping the front. He had released her.

And he was falling, falling, falling. Falling to his death.

Drake hoisted her up, pulling her over the edge of the rope railing and into his arms. She fell into him, the force of her weight shoving them to the wood planks. Drake gathered her against him, holding her close as she sobbed into his chest. She never wanted to let him go. She never wanted to leave his side again. His big hand cradled her head, stoking her hair, soothing her.

"I've got you. You're safe," he whispered.

Once she got her emotions under control, Allanna moved off Drake and climbed to her feet with Eldrin's help. Her brother held a hand down to Drake. When he was on his feet, she cuddled against him.

"Thank you, Eldrin." That deep baritone voice rumbled against her, calming her and she thanked the gods he was still alive and still *hers*.

"I'm sorry I didn't get here sooner. I was detained," her brother replied. "Allanna?"

She turned her head, resting her cheek on his chest. Drake's hand fluttered through her hair. "I'm all right but I thought for certain he was going to take me with him."

"As did I."

"The mage?" Drake asked. "Where is he?"

"I don't know. Even with Marath dead, I doubt he will give up so easily. But the spell seems to be gone."

Drake looked up at the sky and nodded. "Aye the shadows have lifted. Mayhap with Marath's death, the spell was broken."

"It seems so. You'll stay with her?"

"Aye," Drake said.

Eldrin hurried away, leaving them alone. They stood there together, listening to the sounds of the dwindling battle around them. But she didn't want to move from the safe sanctuary of his arms.

"I thought you might be dead, Drake."

"Turin revived me. He has powerful healing magic, I think." He pulled away from her, held her at arm's length. "We must find you something more suitable to wear. And doctor these wounds." He examined her bleeding fingertips and rope-burned arm with a critical eye.

Her gown was ruined. Marath had managed to rip it to shreds in his frenzy to take her for his own. Thankfully, her shift remained somewhat intact, covering her.

"That can wait. What of the Skye Elves? I saw them."

"Lady Talaiel brought her men to help."

"She did? She's here?"

"She insisted on coming." Allanna knew why. She smiled. But Drake continued. "We found Eldrin in the great hall battling the Fomorians alone. They'd backed him into a corner. The Skye Elves killed them. All of them. Her guards are not merely guards."

"What do you mean?"

"I mean they are powerful warriors. They can kill twice as many men as I can. I've never seen the likes. It's because of that we were able to get into the Woodlands and here. By my count, most of the Fomorians were wiped out. Or fled."

"Except for Lorcann."

"Aye."

"We'll have to find him then and bring him to justice."

"In time, princess. For now, we have other more important matters."

"We do?"

"Aye, we do. Like me kissing you."

He tilted her face to his and kissed her. He kissed her as though he would never let her go. And she knew he wouldn't.

Eldrin was certain he saw Lady Talaiel in the mix with her Elven warriors. Fighting. He had never anticipated that from her. She was truly a woman of many surprises. Dead Fomorians littered the bridges. He shoved them unceremoniously off, letting their corpses fall to the ground without a care or thought.

When the fighting began, his people emerged from hiding and took up arms against the Fomorians. Now they stood triumphant, grinning and cheering as he removed the dead one by one. Some even got in on the action and Eldrin had to wonder what those on the ground thought of seeing the dead falling from the tops of the trees.

He was delighted to see there were no Elven casualties. He smiled at that. Not many knew the Skye Elves were never to be trifled with. They had long ago retired to their realm in the sky, having fought for it and won it by right. They were fierce warriors and each one had the strength and skill of ten men.

He had never expected the lady to bring them to his fight though he was grateful and owed her a debt of thanks. He paused at the entrance to the palace and then spotted her at last on the other end of the rope bridge. She gave out orders to her men to clean up the mess they'd left behind and they scurried to do her bidding. When she saw him, she flushed with happiness and immediately forgot her duties.

Desire surged through his veins with her approach. She hurried her steps faster and faster the closer she got. He dropped his bow and held his arms out and they collided, falling together and kissing as though they hadn't seen each other in eons.

"I'm so glad you're all right," Talaiel whispered against his lips before kissing him again. "I worried."

"That's why you came." His fingers tangled in her coppery hair, pushing through the silken strands with ease. "How did you convince the council?"

"I didn't ask them." She giggled, the sound bubbling up her throat. It was like a symphony to his ears. "I came because I love you. I've always loved you."

The words made his heart squeeze. He pulled away from her, cradling her beautiful face in his hands and gazing down into those gorgeous silvery eyes. "Ah, Talaiel. A man could not ask for sweeter words. I intend to marry you if you'll have me."

"Do you now? Does that mean you love me, too?"

"Aye, it does. I burn for you with a flaming desire that cannot be extinguished."

The tips of her ears turned pink as her face flushed a gorgeous pink. "It isn't possible."

"It is possible," he affirmed. "I intended to come back for you. I want you."

"I thought you said you never could because of your duties to your realm."

He couldn't help but to continue to kiss her as she spoke, tracing the edge of her jaw, her cheekbone and nibbling her earlobe.

"Duties be hanged," he said, his breath fanning her skin. Her sweet skin tasted like honeywine on a warm summer's night. "I'll not live another moment without you."

"But...I cannot abandon my realm." Her breath hitched when he tasted the soft skin behind her ear with the tip of his tongue.

"You won't. Nor will I. We'll think of something, my love. That I can promise you. What is your answer?"

Her fingers dug into his shoulders. "My answer?"

"Will you have me?"

"Oh, aye, I'll have you. And, Eldrin, if you continue kissing me this way I must ask you to take me away from this public place at once." Her breath shuddered out of her as she clutched him, pulling her to him.

"That can be arranged, my lady."

He took her by the hand and led her to his chamber. As soon as they were behind the closed door, he barred it. He wanted no interruptions. He wanted to seal their promise to each other.

She wasted no more time. She shrugged off the cloak that rested on her shoulders and went to work on removing her gown. Eldrin removed the sword from his waist, his padded vest and toed off his boots, leaving them all in a pile at his feet. He pulled her to him, kissed her with all his pent-up fervor. His hands were in her hair and cupping her face as he pressed his lips against hers.

Talaiel put a hand on his chest and pushed him away, taking a deep breath.

"Eldrin, wait. There is something I must tell you."

"It can wait." He pulled her to him again, tried to kiss her but she turned her head.

"I cannot. I have to tell you what I did."

He reluctantly released her and she stepped out of his arms, turning her back to him and slumping her shoulders. He feared it must be something awful.

"What is it?"

"When you left Drake and Allanna in my care, I…I did something." She hesitated and he could see she had clasped her hands together. "I probably should not have done it but I knew it was the perfect opportunity."

Eldrin took a tentative step toward her. "What did you do?"

Talaiel turned her head and peered at him over her shoulder. "I arranged for Sir Drake and Princess Allanna to be handfasted."

He blinked surprise and words failed him. She had managed to give each of them what they most desired—each other. All this time Eldrin had told her how impossible it was for them to marry and how she would have to give up all that she was to marry him. And now? What would become of them? With their father ill, would Andahar allow the match? Would he see how suited they were to each other?

She rushed on.

"I did it because I knew of her betrothal and how much she didn't want to marry the man. I, too, didn't want to see her marry him after all the things you told me about him. I thought if I…if I handfasted them the king would surely see how truly devoted Drake is to her and how much they love each other. I had no idea the king was ill." She turned to face him and he could see the guilt creasing her features, marring her beauty. "I tell you this now because I don't want you to hate me for what I did."

He had never been more relieved. He thought it would be something dreadful. Some confession she had to make to him that would utterly destroy them. Hearing she had arranged the marriage of his sister to his friend made him happy. True, he had urged Allanna to give him up because he didn't want to see her leave the realm. To give up all that she was and all that she had though he knew now she would do anything for Drake. Much like he would do anything for Talaiel.

He realized, too, several of his sister's visions had come true— her vision of marrying Drake, the poisoning of the king and the attempted murder of Andahar. Her visions, it seemed, were getting stronger and clearer.

They would have to deal with the fallout once things were back in order. Ultimately, it would be up to Andahar to decide what to do with Drake and Allanna.

"I also thought since you wished to marry me you had changed your mind about the boundaries of realm and duty," she added.

"Talaiel, I could never hate you. You were right—you can't help who you fall in love with. What you did was a wonderful gift."

"So you're not angry with me?"

"No, my love. Far from angry. I told you once I thought the match was a fine one and I still do. Now I'm pleased to know Sir Drake will be permanently part of our realm."

"What about the king? What will he say?"

"Should he recover from his illness, we will deal with it then. In the meantime, Prince Andahar will need to be informed as regent of the Woodlands. But we can worry about that later. Much later."

She heaved a sigh of relief. "I'm so glad you don't hate me."

"No, I do not. In fact I intend to show you how much I don't hate you by making love to you until the dawn."

She flushed a gorgeous pink as her lashes fluttered down.

"All I care about is you, me and this moment. Now let's get this gown off you."

Before he could reach for her, she fell into his arms and kissed him. Kissed him with all the passion she possessed. She slipped her hands under his tunic and over the hard planes of his chest, shoving the material upward as she went. Eldrin stripped it off and discarded it, happy to have the garment gone.

His fingers fumbled with the lace ties down the front of her gown and she giggled. "Let me."

Talaiel took a step back from him, her gaze never wavering from his as she pulled one shoulder and then the other out of her gown. She shimmied out of it, letting it pool at her feet and baring all to him.

He took a moment to drink in the sight of her naked beauty. Her skin was smooth as alabaster. Perfect. Unmarred. Her breasts were topped with rosy peaks, the nipples hardened into pearly nubs. His body had gone rigid, tingling with the want of touching her. His shaft hardened to a painful length in his breeches. He couldn't stop looking at her.

"You approve, my lord?"

"More than you know." So much more than she could ever know.

He could stand there all day mesmerized by her but he didn't. He forced his feet to move, one step in front of the other until he stood before her. Until he could reach for her, until his hands landed on her shoulders and slipped down her arms.

Talaiel pressed her palm against his chest, her fingers cool against his heated skin.

"Your heart is racing," she whispered.

"For you. I worship you."

"Touch me then."

Eldrin wasted no more time as his hands slipped over her breasts, cupping them, feeling the hardened peaks against his palms. When he did a breath shuddered out between her lips.

She backed toward the bed, taking slow steps and keeping her gaze firmly on his. But he stood rooted in place, watching her. At the edge of the bed, she slid across the coverlet and reclined.

"Come to me, Eldrin. Let me feel you." She held a hand out to him.

He shucked his breeches and stepped to the bed, wasting no more time. Now was the time. The time he had waited forever for, it seemed. When he slid on top of her, she welcomed him by opening her legs and wrapping them around his waist. Her core was already damp for him. His shaft already hardened to a thickened length ready to take her.

When he slid inside her, she gasped with a breathy sigh as though she too had waited a lifetime for him. Their bodies melded together in one fluid motion. Her hips vibrated against his as he thrust into her, pulled away and thrust again.

He took her hands in his, lacing their fingers and pushing her arms over her head as he rose up to see her. To see all the glorious skin and the two perfect breasts with peaks that brushed against his chest with every movement. She was his salvation, his heaven, his everything. She embodied perfection.

When she climaxed, she cried his name on a breath. He gathered her to him, cradling her ever so close and knowing he would never let her go.

Chapter 17

Allanna stood at the window, watching as morning pierced the panes of glass and spilled a shaft of light across the wood floor. The light warmed her, pulsing through her. Her stomach was knotted with worry as she stared out at the morning, the high wispy clouds that moved lazily across the pink sky. She knew she had to face today but she didn't want to. She wanted to stay in her chamber, the door barred, with Drake. Alone. Blissfully unaware of the goings-on outside the door. All that mattered was what happened here with Drake.

It contented her to know he still slept, snoring softly. She glanced at him sprawled on his back and smiled. His chest rose and fell with the even breath of sleep. He had a stubbly growth of beard shadowing his cheeks and chin. He hadn't shaved—they'd scarcely left her chamber since she had nearly fallen to her death with Marath.

Drake. Her husband. He had saved her in more ways than one. Not only from Marath but also from a loveless marriage. From isolation. From loneliness.

It had been two days since the battle with the Fomorians, if it could even be called a battle. They didn't seem to fight back very hard when they realized Lorcann had disappeared and Marath was dead. Lorcann was still missing—no one had seen him since the day he had been ordered to find Drake and bring him to Marath. When Marath had threatened to cut him into small pieces in front of Allanna.

In that two days, though, Brom had administered an antidote for the poison the king had swallowed. From what she'd heard, the king was still not conscious. Though she had visited numerous times, he hadn't known she was there.

Andahar was recovering from his near-fatal wound. Turin, the Skye Elven healer, had come from their heavenly realm to assist with the wounded. He had used some sort of healing magic similar to what he used on Drake. Her brother would live, thank the gods. He would return to the throne today and he had asked for her and Sir Drake to appear in court that morning.

She knew all too well what that meant. She would never give him up, no matter what Andahar said. They belonged together.

Eldrin had taken over while Andahar and their father recovered. He wasted no time in marrying Lady Talaiel. He had taken her as his wife the morning following the battle. They announced they would split their time between each realm so that the lady could continue as regent while Eldrin would continue with his duties as ranger to the Woodlands.

Lord Navin was back to guarding the Woodland gates. The remaining Fomorians had been pushed out. The dead had been removed. The gates had been fortified.

And all seemed right in the realm.

Except for meeting with her brother. Her brother who had never really treated her like a sister. Like Eldrin had. In his world, there were rules that had to be followed and she had broken them all by marrying Drake, the human knight.

What would Father say? He would be horrified, no doubt. Andahar subscribed to the same type of rule as he did so it seemed to her that her brother would cast out Drake. They had been handfasted a short while. What if he did? What if he made Drake leave her in the Woodlands and return to the human realm?

It would devastate her. And she would not allow it. She would never live without him. She would return with him whether Eldrin or Andahar liked it or not. That was her plan all along, after all.

"You're awake."

Drake's sleep-thickened voice pulled her out of her deep thoughts. She turned from the window, gave him a smile.

"Good morrow, my husband."

"And you're dressed. Such a travesty." He propped up on his elbows and looked her over.

"I couldn't sleep," she confessed.

She had tossed and turned far too long and finally rose, splashed cold water on her face and dressed. She didn't know how long she had stood at the window. Long before sunrise, that she knew. She'd watched the sky lighten with the dawn.

"Nervous about today?" He sat all the way up, his hair standing in spikes around his head.

It made his devilish good looks even more devilish. It stirred that deep-seated desire inside her as she looked at him. Desire that shoved away the nervous knots that plagued her.

"I am."

"There's no need."

He swung his feet off the side of the bed, stood and walked toward her. Naked. Gloriously naked. It took all her self-control to keep her eyes on his face. When he reached her, he brushed the back of his hand down her face.

"It will be all right, Allanna."

"How can you be sure?"

Her strength wavered with that touch and she wished she still wore her shift. She wished she hadn't dressed in this bloody crushed velvet gown with the fine lace trim at the wrists and neckline. She wished she could rip it to shreds in front of him and let him have his way with her.

She wished.

He cupped her face. "Because Lord Eldrin has already spoken to Prince Andahar."

"But that doesn't mean he won't banish you anyway."

"Lord Eldrin asked to trust him. Do you?" After hesitating, she finally nodded. "Good. I do, too. I daresay he won't banish me."

"I hope you're right."

"Prince Andahar took the news of Lord Eldrin marrying Lady Talaiel quite well, I heard."

"That's because he had lost a lot of blood and was lightheaded at the time. He didn't know what he was agreeing to," she said.

He laughed. "I'm sure he was in his right mind after Turin helped him."

"But—"

"No more buts, my princess. We must have faith." His warm hands landed on her shoulders and he bent to kiss her cheek. "I will be beside you the entire time."

"I'm glad of that. It gives me strength. *You* give me strength."

"As do you."

"Now, will you do something for me?" she asked.

"Anything."

"Will you put some breeches on? I find I'm terribly distracted."

He laughed again. "As you wish, my princess."

Eldrin knocked on Andahar's door and waited.

"Come," was the muffled reply.

He entered, closing the door behind him. His brother sat on the edge of the bed, his breeches and boots on but no tunic. He held an arm against his side, the color washed from his face as he struggled to catch his breath. Eldrin could see the stains of blood on the bandage and immediately went to him.

"I moved too fast I think." Andahar flashed a sheepish smile. His body quaked from the sheer pain.

"Why didn't you wait for me?" Eldrin clasped a hand around his upper arm and pushed him back on the bed while he scooted toward the pillows. "I'll get the healer."

"No. That's not necessary." He inhaled a deep breath but it shuddered out of him in a ragged pant.

"It *is* necessary. It looks as though you may have torn a stitch."

Eldrin stomped to the door, opened and it and called for the healer. Turin arrived a moment later to tend his brother's wound.

"I told you it wasn't a good idea to do this today," Eldrin chastised. "You should be resting."

"Aye, you *should* be resting," Turin said with a nod of agreement. "I told you as much. Yet you insist on getting out of that bed." He shoved Andahar back into the pillows with a firm but gentle hand. "Let me change the dressing and check your stitches."

"I can't rest," Andahar said. "The realm depends on me now. I need to make an appearance to let our people know we are still strong. They need to know I'm still here. And then there's the matter of Aesir—"

"All of that can wait." Eldrin folded his arms over his chest. "I told you that. The people are merely happy the spell has been lifted and Marath and the Fomorians are gone."

"But for how long?" Andahar asked. "How long will they be gone? Lorcann has not been found. There is still a chance he will come back to fight us. To avenge the death of Marath."

"I doubt the mage has any love for the dead man. We can worry about all that later when you and Father have fully recovered."

"You've torn a stitch," Turin interjected. He probed the wound with a fingertip and Andahar sucked in a sharp breath. "Apologies, your highness. At least the tear isn't bad. Hold still while I fix it."

"More stitching. My favorite." Andahar's mouth flattened into a thin line. "Distract me, Eldrin. How is Father?" He asked it between clenched teeth.

"Better, I think. Brom worked up an antidote."

"That bloody Marath nearly killed me." Andahar grunted when Turin tied off the new stitch. "I should have listened to Allanna."

"Aye, we should have all listened to Allanna." Eldrin nodded, thinking of her visions and how they had come true. Mayhap not in the same fashion as she saw it, but true nonetheless. "At any rate, the antidote doesn't seem to be working. He hasn't improved."

Turin placed a fresh bandage on Andahar's side. "What ails the king?"

"He was poisoned," Andahar said.

"With what?"

"Brom thinks it was some type of nightshade," Eldrin replied. "The only evidence he had was a residue in the bottom of his cup of honeywine."

"Take me to him. I want to have a look."

Eldrin glanced from Turin to his brother. "All right. I'll be back for you, Andahar. Stay put."

"I'm fine." He waved away his concern but made no move to stand again.

Eldrin led Turin from Andahar's chamber to the king's, which was a few doors down the corridor. The king's was guarded day and night now, both inside and outside. They had decided not to take any more chances should the mage return.

Lady Talaiel had offered to place wards around the castle walls as well as the gates to keep the Fomorians out. Eldrin had agreed to allow her to do so though he hadn't discussed that with Andahar yet. He thought it would be best to wait. Andahar, after all, didn't need to be burdened with such minor things as wards on palace entrances and exits.

At the king's chamber, Eldrin stood aside as Turin entered. Brom was there, checking on the king. From the doorway, he could see the slow rise and fall of his father's chest as he breathed, showing signs that he still, in fact, lived. Turin entered the room with a purposeful stride, stood next to Brom and looked down at the king. He reached for his wrist, wrapped his fingers around the bones.

"What do you think you're doing?" Brom clenched his fists, as though trying hard not to shove the other healer away.

"Easy, Brom," Eldrin said. "Turin is here to help."

"I don't need his help, my lord. I have done all I could for him."

"Have you?" Turin asked. One brow rose in challenge. "Ashen, clammy skin. Slow and weak pulse. You think this was some type of nightshade?"

"How do you know that?"

"That's what Lord Eldrin said. Describe the residue in the bottom of the cup."

Brom narrowed his gaze, almost seeming to be affronted by the brusque manner of the man. "A whitish substance. Thick. Like muck."

"Did it have an odor?"

"Aye. Sweet. Like a flower." Brom lowered his brow, glowering at the other healer.

"Not nightshade," Turin said. "Baneberry."

Brom drew up straight and tight, angling his body away from Turin. "I've never heard of such a thing." He gave a snort of derision.

"That's because it grows in temperate climates. It's far too humid here."

Something sparked inside Eldrin. "But it could grow near a beach or water. Where the temperatures would remain moderate year round?"

"That's right." Turin nodded.

"Bloody Fomorians. That's where Marath got the poison." Eldrin clenched his fists.

"I...had no idea."

"Nor would you, Brom." Eldrin patted him on the shoulder to console him. "I wouldn't know either." Then to Turin, "Can you help him?"

"It may be too late but I will do what I can."

"Brom, work with Turin. See what you two can come up with together."

Brom nodded. "As you say, my lord."

Eldrin left the two healers as they put their heads together to come up with some way to save the king of the Woodland Elves. Brom, though, still seemed reluctant but at least he acted as though he was willing to work with Turin.

He headed back to Andahar's chamber. When he entered, his brother had managed to stand and pull on a tunic as well as strap his sword to his side. He stood near the bed, his hand on the bedpost and leaning into it, as though he were trying to catch his breath.

"I told you to stay put." Eldrin didn't hide his sharp tone as he rushed over to him to brace him with a shoulder under one arm.

"I don't follow orders well," Andahar replied. He gratefully allowed him to help. "Get me to the throne room, will you?"

"You're mad, you know. If you rip another stitch Turin won't be as gentle."

"*As* gentle?" Andahar snorted. "As though he had a gentle hand this last time. I'll need a lot of honeywine to get me through today. Mayhap something stronger."

"You'll be drinking no honeywine or ale. You should be resting. Not playing ruler."

"And leave all the fun to you, brother? I should think not. Now stop mothering me and get me to the throne room."

Eldrin didn't hide the roll of his eyes as he walked slowly from the chamber to the throne room. It seemed like an eternity at their unhurried pace. But he didn't want to hurry and risk hurting him again. At the throne room, Eldrin delivered him to their father's chair. Andahar sat with a grunt. He pressed his hand against his side as though holding the bandage in place.

"Do you need the healer?" Eldrin asked.

"No." He waved him away. "Bring in the prisoner."

Eldrin took his place next to his brother and waited as Aesir was brought before them. The guards had shackled his wrists to keep him from escaping, though the man hadn't exhibited any sort of violent behavior. He had been found in one of the empty chambers shortly after the battle.

"Aesir, you stand accused of crimes against the crown," Andahar said. "You, along with your lord-regent, conspired to kidnap and kill the princess, as well as the entire royal family. What say you?"

"Your highness, forgive me, but I accept no guilt in the matter."

A muttering went through the room. Andahar leaned forward a little, his elbow on his knee as though to intimidate the man. He winced, clearly in pain.

"You have no guilt?" the prince asked. "Explain why you should be exonerated."

"Lord-Regent Marath did not share his plot against the crown with me until it was far too late. Until he had called the Fomorian mage, Lorcann. I knew nothing of the plan. You have my word on that," Aesir replied. "I complied with his wishes because I valued my life. Nothing more."

Andahar glanced at Eldrin, a question in his eyes. The ranger gave a swift shake of his head as if to say he didn't believe the man.

"But you knew Marath had called the Fomorian," Andahar said.

"I knew he had called Lorcann. I did not know he called the others until they had arrived. I did not know he had invoked the dark magic until it was too late to stop him."

"But you knew he *had* invoked the magic," the prince said.

"As I said, I didn't know until it was too late. I didn't agree with his decisions, your highness."

"And so you believe yourself to be innocent?" Eldrin shook his head again. "You stand as guilty as the lord-regent himself."

"I have but one request, your highness." Aesir didn't look at Eldrin as he spoke. He kept his gaze trained on Andahar.

"And what is that?"

"That I return to my home."

"If you mean Lord-Regent Marath's home, that is now property of the crown," Andahar said. "The land is hereby confiscated. I will decide what to do with it later."

"No, your highness. I do not mean his home. I mean *mine*. Before I worked for Marath, I lived in relative peace in the eastern Woodlands. I should like to return there."

Andahar sat back in the chair and ran a contemplative hand over his chin. "And you intend to stay there?"

"You will never hear from me or see me again, your highness. You have my solemn oath."

He sounded so sincere, Eldrin nearly believed him. He glanced at Andahar, who looked as though he considered the man's request. Surely his brother didn't think he was telling the truth? He had also played a part in the conspiracy.

"Why should I let you go? You are nothing more than a traitor."

"I am nothing more than a man," he replied. "A man who was forced into those evil deeds against his will."

"You expect us to believe that?" Rancor sharpened Eldrin's voice as he glared at Aesir.

"I am sorry, Aesir," Andahar said. "But I cannot let you go so easily. You will be put in the dungeon waiting execution."

"Execution?" He actually sounded surprised, as though he were convinced Andahar would let him leave and return to his home in the eastern Woodlands. "You can't mean that."

"I can and I do. Guards, take him away."

Eldrin blew out a breath as he watched them lead Aesir from the throne room. "A wise decision, brother. I feared you were going to let him go."

"Do not take me for a fool. Now, fetch our sister and the human knight. It is time for her to face her own fate."

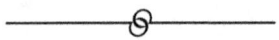

"It's time."

Eldrin's announcement was not a welcome one. Immediately, Allanna's palms turned into slick pools of hot sweat. She cleared her throat, trying to stave off the empty feeling in the pit of her stomach. She hated facing her brother like this. She was fearful of what he might say or do.

"Come, my princess. All will be well." Drake held his arm out to her.

"I'm coming, too." Lady Talaiel gave her an encouraging smile. "You're not alone, Allanna."

She quite liked the Lady of the Skye and was grateful she was her new sister. She'd never had a big sister though if she did, she imagined she would be something like Talaiel.

"I'm ready."

She took Drake's offered arm and followed Eldrin into the throne room. It wasn't bad enough she had to face her brother, Andahar. But it was made worse when she saw the gathered nobles in the room. All staring at her and Sir Drake with wide eyes, curious eyes. Wondering what she could possibly see in the human. The human who had nothing in common with the Elves.

How wrong they all were. He was her everything. Should Andahar decide to banish him from the Otherworld, she would go, too.

They halted in front of Prince Andahar, who slid to the edge of his seat. Allanna noted he tried his best to look as though he were in charge. As though he were the reigning authority in the realm. And she supposed he was, since their father could be dying. A fact she didn't want to think about yet.

"Prince Andahar, I present to you Princess Allanna and Sir Drake Attenborough of the human realm," Eldrin announced, sounding official.

Another thing Allanna didn't like. Eldrin turned to face her and gave her a surreptitious wink before taking the seat next to Andahar. As if to say all would be well. She hoped he was right.

"Princess Allanna, I understand you and this...human are handfasted," Andahar said. His voice was strained, thin.

She held her head high, looking down the slope of her nose at her brother. "We are."

"Forgive me, your highness." Talaiel stepped next to Allanna and did a deep curtsey. "I feel it is my duty to explain."

"You, Lady Talaiel? What do you have to explain?"

Clearly Eldrin hadn't told Andahar any details. He sounded as confused as the rest of the nobles looked. Allanna did a quick survey of the room to see all eyes pinned on them and watching with great interest. Listening to every word and salivating for the final outcome.

"Aye, your highness. It was I who arranged their handfasting in the Skye Realm," she said. "I, alone, take full responsibility for arranging the marriage."

Andahar raised his eyebrows in curiosity. "Why?"

"Forgive me for asking, your highness, but have you ever been in love?"

The prince shifted in the chair and cleared his throat. "I don't see what that has to do with anything."

"It has a great deal to do with everything," she said. "When two people are in love..." She paused, glanced at Eldrin, smiled. Blushed. "Well, there's no stopping those feelings between two people, your highness. It's nigh impossible."

"And you're telling me this why?" Now he sounded annoyed.

"Because the betrothal between the princess and Lord-Regent Marath was not a good match and anyone could see that. Why the king agreed to it is beyond me." She folded her arms to press her point.

Gasps and murmurs filtered throughout the room. Even Allanna couldn't believe she had the courage to speak to Andahar in such a way. Though she applauded her silently for it.

"As it turns out Marath proved he was not a good man. He turned into a Dark Elf."

"And he died for it," Andahar practically growled. "That has nothing to do with Sir Drake or my sister, my lady."

"It has everything to do with them, your highness," she retorted. Clearly unflustered by Andahar's abruptness. "I had them handfasted because it would force the king to eradicate the ridiculous betrothal. Do you not recall the old Elven law? Once handfasted and consummated the king must recognize the marriage as valid."

Allanna blushed. Drake cleared his throat.

Andahar stared at her with unbelieving eyes, his mouth slightly agape. As though he had no idea what to say. He finally clamped his jaw shut. "That ridiculous betrothal was broken days ago. My father ordered it and I saw it was done immediately. And as I recall, the couple is to remain together for a year and a day for the handfasted marriage to be valid."

"Aye that is why I urge you to allow them to remain here in the Woodlands together."

Allanna spoke up and tried hard not to sound timid. "If you banish Sir Drake from the Woodlands, Andahar, I shall follow him. If you send him back to the human realm, I will go. I love him. I will not give him up."

Her brother turned his gaze on her, eyeing her not with derision but something else. Compassion and amazement. And maybe a little bit of envy and admiration. He held himself rigid and tight as he looked at her. As he contemplated their situation. As he held their fate in his hands.

"Your visions came true," he said then. "Your visions of me and Father. I should have listened to you. I should have believed you."

Her heart seemed to freeze in her chest at the admission. Her blood rushed through her veins in a quickened tempo. She couldn't believe it. Had she heard him correctly?

"For that you have my apologies, my sister."

She blinked surprise, her throat constricting and tears threatening. Andahar turned his gaze on Sir Drake then.

"And do you feel the same as she? Will you not be parted from her should I order you back to the human realm?"

Allanna implored Drake with her eyes, looking at him the way he said drove him mad. She even managed to flutter her lashes a bit. He smiled a warm smile at her when he answered.

"I am no longer complete without her."

More murmurs throughout the room. Allanna didn't care. The Elven nobles, no doubt, had ideas of their own about what they thought of her and Sir Drake. Whatever Andahar decided they would not question. It was her father she was worried about.

"You saved my sister from certain death. More than once. You kept her safe in the Skye Realm. You nearly died for her. There is no greater honor. You are a true noble knight and hero, Sir Drake."

"Thank you, your highness."

Even Drake sounded as though his throat was tight as he choked out the words. She was too scared to look up at him again for fear she would lose her composure altogether and break into racking sobs. Too many emotions cascaded through her. Did her brother mean to send him away? Or let him stay? Her heart skittered in her chest as she waited for Andahar's next words.

"Because you have demonstrated such bravery and devotion to the princess, I find there is no better man suited for her. Therefore, I approve of the handfasting. I welcome you to the Woodlands, Sir Drake, as one of our own. I grant you permission to stay within our realm and live as one of us." Then his gaze flickered back to her. "I should hate to lose my little sister to the barbaric human realm. No offense, of course, Sir Drake."

"None taken, your highness."

And Drake was smiling. Smiling with all the joy she felt pumping through her body. Heat radiated through her chest. She gasped, trying to gulp air into her lungs and keep from crying.

"There is one more matter to attend to," Andahar continued. "And that is of your mortality. I will consult the High Druid to see if there is any way to give you an immortal life."

Allanna sniffed. "You mean that, Andahar?"

"I do. The High Druid will know what to do. If you approve, Sir Drake, we shall go at once."

"Oh, I do. I approve."

Cheers broke out in the throne room. That was the one thing that worried her. The one thing that kept them apart—he would die and she wouldn't. But Andahar and the High Druid would make it so they could live together forever. They would truly never be parted.

Allanna could no longer hold in the tears that had threatened. Drake pulled her to him in a fierce hug and kissed her with unabashed passion in front of Andahar, Eldrin and everyone. She welcomed his kiss. She wrapped her arms around him and held him tight.

"Are you happy?" He brushed away the tears that dampened her cheeks.

"Deliriously so." Her throat clotted around the words.

He kissed her brow. "So am I. I'm glad to know you don't have to give up all that you are."

"I would have."

"I know. I love you for it. Welcome home, my princess."

Realm of Honor Cast of Characters

The Humans
Sir Finian "Finn" McCullough: Scottish knight
Maggie Chase McCullough: Finn's wife
Sir Drake Attenborough: English knight and jousting hero
Henry Chase: Maggie's father

The Fae
Princess Elyne: crown princess of the Fae Otherworld
Lord Derron: Knight of the Realm, Protector of the Otherworld
Queen Maeve: ruler of the Otherworld and the Seelie Court
Lord Roderick: member of the High Council
Lord Aldun: member of the High Council
Lord Vaughan: member of the High Council
Seamus: healer for the Fae
King Adhamh: the queen's husband who was murdered
Morrigan: Goddess of War
Lord/Dark King Kieran: dark elf bent on human and Otherworld domination
Lord Gawaine: Queen Maeve's high councilor
Dark King Fergus mac Delbaith: dark king of the Unseelie court
Lord Pwyll: Guardian of the Stone of Destiny
Lord Malcolm: Guardian of the Sword of Light and Derron's father
Lord Llewelyn: Guardian of the Club of Dagda
Lord Udrich: Guardian of the Spear of Lugh

The Elves

King Urdithane emar'Rudul: ruler of the Wood Elves

Andahar emar'Rudul: crown prince of the Woodlands Elven throne

Leopold: Wood Elves royal advisor

Eldrin emar'Rudul: brother to Andahar, Elven ranger

Allanna emar'Rudul: sister to Andahar and Elven Princess

Lord Navin emar'Rudul: brother to Andahar, Woodlands Gatekeeper

Lord-Regent Marath: Wood Elves liege lord

Lord Randir: Fire Elf and Laerwen's betrothed

Laerwen emer'Aranhil Bloodfire: Fire Elf and Princess of the Hin'dar Rhule

Hiram: Laerwen's royal advisor

Lady Talaiel: ruler of the Skye Elves

Turin: healer for the Skye Elves

Brom: healer for the Wood Elves

Lord Malack: one of the noble Wood Elves

Queen Lucinda and King Aleron: ruler of the Fire Elves

The Fomorians

Cormac: Fomorian mage forced to help Kieran

Lorcann: Fomorian mage

The Dragons

Ambrielle: the emerald dragon

Aura: the azure dragon

Luna: the silver dragon

Nero: the black dragon

Moon dragons: silver dragons of the Skye Elves

The Realms
Fae Otherworld: home of the Fae, includes Seelie and Unseelie Courts

Woodlands: a humid forest region and home of the Wood Elves
Hin'dar Rhule: dry, arid volcanic region and home of the Fire Elves
Skye Realm in the clouds: home of the Skye Elves and the moon dragons

Human Realm: home for Maggie and Finn

Underworld: where Morrigan was banished

The Races
The Fae: also known as Faeries, a race of magical beings who can alter time and travel from their realm to the human realm.

Fire Elves: Elves who live in the volcanic realm known as the Hin'dar Rhule. Their bodies can withstand the hottest heat of the fires, but the lava is still deadly to them. They seek help from the Wood Elves when the Fomorians destroy their home.

Fomorians: an ancient race of vile creatures who wreak havoc. They were banished to a watery prison but one powerful Fomorian mage managed to break out and free his people so they could rampage once more.

Skye Elves: a reclusive Elven race living among the clouds with their moon dragons. The legend of the Skye Elves says one is as strong as ten men and they are undefeatable in battle.

Wood Elves: Elves who live in the trees of the Woodlands and who had a long-standing Treaty of Separation with the Fae, dividing the two races. The Treaty has since been abolished, uniting the two and allowing them to work together to defeat the evil in the realm.

ALSO BY MICHELLE MILES

Age of Wizards (Epic Fantasy)
In the Tower of the Wizard King
On the Hunt for the Wizard King

Dragon Protectors
(Paranormal Shifter Romance)
Desiring the Dragon Lord
Seducing the Dragon Knight
Tempting Her Dragon Bodyguard
Dragon Protectors Book Collection (Books 1-3)

Dream Walker (Urban Fantasy)
Call of the Dark
Blood and Bone
Flame and Fury
Smoke and Ashes
Light of the World
Dream Walker Collection (Books 1-5)

Dream Walker: Origins (Fantasy)
Provenance

Enchanted Realms (Fantasy Romance)
Once Upon a Midnight Clear
Once Upon True Love's Kiss
Once Upon an Enchanted Kiss

Five Towers (YA Fantasy)
The Sorcerer's Daughter

Highland Destiny
(Fantasy Historical Romance)
Desiring the Highland Laird (Coming 2025)
Loving the Highland Warrior (Coming 2025)
Captivating the Highland Rogue (Coming 2026)

Ransom & Fortune Adventure
(Time Travel Action/Adventure)
Highland Fling, Vol 1
Dead of Winter, Vol 2
The Citadel, Vol 3
Lord of the Underworld, Vol 4

Guardians of Atlantis (Fantasy Romance)
Tempting Eden
Seducing Eve
Ravishing Helene
Guardians of Atlantis Box Set

Realm of Honor (Fantasy Romance)
One Knight Only
Only for a Knight
A Knight to Remember
A Knight Like No Other
Shadows of the Knight
Realm of Honor Collection (Books 1-5)

Shorts and Anthologies
A Dance Among the Faeries, Short Story
Eorwulf, Short Story
The Soul of Sharah, Short Story
Flights of Fantasy: A Collection of Short Stories

Watch for more at www.michellemiles.net

About the Author

MICHELLE MILES believes in fairy tales, true love and magic. She writes heart-stopping urban fantasy, epic fantasy and paranormal romance with an action/adventure twist that will leave you breathless. She is the author of numerous series that includes everything from angels and demons to fairies, dragons and elves.

She is a member of Romance Writers of America (RWA) and Science Fiction and Fantasy Writers Association (SFWA). A native Texan, in her spare time she loves reading, listening to music, watching movies, hiking, and drinking wine. She can be found online at Facebook, Instagram, Pinterest and Goodreads.

Your Adventure Awaits

Read more at www.MichelleMiles.net